Torchlight in Berlin
Daniel Fludgate

(The second book in the Dmitri Romanov series)

Published in 2021 by FeedARead.com Publishing

Cover image reference 776495920, through Shutterstock

Cover font of Aprille Display Caps SSi, through wfonts.com

A CIP catalogue record for this title is available from the British Library.

PROLOGUE
January 30th, 1933.
Berlin.

11am.

A NERVOUS Adolf Hitler paced around the hotel room.

The chef had provided a vegetarian lunch, even though it was still only late morning. Hitler's advisers insisted their leader needed to eat something before the busy day ahead, but the Nazi Party leader left his food untouched. It was a momentous day for him, and one a long time coming.

The promises of socialism had failed, with seven million Germans unemployed; this benefitted him and his followers.

The revolution from the communists had not materialised, but had caused the industrialists to fear for their positions and wealth; this had benefitted him and his followers.

The economically crippling Versailles terms accepted in defeat by the Weimar government, and the occupation of the Ruhr by France and Belgium ten years before, were national humiliations still resented by the populous; this had benefitted him and his followers.

These events had given his movement its strength, and they would soon give Hitler power.

The leading statesmen in Germany were arrogant, but they couldn't ignore the seats in the Reichstag won by the Nazis. Hitler knew they thought of him as the little Austrian corporal who could be tamed, so they didn't fear him. This placed Hitler exactly where he had dreamed of being.

In less than an hour he would be chancellor of Germany.

One of President von Hindenburg's adjutants arrived; he'd been sent to remind Hitler that it was well past time for the Nazi leader to travel to the presidential palace. He found Hitler calming his nerves by whistling a favourite tune. Being a fellow Beethoven aficionado, he recognised Allegro Ma Non Troppo. The adjutant approached Hitler. The room was crowded with senior Nazis shuffling nervously and muttering like small children being kept waiting for their presents on Christmas morning.

The adjutant had never met the Nazi leader before. All reports received from the president and other statesmen indicated that the former lance corporal was nothing more than a ham actor desperate to take on a leading role for which he was woefully ill-suited. The adjutant, a veteran of the Great War himself, albeit from the comfort of a commander's tent rather than the trenches poisoned with mustard gas that Hitler had carried messages through, was pleased that he had something in common with the soon-to-be chancellor. A man who likes Beethoven cannot be all bad, he thought whimsically.

"Herr Hitler, you enjoy Beethoven?" asked the adjutant.

Hitler said nothing. He continued to whistle.

"If I may, sir," continued the adjutant, "I believe you were incorrect there in the second movement."

Hitler stopped whistling.

The room fell silent immediately.

"It is not I who am whistling it wrong," replied Hitler, "but the composer who made a blunder there." A malevolence to his expression arrived quickly. Everything about the Nazi leader's tone and body language indicated to the president's adjutant that this comment had not been made in jest.

Dr Goebbels limped over. He handed Hitler's raincoat and trilby hat to his leader; the propaganda chief had stage-managed the entire day and didn't want to risk his principal player making a mistake.

Hitler held his stare with the adjutant until the colonel dropped his eyes in submission. Hitler then took the coat and hat from Goebbels.

Minutes later, and smiling broadly, Hitler emerged from the Kaiserhof Hotel to cheers from the brown-shirted stormtroopers waiting outside. His chauffeur, Erich Kempka, held the rear door of the Mercedes Nurburg 500 cabriolet open for his leader. The two men exchanged a salute, each raising their right hand; the crowd responded with the same gesture, something that had become a reflex action to them.

A young girl at the front of the throng dropped her porcelain doll into the footwell of Hitler's car. She tried to quickly ease back into the crowd, but the forward motion of the Nazi supporters prevented her escape. She was trapped next to the vehicle. Noticing the doll, Hitler picked it up and reunited it with its owner, patting her on the head. With a shaking hand, she quickly reached inside the doll's dress to find the concealed wire and disconnect it from the explosive.

The car drove away before the president's adjutant could push through the crowd. He had intended to join Hitler for the short journey to where President von Hindenburg had been waiting impatiently for some time to meet the man he had been advised to swear in as chancellor, against his own better judgement.

Without knowing it, the adjutant had already dispatched his last official duty for his country. Chancellor Hitler, as the man in the back of the Mercedes would soon be known, would make sure the colonel who had corrected his whistling would receive an envoy later that afternoon thanking him for his service to the Reich, assistance that was no longer required.

5pm.

IN PRESIDENT von Hindenburg's office the new cabinet was sworn in. Chancellor Hitler wiped a tear from the corner of his right eye. A few hours earlier he had made his own oath to the handle-bar moustached hero of the Great War. Hitler had sworn to employ his strength for the welfare of the German people, and to conduct his affairs with justice for everyone.

Now he was Führer over Germany, and those constitutional promises no longer mattered.

He had power, legitimately.

The collection of men making similar promises of honour and respect for Germany included two of his own Nazis. They were all now the Führer's marionettes to manipulate in the final few gestures of a democracy that had become nothing more than a puppet show. The old guard mistakenly believed themselves to be the puppet masters, and the new chancellor their Pulcinella, a coarse bumpkin who would be kept from rising any further above his station.

They had miscalculated.

Hitler and his Nazis were no court-jesters.

Dr Goebbels encouraged the new cabinet to present themselves to the news cameras he'd assembled in a reception room.

None of the men congratulating each other had any concept of the brutal abyss their Reich had just plunged itself into. Nor did they understand that future generations would note with such significance the ceremony which had just taken place.

11pm.

FROM BEHIND a window, President von Hindenburg leant on his cane with one hand, with the other he waved at the crowds in the street below.

From a nearby window, this one open, Hitler and Goering stood in the light of a bright lamp to be seen more clearly.

They took the salute of their followers.

These massed ranks had been parading through the streets of Berlin for over two hours already. They carried lighted torches and swastika-emblazoned flags in jubilant procession from Tiergarten, through the Doric columns of the Brandenburg Gate - built to represent peace - across Pariser Platz, and down Wilhelmstrasse. They sang the Horst Wessel song with relief that the years of national humiliation would now be over: "Clear the streets for the brown battalions; clear the streets for the storm division!" they sang.

Thousands marched in disciplined columns.

Many more stood by the side of the road cheering the Nazi troops. And yet more cluttered every balcony along the route, waving, cheering and throwing flowers.

Most were celebrating.

Some who watched were curious, cautious, optimistic that the brutish election tactics of the Nazis would be tempered now that their leader was chancellor. They hoped that the roughness would receive a polish.

A few were wide-eyed with fear and hatred. They shuddered at every thump of jackboot on cobbled street, and felt revulsion at every 'sieg heil' hollered in triumph. A doctrine of brutality had been legitimised that day, and this last group of spectators, by far the smallest, seemed to be the only ones who understood that.

Two floors below Hitler's window a young woman was lifted on the shoulders of others. With her arm outstretched she tried to reach up to her Führer and deliver to him the single red rose she'd bought from a florist earlier that day. She couldn't quite reach, and Hitler didn't see her. He turned to Goebbels, who had slid in next to his leader.

"It's almost like a dream, a fairy-tale," Goebbels said. "The new Reich has been born. Fourteen years of work have been crowned with this victory."

Hitler nodded and smiled.

The Nazi era had now begun.

I

30th January 1933 (the same day).
Kitzbühel, Austria.

THE NORTHEAST face of Hahnenkamm, in the
Austrian Kitzbühel Alps, was one of the most demanding
downhill slopes Prince Dmitri Andreevich Romanov had
ever attempted. This was especially so in January, when
that face of the mountain is in shade.

Overcast, foggy, and with 'flat' lighting, the course
required a high degree of technical skiing. Fall-away turns
with limited visibility combined with gliding sections so
that Dmitri was tested beyond any previous ski adventure.
Nevertheless, he had achieved it that morning. Now,
feeling elated by that accomplishment, the playboy émigré
Russian prince spent the afternoon in a more relaxed
fashion. He skied the rest of the circuit around the three-
peak mountain range that had become his regular winter
haunt.

Nourished by a lunch of goulash soup and a warm
cocoa from one of the many ski-in, ski-out family run
chalets that dotted the slopes, Dmitri weaved his way
around the mountains, taking in the dramatic scenery.

There was something magical about being nearly two-thousand meters up, alone, and traversing fresh snow unmarked by any other tracks. The closeness of the sun, the vivid blue sky, the pleasant coolness of the temperature, and the calming stillness of the mountain air created an other-worldly feel.

The pretty cobbled streets of the medieval town far below were pleasant, but it was the solitude and magical escape of the high mountains that brought Dmitri back to the Austrian Alps every winter.

But this year was different.

Waiting for him at the hotel were his sister and father, both discharged from the sanatorium in Paris, and grateful for the holiday Dmitri had encouraged them to join him on. For his father, Grand Duke Andrei, this journey was the first since his evacuation from the Crimea fifteen years before, fleeing from the Bolsheviks.

The old man was by no means fully recovered of his faculties. After so many years in the mental catatonia the news of his wife's death had imprisoned him in during that evacuation, his recovery would take time. But his daughter's rescue several months before had done what the years of Dmitri's care had not achieved – their father had emerged from his mental solitary confinement.

Unlike every year before in Kitzbühel, there would be people Dmitri cared about waiting for him when he skied back to his hotel later that afternoon. This year he was spending time with his family, not just mingling with those of the international set he forced an acquaintance with, often just because of the access to the former Romanov jewels this high-society group facilitated.

The remaining list of precious items the aging grand duchess in Paris, his co-conspirator, required Dmitri to steal back had been shortened through his recent efforts but was not yet a task considered complete.

Also staying in the Austrian resort was a member of the Japanese imperial family, someone who had recently purchased from a Soviet agent an engagement gift for his betrothed. The diamond and sapphire gem-set gold ring had once belonged to the assassinated tsarina, having been given to her by her mother-in-law for her coronation. The presence in Kitzbühel of the Japanese prince and the Romanov ring was a contributory reason to explain Dmitri's choice of the Austrian Alps for a skiing holiday. Dmitri had skilfully taken back the heirloom, and the Japanese prince would now be sailing to Tokyo with a worthless piece of copper and glass in his luggage. This made Dmitri's relaxing afternoon on the slopes even more enjoyable as he navigated the twists and turns.

THE ACOUSTICS of the high mountain distorted the sound of the gun shot. But Dmitri recognised it as such, nevertheless.

The bullet missed Dmitri's head by inches; it splintered part of a tree branch, sending a large dollop of snow to the ground. The bang that Dmitri was used to hearing when a gun was fired at him, an all too frequent occurrence in recent years, sounded more like a crack because of the mountain conditions.

His mind and body reacted immediately, and he turned sideways into the forest.

Dmitri was unarmed.

In the canvas daypack slung across his shoulders he had spare metal edge segments, a screwdriver, screws and glue for field repairs on his hickory segmented steel-edged skis, but no gun.

Nor did he have time to wait for the person shooting at him to emerge into view.

He was, for now, safest in the forest of fir trees trying to evade a second shot, and so he pushed off down the slope.

The Bolshevik spies in Paris had made several attempts to kidnap him recently, so the presence of an assassin here was not a surprise. When in Paris, Emile-Jacques of the *Deuxiéme Bureau* had provided the necessary protection for Dmitri and his family. Travelling to Austria under false names had seemed sufficient a precaution to enjoy an unhindered short break. Dmitri had been wrong.

The going was slow and careful.

Dmitri dragged the steel tips of his poles along the ice and snow to help brake quickly as he changed direction multiple times, trying to disorientate his pursuer, and still get to the open slope he was aiming for as quickly as possible. Even one small mistake would throw him against a tree, giving him serious injuries, and leave him ready to be killed like a defenceless animal by the armed hunter behind him.

His tapered tweed trousers and wool-lined coat were perfect garments for a casual downhill run to keep Dmitri dry and warm. The outfit was inappropriate for the new route taken, which was like a workout at a gymnasium, requiring frequent exertions to twist his body and equipment through the trees, across the slope, and back again in a circuitous path to confuse the assassin following behind. He undid the storm button that had closed the neck of the jacket completely, and let some heat escape out across the white turtleneck of his sweater.

What he was attempting was dangerous, but the alternative of stopping, or moving out to the exposed slope too early, was more so. There was no room in his mind for fear or hesitation. As with the Streif slope that morning, Dmitri had to attack the mountain and rely on the instinct of his body and the skiing experience of his mind to get him through the obstacle course of the forest safely.

No further bullet came his way, nor did he see anyone closing upon him.

Emerging from the forest onto the clear slope, he was momentarily unsettled. This switch in terrain made him hesitate, and one ski caught on the powder as the other moved onto ice. He could feel himself about to fall, whilst still gathering uncontrollable speed that could rip his legs apart. Resisting the fall would lead to certain injury, so Dmitri relaxed his body, allowing it to go with the momentum of the tumble rather than fighting against it.

He moved the weight of his body down and to the side of the skis, extended his legs before his rear touched the ground. He kept his hands clear of the snow to avoid a broken wrist. His loose body bounced and rolled through the powder of the snow as he became disorientated and fearful of injury.

His body came to a stop.

Testing his limbs, nothing seemed broken, merely bruised, but Dmitri was exhausted. For the briefest of seconds, he considered staying where he was, taking cover back in the forest, and hoping the threat had been lost, while his muscles recovered. But unlike his previous escapes from jealous husbands, swindled jewellery collectors, and Bolshevik spies in the cities and countryside of Europe, snow was an unforgiving environment that favoured the chaser rather than the chased. His ski tracks provided a map that, easily followed, would bring his would-be killer directly to his hiding place.

Hearing voices in the forest behind him, Dmitri knew he had to move.

He angled the skis across the slope, sat close to his heels, pushed against the lower ski as he rolled his knees above his feet, and pulled forwards on the poles planted uphill. He was up and moving.

The clear slope required a change in approach. Now, all that mattered was to get down the mountain as fast as possible. The new tactic was to outrun, rather than outmanoeuver, whoever was behind him.

He found the fall line, being the most direct route downhill, and the young exiled Russian prince focussed his mind and body to achieve the fastest descent possible. His skeleton, ligaments, muscles and limbs all aligned to avoid any twisting. With a high, relaxed posture, and legs slightly flexed, Dmitri let the hickory, steel-edged skis glide across the snow in long, graceful smooth movements rather than the short radial turns he'd used in the forest. With effective forward motion, his movements carved a shallow s-shaped wave-like path down the slope.

Only once did he allow himself a glance behind, which confirmed that the threat, being two men, was still present. The assassins could stop where they were and take a carefully aimed shot, but would risk missing and then losing their target, or they could keep the guns in their belts and not allow the Russian prince to get too far ahead, hoping for a mistake on his part that would switch the small advantage he had back in their favour.

Dmitri let himself go, suppressing every human instinct of caution and due care.

The small bumps that sent his skis off the ground for a second or two risked throwing him off balance when he landed back on the ground. He tried to soak up these moguls and push down with his legs to keep in contact with the snow as much as possible while his upper body stayed relaxed.

Each slight turn was executed at a dangerous speed, knowing that pushing the tail of his ski out, or moving his weight slightly from one leg to the other could cause a catastrophe. The square-toed leather boots, custom made for him by an Austrian cobbler, kept his feet in control, and the Kandahar bindings forced his heels down onto the skis giving him expert handling. The tightness of the bindings meant that a crash at this speed would almost certainly result in broken legs or ankles, and he'd be unable to get back up and continue his escape. But there could be no consideration of caution in his skiing; he had to get down to the safety of the medieval town as quickly as possible.

Coming to the faster sections of the slope, Dmitri streamlined his body into a low tuck to increase the speed still further. Sitting low over the skis with his poles and arms parallel, Dmitri compressed his torso right down between his splayed legs as his egg-like shape reached sixty, seventy, then eighty miles an hour. There would be no splintered legs or ankles from any crash at this speed, only a broken neck. Despite the danger, he felt the full thrill, the inhuman speed, and the perfection of his skiing. It was exhilarating, almost superhuman. Knowing he was one misplaced centimetre of a ski away from death only increased the euphoria.

The assassins couldn't compete with Dmitri's speed. They needed him to make a mistake.

He saw the cable car in the distance. The slope was on course to join up with a commercial route busy with other recreational skiers, and to safety.

Dmitri eased his body out of the tuck, inch-by-inch, taking care that each tiny movement didn't disrupt his balance; he was not out of danger yet.

Regaining his high posture, feeling his speed reduce, and the danger of catastrophe ease, Dmitri brought his skiing out of the virtually vertical path and into a wider curve. He stemmed the skis to slow the speed and ready himself to join the vacationing skiers.

He merged himself into their ranks and checked behind. His assassins were still there, themselves preparing to join the merry holiday makers, but Dmitri was safe, for now.

Kitzbühel could be seen below. There, Dmitri could lose himself and leave no track. But it wasn't just him to think about now. At the hotel, his sister and father were in danger.

If the Bolsheviks had found him, they could easily find his family.

II

ANNA HADN'T skied for seventeen years. The last occasion had been a family holiday to Norway in 1915; she'd been twelve years old. She was now approaching her thirtieth birthday and had neither the desire nor the intention of trying the sport again, at least not this year.

Anna was not yet fully recovered from her years of mistreatment in Russia.

The weeks spent by her father's side in the Paris sanatorium had helped her start to rediscover the person she had once been. But the fifteen-year-old princess who had clung to her older brother's arm when revolutionaries stormed their Petrograd palace after the February Revolution was lost completely.

More than a decade in a labour camp had strengthened one side of her character whilst weakening the other. She was now independent, but mistrustful of happiness, and unable to relax fully. Experience had taught her it could all be taken away easily. This had created a barrier between her and the brother she had once idolised. But her father was different. He needed her in a way that Dmitri didn't.

Without her by his side, Anna feared her father would slip back into the catatonia he had been in when she was reunited with him months before. She worried that the fragility of her father's recovery would be threatened if she didn't embrace the role of caregiver wholeheartedly. Her new life seemed built on fragile foundations, preventing her from really enjoying them. Anna lived entirely for her father, for the old man whose gaze would often become vacant, his mind having to shut itself down every now and then to cope with the remembrance of the wife he had lost and the humiliation of his wider family's ruin.

That occasional vacancy of her father's expression was something Anna had learnt well to recognise. It emerged again during lunch on the terrace of the Austrian hotel Dmitri had chosen for their holiday, and Anna knew it was time for her father to rest. She was assiduous in her perceived duty to not let her father's condition become noteworthy to others.

"Marc, I think father needs a rest," suggested Anna to her other lunch companion. Marc Vallan, a *Deuxiéme Bureau* officer Captain Emile-Jacques Brossard had assigned to the family for the trip, hadn't yet finished his large lunch. He was a burly man with a big appetite, but Anna's interruption of his meal suggested the rest of the pig-blood sausages and dumplings would have to be left, and the strudel he'd already ordered, relinquished.

Emile-Jacques had adopted the Romanovs as if they were his own family since rescuing Dmitri and Anna from a jail cell in Istanbul. He had specifically chosen Marc, as the broad-shouldered young detective had also been an army medic and could competently carry out both medical and security duties as required. There were worse assignments than a stay in a luxury alpine hotel, Marc had thought when receiving his instructions from his boss.

Anna and Marc each took an arm of Grand Duke Andrei's and supported the old Russian prince inside the hotel, and up to the first-floor bedroom that formed part of the luxury suite of rooms Dmitri had taken for their week-long holiday.

"I'll head down to the town and check for messages," suggested Marc, leaving Anna to finish putting her father to bed for an afternoon rest. Those close to the family in Paris had been asked to send messages via the post office rather than the hotel as a further security precaution.

"Take your time," Anna replied, "I expect my brother will be back soon, unless Mitya finds another distraction aside from skiing." She smiled; both she and the detective were aware of Dmitri Romanov's playboy reputation, and the higher-than-usual concentration of rich, bored women making themselves available for bedroom-based après ski adventures in Kitzbühel that season.

Now that her father's needs had been attended to, she was glad to let the policeman have some time to himself. She would also take the opportunity of a rest; she tired much more easily than a twenty-nine-year old single woman should, but that was yet another legacy of the years of exhaustion suffered at the mercy of her Bolshevik gaolers.

WHEN IN the hotel room at odd times on other days Anna had become used to the quick, light, perfunctory knock at the door to the suite immediately followed by the entry of a chambermaid coming to clean the room, not expecting any guests to be present. Therefore, the louder, purposeful knock on the door, and the delay in any master key being inserted into the lock gave Anna reason to pause as she woke from her nap.

She dismissed the concern as irrational, a further legacy of her own expectation of catastrophe at any moment. She opened the door.

"*Entschuldigen Sie mich,*" apologised the pretty blonde chambermaid. She backed further into the corridor, as if to make her way to another room.

"Please," said Anna, "come in." She stood aside. With one hand Anna held open the door, the other she combed through her mousy-brown hair flecked prematurely with strands of grey, and which had become disorganised during her light nap on the sofa outside her father's bedroom.

19

"Thank you," replied the maid. She performed a small curtsey and carried her basket of linen into the Romanov suite. Anna settled herself down at the writing desk to catch up with her correspondence. It was only the grand duchess and Dmitri's American friend, Sable, with whom she'd made any meaningful friendships since her return from the grave of Soviet Russia the previous summer. Nevertheless, she knew her brother would not write to either friend, so she took on this family duty also.

Watching the maid change the linen on the unoccupied beds and clean the furniture in the communal rooms made Anna feel uncomfortable. It had only been months before when she had been forced to carry out such tasks for Gennady and Valentina Bunin, her family's former chauffeur and laundress, who had been elevated in status by the Revolution.

Anna still felt more like the version of herself who had slept in a corner of their kitchen in Yalta, suffering the humiliations of being made to clean for others, than she did the princess who used to change outfits three times a day and leave the discarded gowns on the floor of her dressing room for others to pick up.

She abandoned the letters to step out on the balcony so that the maid could continue her work without being watched.

The early afternoon temperature was hovering around freezing, but she was accustomed to the cold. Even the night-time drop of five or more degrees below zero didn't discomfort Anna. She reclined on one of the balcony chairs. She was without a coat and the chill kept her alert, so she didn't drift back into a light sleep despite still being tired.

The sound of something crashing to the floor made her sit up, but she stifled her instinct to rush to check on her father. If the maid had accidentally broken something, the last thing the girl needed was a guest blustering into the room with a panicked expression on her face. Let the maid come and find her when she was ready, or leave the room in guilt. Anna would happily take the blame for the breakage rather than bring any penalty on the young woman working for what was likely to be little pay.

But Anna couldn't relax back in her chair.

Her instinct had told her earlier that the knock at the door which anticipated someone being inside despite the peculiar hour of the day was unusual. The crashing sound had made her sit up and start to rush to her father's aid. In both cases she had suppressed her reflex, but the feeling of there being something more to both incidents than merely an unprofessional maid wouldn't dissipate.

She stepped through the curtain, ready to accept the maid's apology for the breakage with grace and charity, but instead she saw the young blond woman and her father wrestling on the bed. The maid had a pillow pressed over the old man's face as he writhed under the force of her grip. The crash had been the bedside lamp getting knocked off in the struggle.

What Anna saw didn't make sense, but it didn't need to.

She obeyed her instinct on this occasion and was across the room in a second.

Anna launched herself at the body of the woman who hadn't expected the sick old man to have as much strength to resist her as he did. Both Anna and the maid crashed against the heavy wardrobe near the bed.

Anna was on her feet first, winded by the fall, and bruised by the collision with the furniture. She grabbed the maid by the bunches of her blonde hair and dragged the woman across the polished block-work floor. Anna wanted to get her clear of the bed and a possible renewed attack against her father, who was coughing and trying to gather his senses after the surprise suffocation.

21

The maid looped her foot around a leg of the bed, halting her progress across the floor.

As Anna stepped towards her to unhook the impediment, the maid swiped her free leg sideways, smashing against the back of Anna's knees. The Russian princess collapsed to the floor as the Austrian maid regained her own footing. She delivered a firm kick to Anna's stomach to ensure the woman couldn't quickly resume the attack, but she'd misjudged Anna's toughness. Anna had spent her late teenage years in Siberia enduring more than a gut-kick; she had learnt to receive much worse and show no reaction to the violence.

She uncoiled herself quicker than her attacker had expected and surprised the maid by grabbing both white-stockinged ankles and pulling the Austrian girl down.

Both women tussled with each other on the floor of the hotel room in a confusion of limbs struggling to gain an advantage over their opponent's. Anna reached for the maid's neck, but her grasp missed, and she tore at the high-buttoned white blouse of her uniform. The torn collar revealed a line of white scar tissue around the maid's throat, raised flesh of heeled skin from a rope burn. Instinctively the maid reached up to cover the scar with her blouse. This allowed Anna to push herself free.

A bullet exploded across the room, embedding itself with a thud in the upholstery of an antique armchair.

Andrei, with a shaking hand, aimed the gun he'd taken from the bedside cabinet drawer at the maid for a second shot, but the weapon was too heavy for his frail arm that usually struggled even to lift a fork to his mouth.

The gun fired again, once more missing its target.

Anna was by now on the bed with her father. She reached for the weapon. When she took it from his bony hand and turned, intending to scare the maid off rather than shoot her, the target had already regained her footing and was making for the door.

Anna lowered the gun.

III

"HOW DID they know we were here?" asked Anna of her brother.

"I don't know, Annochka," Dmitri replied. He'd met Marc in town and hurried back to the hotel.

Marc employed his medical training to examine their father in the bedroom.

Whenever he'd escaped from such a threat previously, Dmitri had generally been left elated by the experience. His safety being in jeopardy had been like a drug, and each time he needed more risk to achieve the same rush of feeling. However, realising how close his father, and the sister whom he'd only recently been reunited with, had come to danger made him feel angry and unsettled.

Marc emerged from the bedroom and closed the door carefully behind him.

"His Imperial Highness is restless," he said, "I shall administer something to help him sleep." He went over to his medical bag for a syringe and a solution of barbiturates.

Dmitri gave his sister a large glass of whiskey. She was reluctant to accept it, but her brother forcibly clasped her hand, still rough and scarred from years of hard work, around the glass. He held her hand steady while she drank.

"I don't know how they found us," said Dmitri. He'd made extensive precautions for their holiday. He hadn't even told his travelling companions which hotel they would be staying at until the group was already en route across Europe for Austria. He'd sent a telegram from the central cable office in Paris under a false name to make the hotel and train reservations and had kept his true identity concealed whilst in Kitzbühel.

His past exploits as a playboy had received some press attention over recent years, so it was possible that he'd been recognised by a fellow skier. Any such diligent magazine reader would have to deliberately contact the Soviets, who would then need to assemble the assassins who had that day tried to kill him and his family. This seemed unlikely.

What he did know was that he and his family were no longer safe in Kitzbühel.

"Marc!" barked Dmitri, as the detective was about to open the door to the bedroom with the barbiturate-loaded syringe. "We need my father awake."

"Mitya, no!" implored Anna. "Papa's had such a shock. He must rest."

"We're leaving Austria. All of us," urged Dmitri.

Marc and Anna looked at each other, themselves both aware of the danger they were all in, but undecided about the best thing to do. To Anna, now in the hotel suite with her brother and their armed detective, she felt safe. Marc could see Anna's reluctance, and he too felt like remaining. He could protect them better here than on a train.

"Now!" exclaimed the Russian prince.

"I could wire to our people in Vienna for more detectives," suggested Marc. "They'll liaise with the local police here."

"Maybe it's safer to stay than to leave, Mitya?" asked Anna. "At least until we know more about who these people are."

"We know who they are, Annochka," replied Dmitri, adding, "Bolshevik assassins. And we know what they want."

He and his sister found that they argued often now. Their markedly different life experience, at least in adulthood, often separated them on practical matters, even if emotionally they were rebuilding bonds. As someone who'd been forced to obey every instruction in the labour camps for fifteen years, Anna, now free, was unwilling to defer to her brother, or anyone, without an argument.

The door to Grand Duke Andrei's bedroom opened slowly. The unexpected creaking interrupted the sitting room discussion. Grand Duke Andrei held onto the doorknob with one hand for support, in the other he was holding his overcoat. He was wearing a fresh shirt, had smoothed down the wispy semi-circle of grey hair around his bald patch, and combed his grey beard.

"Well, what are you all waiting around for?" asked the old man in a croaky, yet commanding voice. "Let's go."

The head of the family, revived by the attempt on his life rather than fatigued by it, had decided they were to leave.

DMITRI INSISTED that the French detective ride in the first sleigh with Anna. Marc kept his revolver in his hand and concealed in a coat pocket. Dmitri and his father followed in the second sleigh. The luggage would come separately. If it made it in time for the train to Paris, fine, if not, then so be it, thought Dmitri.

He'd directed the sleigh drivers to turn left towards Kirchberg Tirol station, rather than right towards the much nearer Kitzbühel terminus. The sudden departure from Austria of the Romanovs could easily be predicted by those who'd failed to catch their targets that day, and any informer on the Bolshevik's payroll at the hotel could easily phone ahead to make sure the assassins were waiting to board the same train for Paris. Kirchberg was one stop after Kitzbühel, so hopefully the assassins could be outfoxed into waiting for passengers that would never arrive.

The bells of Liebfrauenkirche, the baroque church in the centre of Kitzbühel, could be heard ringing, informing those in the sleighs that it was now five o'clock. Dmitri hoped they wouldn't be too late for the Paris train. They had thirty minutes to reach it.

Marc had given Dmitri a telegram he'd collected from the post office whilst out of the hotel that afternoon. The Russian prince now scanned its contents hurriedly for the first time as the pony pulled their sleigh along the icy road, and the smoke from their Tirolian driver's pipe wafted back over his passengers.

Dmitri took out one of his special Syrian-leaf cigarettes from its tortoiseshell case and lit it with his gold-plated Dunhill spin-wheel lighter. Grand Duke Andrei, wrapped up in a fluffy dark brown Motoluxe deep-pile Alpaca fur coat that gave him the resemblance of a noble-faced teddy bear wearing a Homburg hat, had been cured of his smoking habit by his years in the Paris sanatorium, so no cigarette was offered to him.

"What does it say?" asked the old man. His son crumpled the telegram into his own coat pocket.

"It's from an old friend," replied Dmitri.

"Who?" asked his father.

"Don't worry about it, Papa."

"Tell me," urged the old man. His breath came forth only with some effort after such a long period of time spent unused to talking. In the recent weeks of his

28

recovery, both his son and daughter had learnt that the abruptness of speech did not accurately reflect the tenderness in attitude of the man who was so surprised to find himself a father to two children once again. He was fascinated by every aspect of their lives which had, in his fractured memory, moved directly from their teenage years to adulthood, with no period of youth in between.

"It's from Berlin. Sergei Vasilyevich has forwarded it on."

Count Sergei Vasilyevich Mishukov, the grand duchess' equerry in Paris, now acted as adjutant to Andrei's branch of the Romanov family also; it was a service the former official of the Imperial Court undertook with great devotion. The resurrection of Anna had encouraged all Russian émigrés, including the count, in the hope that there might be more relatives thought dead who could be restored to them from the living graveyards in Siberia.

Count Mishukov acted as unofficial messenger for the Russian court in exile, weaving together the strands of a now dispersed, and sometimes disunited, community with the delicate skills of an expert courtier.

"A friend in trouble?" asked the grand duke. Now freed from his mental imprisonment, Andrei soaked up news of any kind. He read several newspapers daily, so the mention of Berlin suggested bad news rather than good.

"Unfortunately, it seems so," sighed Dmitri.

The road was clear of traffic both ahead and behind their two sleighs, apart from two middle-aged cyclists wrestling with the icy conditions that were ill-suited to bicycles. Once these had been overtaken, Dmitri felt more relaxed that there was no immediate danger that required a heightening of his attention.

"Do you remember Erich Arnheim?" he asked of his father, resuming the discussion about the telegram. Andrei took a second to think.

"Your music tutor?" he asked.

"Yes."

"He's Jewish," said Andrei. There was a tone of concern in his voice. He began to guess what the nature of the call for help from the German capital was. The reports of aggressive Nazi election tactics, and references to their racial ideology, had been closely followed by the grand duke in recent weeks. Only the day before, a foreign correspondent had reported in Le Figaro about the Berlin fire-fighters under pressure from Nazi aggressors, being told to leave a synagogue deliberately set ablaze to burn to the ground and save only the neighbouring buildings from destruction.

"He is, but Erich isn't concerned for himself. My old friend Pavel Darensky seems to have got himself arrested. Erich needs money to bribe officials for Pasha's release before things get too rough for him."

"Darensky." Andrei repeated the name to himself, searching through his cob-webbed memory for the reason why the name seemed familiar to him. "The orphan boy?"

"That's him," confirmed Dmitri. He raised himself up alertly in the sleigh as he saw his sister's carriage getting ready to pass a group of walkers carrying skis over their shoulders; anyone could be a threat, thought Dmitri.

"His father was Vice-Admiral Darensky," said Andrei, pleased that his long-dormant mind was still able to recall such details. "He resigned his commission and enlisted as a private when Cousin Nicky refused to let him leave the Court for war in nineteen-fourteen. He died at Tannenberg with the Second Army."

"And Pasha's never forgiven him for it." Dmitri settled back again once they'd passed the skiers.

"Forgive him?" queried the grand duke.

"For choosing Russia and the war over him. Pasha was only eleven when the admiral died. He was left with no one. I think living in Germany, under the presidency of the general whose army killed his father, is Pasha's attempt at revenge."

Andrei furled his mouth in thought at what his son had said, as if a problem had just been presented to him that required a solution. Dmitri lit himself a fresh cigarette from the glowing remains of the previous one, which was then discarded into the snow at the side of the road.

The change in pace of the chimes from the cowbell slung around the neck of the sled pony pulling their sleigh indicated they were slowing down. The Kirchberg station was just around the next bend.

"You must go to Berlin," said the grand duke after a few moments of silence. He'd organised his thoughts and come up with a solution for a problem Dmitri had not even asked for help with.

"Papa, I can't," said Dmitri. "I'll wire some money to Erich when we're all safely back in Paris."

"No, Mitya." Andrei took a deep breath, determined to get out all he had to say. "That young man, as you say, was left with no one." Andrei took hold of his son's hand and continued, "You must go to Berlin. You are a prince of Russia, and he's Russian; it's what we do. If his father were still alive, or he had a brother, they would go. You must be his brother now, Mitya."

"No, Papa," said Dmitri quietly. He hadn't had a father to defer to for any of his adult life, and he was unfamiliar with showing such obedience.

Once the sleighs had stopped, Marc and Dmitri hurried their companions into the train station, to enquire about the Paris train. They hadn't missed it.

"What about the luggage?" asked Anna.

"Mitya can ensure it is sent on," replied Andrei, "he's not coming with us."

"Papa, I'm making sure you all get safely back to Paris," said Dmitri. His father shook his head. The train pulled into the station.

"Yes, Papa, we need Mitya." Anna touched her father's arm as she spoke, hoping to help reassure his confusion. Andrei shook his arm free from the coddling.

"He has a royal duty to someone else, in Berlin. We can take care of ourselves." The grand duke stepped forward and kissed his son on both cheeks. The affectionate gesture, something Dmitri had been used to as a child, but had never received since, silenced any further disagreement.

IV

DMITRI WENT BACK TO KITZBÜHEL in the sleigh that arrived with their luggage. His family's cases and trunks were left with the Kirchberg station master to put on the morning train for Paris. Wrapped in a pair of ski mittens buried in one of the cases were those Romanov jewels reclaimed from the Japanese buyer, and which Dmitri would send a telegram to Count Mishukov about.

Regardless of Pasha's situation in Berlin, Dmitri now saw the benefit of him and his family splitting up to confuse the Bolshevik spies. He wondered whether this had been part of his father's reason for insisting on the change in travel plans all along. The grand duke had been a master tactician of the Imperial Cavalry in his younger years, and had continued the habit of treating everyday life as a chess game during Dmitri's childhood.

The last Berlin train had already left. The station master at Kitzbühel told Dmitri he could catch the train coming in from Salzburg leaving in two hours' time and change en route. Dmitri decided that he would send the telegrams to Emile-Jacques and Count Mishukov in Paris, then have an early dinner before the train journey.

The Reisch restaurant was near the station; it was busy enough to seem safe for Dmitri to rest in while he waited to leave Austria.

Without his family in immediate danger, the risk from the Bolsheviks lifted his spirits; he enjoyed such an adventure.

Having changed out of his ski wear into an off-white cable-patterned Aran jumper and wool flannels, the young Russian prince swept a hand through his dark-blonde hair and ran a finger across his pencil-thin moustache; this had become a habit, a cue that signalled to the rest of his mind and body that he was ready to join society as the playboy prince.

With a demeanour of fierce grace and extraordinary ease, he walked through the middle of the busy restaurant to the bar. He was aware that many eyes were looking up from their meals.

Dmitri was certainly good looking, but that wasn't why he found himself so desirable to women, and so hated by their husbands. His long stride had a feline smoothness to it; the rhythm of a dancer, and the determination of an athlete. Dmitri was very aware that his body in action could communicate far more than any words. It was a piece of well-planned choreography to cross the crowded room and take up his place at the bar with one hand slipped into a pocket and the other slowly taking the cigarette out of his mouth to order a drink. The success was in its understatement, which made it so hard for other men to copy. Dmitri's physicality had power and elegance because it quietly announced his presence, rather than shouting it; that whisper of a thrill made people, especially women, pay attention.

He was quickly joined at the bar by a young woman whose clothes and jewels screamed for attention, as well as announcing boldly that she had money and was keen to spend it. Dmitri had seen her type many times before:

daughters of rich neglectful parents. They knew they were beautiful and wanted to conquer the men they found. She held an unlit cigarette to her plump blood-red lips and waited for Dmitri to follow her cue for his entry into the scene she had rehearsed with many men before him.

She wasn't wearing a wedding or engagement ring, he noticed, and he never entangled himself with single women. Such women always expected more than he was prepared to give. He was best suited as the other man, not the primary one.

Dmitri let her wait.

He had no intention of reaching into his coat pocket for the Dunhill lighter with his initials engraved on it to light her cigarette.

The young woman didn't look at him, but he could see her hand was beginning to tremble slightly with impatience, perhaps even worry that she'd be rejected.

"That's a bad habit," he said. The comment was deliberately loaded with double meaning.

Hearing her cue at last, and misunderstanding the nuance of it, she turned her head slowly, feeling pleased that she had him.

But Dmitri was already walking away as she completed her flirtatious movement. On the bar in front of her Dmitri had left an open matchbook. The paperboard cover was tucked behind a comb of blazing matches that he'd lit in one stroke against the coarse striking surface of another matchbook.

"The fire went out," said the woman in a husky tone. She stood over Dmitri, who'd taken a seat at a nearby table. She dropped the paper-fold of burnt matches in front of him. He looked up to find her holding the cigarette between her fingers expectantly, it still being unlit.

She was well-made but not masculine. Her accent was Germanic but had a girlish softness to it. Her blond hair was tightly woven into a traditional alpine style. Her physical appearance suggested there was more substance to her character than the clothes and jewellery suggested. Dmitri had over an hour to wait for his train, and the woman's persistence intrigued him. He took the Dunhill lighter out of his trouser pocket, stood up, and lit the cigarette for her.

As they chatted and drank their way through a bottle of passably decent local wine, the girl's demeanour became unguardedly clumsy. Dmitri guessed she had learnt some tricks of flirting but hadn't yet the experience to keep up the character of coquette for too long; this endeared her to him more.

She introduced herself as a Swiss countess on holiday, and Dmitri told her he was a French freelance reported stopping for a few days of skiing en route to Istanbul; it was obvious neither believed the other. Over a fondue blend of gruyere, appenzeller and Emmental cheese, they dunked cubes of bread, laughed about the comic characters of other skiers in Kitzbühel that season, and commented on the quality of the snow.

He engaged his body in the game of seduction. With a careful roll of the shoulder, a smile that showed he was pleased with himself but still courteous to his companion, and a tone of voice as smooth as the best whiskey, he deployed the full arsenal of weapons effortlessly. With eyes that devoted their attention on the other person, Dmitri attacked the woman's defences through animalistic communication. If she'd thought this game was hers to control, she was wrong. Dmitri would soon have her ready to do his bidding on terms he would dictate, instead of by the rules she may have thought were hers to set.

Dropping her cube of bread in the pot, the 'countess' accepted her forfeit and kissed Dmitri. This quickly led to them drinking large glasses of kirsch brandy by the fire, and then they were outside pressed up against each other in one of the narrow alleyways of the medieval town. Dmitri could tell she was more experienced at kissing than at pretending to be a countess, but the quickness of her frozen breath being released into the cold air in small puffs between kisses showed how nervous she still was.

Even though her clumsy flirting by the bar ranked her lower down the professional league of bored wealthy women he was normally only happy to have some fun with, Dmitri decided that the train journey would separate them soon, so there was no harm in breaking his rule of only having fun with women already spoken for by a fiancé or husband.

He kissed her lips, then her cheek. Dmitri reached a hand up to slide the frilly collar of her blouse down, so he could expose her neck to kiss it. Hypnotised by the touch of his mouth, she was too late to react and prevent the collar being pulled back. He saw the ring of scarred flesh that his sister had described. The rest of Anna's account of the female assassin at the hotel matched the woman he was now pressed up against.

The sound of snow creaking beneath a heavy step close behind him warned Dmitri of more danger, just as he began to move his head away from the woman's neck. The sound had betrayed his attacker, and Dmitri pushed himself off the woman in time to get clear of the heavy iron workman's clamp that would usually hold sections of wood together while skis were being glued. The object knocked a chunk of masonry from the wall of the building Dmitri had been leaning the girl up against. She ran off. Dmitri pinned his attacker's arm firmly against the wall until the pressure forced him to drop the clamp. Dmitri turned the man around.

He was looking at a familiar face.

Dmitri had last seen Basil Calloway, the former English actor and current Bolshevik spy, when the middle-aged Englishman had been disguised as a taxi driver picking up Dmitri as he left Sable's Paris flat. Dmitri had managed to jump free of the vehicle then but had hoped he'd see the agent again for a chance at revenge against the man who'd kidnapped Anna from the Grand Bazaar in Istanbul whilst pretending to be Major Willoughby, yet another one of the actor's disguises.

Dmitri's surprise at recognising his attacker gave Calloway an advantage, managing to get his fist in movement first. The blow to the chin knocked Dmitri down onto the cobbles that were iced over with impacted snow. He twisted his knee painfully. Dmitri blocked a kick to his gut, and twisted Calloway's boot until the Bolshevik spy was thrown off balance. As Dmitri stood up, his damaged knee gave way. He slipped on a patch of ice and cracked his head on the brick wall.

The face of Basil Calloway became blurry.

COMING TO his senses, Dmitri found himself in a small room that smelt familiarly of the varnish he used for his skis. Calloway was there.

"Hello Mister Romanov," said the smiling Englishman as his prisoner opened his eyes. It amused Dmitri that communists really seemed to enjoy making a point of not referring to him by his princely title, not realising that Dmitri cared neither one way nor the other what name he was called by; such things always seemed more significant to people who didn't have a title, than those who did.

Dmitri's wrists were tied behind the back of the chair he was sitting on, but it was a chair which wobbled significantly as he moved. This instability didn't surprise him, as everything in the workshop looked antique. His legs weren't restrained, but the Englishman had the iron clamp in his hand as a warning for his prisoner not to try an escape. Dmitri had every intention of escaping, regardless of such signs that he ought not to.

"I'm glad to see you again, comrade," replied Dmitri.

"Really?" asked Basil. "Why is that?" He stepped closer to Dmitri, palming the iron clamp menacingly as he approached.

Dmitri just needed Calloway to make two more steps towards him.

The Englishman approached further.

Dmitri pushed off from his feet, throwing himself backwards. He tensed his neck to stop his head hitting the floor too hard.

As the chair lifted backwards, Dmitri brought his right leg firmly up between Basil's legs, connecting with an area of such male sensitivity that the iron clamp was dropped, and the Englishman rendered momentarily defenceless.

Dmitri was lucky. As he'd hoped, the old chair broke apart as it hit the ground, and his hands were free, albeit still tied together. But this didn't stop him charging forwards against Basil, knocking him against a wooden partition. It gave way under the force and Basil fell through to the basement below.

Dmitri wriggled free of his bindings and picked up the iron clamp. He considered descending the stairs to finish off the Bolshevik spy, but a quick glance at his watch changed his mind.

He had a train to catch.

THE BURGUNDY livery of the Mitropa train to Innsbruck, the one Dmitri needed to be on to get away from Kitzbühel, a place where the Bolsheviks had infiltrated, was gathering speed as Dmitri approached the train station. He ignored the pain from his twisted left knee as much as possible, focussing instead on the yellow lettering of the stylised eagle logo that was supposed to resemble an 'M' for the name of the luxury Central European train operator. By keeping his attention on this logo, Dmitri was able to judge his own speed as he ran along the platform chasing the departing train.

The carriage was getting away from him.

He wasn't fast enough.

But Kitzbühel was now a nest of Bolshevik assassins.

He had to reach the train.

"Move!" he screamed. Passengers waiting on the platform, hearing his shouts, stood aside to give him a clearer path.

The train conductor, in an unusually charitable mood, had opened the last door and was extending a hand down to the man half-running, half-limping desperately along the platform, the end of which was rapidly coming into view.

Heads now poked out of the carriages to watch the race between man and machine; a few willed him on to succeed, most were enjoying watching the inevitable failure. The majority were to be disappointed.

With a burst of additional speed that even Dmitri didn't know he had, he accelerated enough to get a hand to the conductor. But even this wasn't sufficient, and their hands were about to unclasp when the conductor saw in Dmitri's desperate eyes an indication of what the runner was about to do, it was the only option left if he wanted to reach the open door, but one which, if unsuccessful, might cast him under the huge churning wheels of the locomotive.

Dmitri jumped.

The conductor pulled.

Dmitri's foot missed the stone barrier marking the end of the platform by inches as he dragged himself forward on his belly into the train vestibule.

"What time to we reach Salzburg?" asked Dmitri. The conductor, knowing the train had left from Salzburg a couple of hours before, looked horrified at the thought he'd helped someone risk their life to get on the wrong train. Dmitri cast him a broad smile and slipped a generous tip in the top pocket of his tunic. "Only kidding," he said. The conductor's shoulders relaxed. Dmitri added, "Although I could do with you directing me to the bar please, my dear fellow."

V
Berlin

THE TRAIN arrived at Anhalter Bahnhof through a heavy fog.

The downward-pitched platform lights of the gigantic Berlin station created columns of hazy visibility, in and out of which weaved porters and passengers. There was a conspiratorial quality to the murkiness, allowing people to disappear quickly from sight, and reappear elsewhere. The iron and glass roof of Berlin's flagship station stretched over one-hundred-and-seventy meters and across six platforms. A train left every five minutes, bringing in and sending forth over forty thousand passengers every day.

Dmitri was glad to arrive unmolested by any Bolshevik spies since he'd left Kitzbühel the evening before. He'd taken a deliberately circuitous route, changing trains at Wörgl, Munich, and even Leipzig, although the Munich train would have brought him directly to Berlin. This unorthodox route assured himself as much as possible of having lost his Moscow-sponsored shadows; hopefully, his family was similarly free from the spies en route to Paris.

He had last been in the German capital almost three years before. He'd come to see Marlene Dietrich's intoxicating portrayal of Lola-Lola in 'The Blue Angel' premier. Dmitri had hoped to meet Dietrich, but after the curtain calls, she left immediately to board that night's boat train to Hollywood. High and low Berlin society had turned out in force to see the film, reviewed the next day as portraying Sodom on the eve of destruction.

Dmitri had enjoyed the film, but he was no fan of Berlin.

The Russian prince felt at home when surrounded by the exotic adventure of Tangier, or amongst chattering society in Paris. His sexual game of choice was adultery, undertaken discretely with a wink, a series of subtle gestures, and enjoyed with a bottle of expensive champagne in a luxury hotel suite. By contrast Berlin was sleazy, seething, grimy; its sexuality was scandalous, amoral and despairing.

Dmitri's behaviour labelled him as a playboy, a cad, but never a pervert. Attached women would seduce him on a beach or in a cocktail bar, thinking themselves the corrupter of a bachelor, but always returning to their husbands after their taste of adventure, as was Dmitri's intention. In his sexual encounters, the chase was far more important than the conquest.

But in Berlin, sex was a commodity, and the most readily available one in a society living on the brink of ruin, still feeling the effects of war-time humiliation and the Wall Street Crash three years before.

To Dmitri, a young man engaged for many years in a love affair with the sparkling city of Paris, Berlin was a city of grime, of unpleasant architecture, a set-piece depicted in grey tones.

The fog seemed appropriate.

For Dmitri, Germany still carried a stain as the chief belligerent of the Great War, and the legacy that campaign had on his family's dynasty and his own destiny. Had the Kaiser not declared war on Russia in August 1914, the government of his godfather, the tsar, might not have collapsed two-and-a-half years later. The rulers of Russia and their children, who had been Dmitri's playmates, would not have been massacred. The monarchy would eventually have ceded political decision making to representational government even without the war, but it would not likely have led to the Bolshevik despots taking power eight months after the tsar had abdicated, something almost accidental due to the provisional government's failings.

The life of His Highness Prince Dmitri Andreevich of Russia, now an émigré, jewel thief, and playboy, would have been quite different were it not for the Germans. His mother might still be alive.

Germany had been, and was still, enemy territory for Dmitri.

He'd read the morning papers on the train from Leipzig. They reported on the rise to power of the country's new chancellor, sworn in the day before, despite seemingly ill-suited to the role of statesman. This development did not encourage the Russian prince to change his opinion of the Reich his father had now sent him to as a Romanov emissary.

Dmitri would have preferred to send his former tutor some money to help Pasha, and return to Paris, but Dmitri knew his father had been correct in encouraging him to come to Berlin himself to help. He could hardly grieve anew for one set of murdered childhood friends, the tsar's children, without doing everything he could to help Pasha, another companion of his youth, and one still able to benefit from his assistance.

When he'd arrived at Anhalter Bahnhof three years before for the film premier, his expected arrival then had been advertised. Being a member of the Russian royal family, albeit deposed, his train carriage was approached by a red carpet and city and train company officials greeted him. His exit from the vast station had been facilitated with ease through the lounge and special exit specifically reserved for visiting foreign royalty.

No such announcement had been made for this arrival, nor was there any pomp to greet him, thankfully.

Dmitri tried to keep track, through the fog, of the elderly porter wheeling his luggage circuitously through the throng of passengers who were, like Dmitri, disorientated by the mist which had even infiltrated the concourse. He lined up for a taxi with the other passengers, queueing by the façade of the station which was topped by the zinc structures of male and female figures representing night and day; he couldn't tell by the fog which it was, but his watch told him it was two o'clock in the afternoon.

The queue was moving too slowly so Dmitri picked up his two cases and crossed Askanischer Platz.

Approaching the Hotel Excelsior, he saw a vehicle waiting which had the chequered stripe of a taxi liveried around the bodywork.

"*Frei?*" asked Dmitri. He reached into the driver's section of the taxi and prodded a meaty shoulder to wake the sleeping man. The thick-set driver lifted the peak of the cap which had been covering his tired eyes. He assessed the wealth of his potential fare. Deeming it possible to over-charge the well-dressed man, he nodded and started the taxi's engine.

"*Wohin, bitte?*" asked the driver.

"*Winterfeldstrasse,*" replied Dmitri. He climbed into the enclosed rear passenger section of the taxi, then checked the address for his former tutor in his notebook, hoping it was still Erich Arnheim's residence. As the taxi drove off Dmitri added, "*Nummer sieben, bitte.*"

He'd slept only intermittently on the three trains taken to bring him to Berlin during the night and morning, so he was easily hypnotised by the city passing quickly by. He drowsily watched the passing dreary vista of headlamps reflected on damp tarmac, gaudy neon lights from some of the hundred cinemas in the city, and the lines of huddled people emerging into the gloom at street level from the U-Bahn stations.

Dmitri didn't know the city well, so he gave no rebuke when the driver took a circuitous route up to the throbbing commercial hub of Potsdamer Platz, along the southern border of Tiergarten through the diplomatic quarter, before coming back south across the Landwehrkanal, and down to Nollendorfplatz.

The contrast between the embassy district, protected from economic misfortune by the desire for foreign governments to project an image of power, and the shabbiness of the streets south of the canal was marked. The southern inhabitants, the middle-classes, had been made bankrupt by the American stock market crash three years before. The collapse of that financial system, in which they had invested everything they had, left the residents with little money for the upkeep of their properties, buildings which now showed the signs of neglect.

Winterfeldstrasse matched the unkempt trend of the southern district.

Erich's property looked particularly scruffy. The hand-written sign in the window nearest to the front door, advertising rooms for rent at a cost of sixty marks per month including food, only emphasised the dishonour of this building even more.

"SCHÖN, SIE wieder zu sehen, Frau Renfeldt." Dmitri was lying, it was not good to see his friend's housekeeper

again. She was a woman who treated everyone as if they were an irritation.

Frau Renfeldt's expression of displeasure, one permanently fixed on her craggy, plump face, was exactly as it had been when Dmitri last saw her almost three years before.

After a second or two staring at the young man who'd spoken to her in a peculiar accent, someone who clearly recognised her, but whom she couldn't immediately place, her memory caught up. Upon recognising the prince, she dropped into a deep curtsey that had become habit during the years of accompanying Erich around the palaces of Europe's noble families. She had looked after the music teacher while he tutored the aristocratic children. Everyone suspected her to be Erich's mother rather than just his housekeeper, but the charade, if it was, had been mainatined for so many years that no one now queried it. As they both aged, the two German-Jews began to look more and more alike: dark haired, broad of face, and equally substantial in body.

"Your Highness," she replied, "Herr Arnheim did not warn me to expect you." She stood aside to let him enter. She closed the door after checking whether anyone in the street was paying attention to her royal visitor.

"Erich doesn't know," said Dmitri, somewhat apologetically.

She led him down the hallway to the dining room, past other doors which were, unusually, closed. She reached under shades to switch on table lamps, the tassels of which were frayed. The bulbs were barely able to brighten the dingy dust-laden lighting of the once-grand entertaining space. It was half stripped of furnishings. What remained had been carefully moved around to disguise the losses of cabinets and tables. Empty spaces on walls were marked by lines of discoloration where sections of the wallpaper, long-covered by framed pictures, now showed the original shade of green.

"Herr Arnheim is expected back soon," advised Frau Renfeldt, "he's teaching." She announced this with pride, just as a mother might. She indicated that Dmitri should seat himself at the dining table. "Have you had luncheon, sir?"

"No," replied Dmitri, "but please, don't trouble yourself, Frau Renfeldt." He noticed that the table was still cluttered with the remains of a lunch that presumably the paying house guests had already finished. Nevertheless, she returned a few minutes later and placed a serving of luke-warm lung soup and horse meat leftovers in front of him; he regretted immediately telling the truth about not having eaten yet.

As Frau Renfeldt cleared away the dirty dishes, Dmitri forced down the meal which he realised would only taste worse the colder it became. Having finished, and his plate having thankfully been taken away by his hostess, he lit a cigarette to lessen the damage to his palate that the inedible concoction had left. He offered the cheerless housekeeper a cigarette, only to see her expression change from one of sullenness to horror at the suggested breach in protocol; a housekeeper could not socialise with a prince.

Time passed, and Erich did not return home.

Dmitri became uncomfortable sitting by himself in the dining room while the housekeeper carried out her duties, trying to maintain a house that was falling into disrepair faster than she could keep up. Stepping past the visitor's suitcases in the hallway, Frau Renfeldt also felt the awkwardness of the situation. She regularly checked on the guest, with a smile of embarrassment from a woman for whom smiling had seemed like an activity long ago forbidden by some decree of her birth. Several times she noticed Dmitri had his eyes closed, as the lack of sleep from the train connections the night before caught up with him.

He was awoken from his seated doze by the sound of the front door slamming shut. A key jingling in the door to the sitting room was followed by that less solid door also being thrown closed behind the person who'd entered. Frau Renfeldt waddled hurriedly down the hallway past the room where Dmitri was waiting. She also closed the door to the sitting room behind herself.

Dmitri heard raised voices, but the walls of the nineteenth century German townhouse were substantial enough to muffle what was being shouted. Then the noise abruptly stopped.

"Good heavens!" exclaimed Erich. He rushed into the dining room to greet his friend and former pupil. "This is unexpected."

"Pleasantly so, I hope," replied Dmitri, hinting that he'd heard the argument between his former tutor and the housekeeper.

"Of course, of course." Erich ignored Dmitri's subtle attempt to elicit an explanation for the yelling, which the announcement of the prince's presence in the dining room had no doubt interrupted. "When I sent the telegram, which I did reluctantly, I never expected you to come personally."

"My father reminded me about the meaning of friendship," explained Dmitri, "and I'm glad he did, old friend." He smiled.

"The grand duke?" asked Erich. He was surprised by this comment, as his last letters from Dmitri had not referred to his father. Erich, as a younger man teaching at the Russian Court, had been in awe of the stately presence Grand Duke Andrei projected.

"Erich, we have a lot to catch up on, not least that Annochka has been returned to us."

"I can't believe it!" Erich embraced his friend in a crushing vice. Music would be almost the last profession anyone would guess as being Erich's, a man with the physical presence of a wrestler; this made the mastery with which he could control a delicate instrument such as the violin seem even more extraordinary, but it also meant that a hug from him could be suffocating. "I never thought it possible…"

"Neither did I," interrupted Dmitri, "but it's an awfully long story."

Erich, holding Dmitri at arms-length, assessed the appearance of his former music student.

"You are looking well, Mitya," he said happily. Dmitri couldn't say the same of his German friend, whose face, complexion, and bearing, seemed strained and weary.

"How's Pasha?" asked Dmitri.

"Some friends managed to get him released from prison."

"That's encouraging."

"Far from, I'm afraid," interrupted Erich. "Under the current political climate, I fear he would have been safer in jail."

"How so?"

"Mitya, Pasha has joined the Communists."

VI

ERICH DECIDED it would be easier to show Dmitri how things in Berlin had changed since his last visit, rather than trying to explain them over one of Frau Renfeldt's watered-down coffees.

The fog had cleared, but the early evening still cast a grey canopy over the drab city. Erich led Dmitri on an excursion by tram, bus, and S-Bahn train. They arrived at Bülow Platz in the north-east of the city.

"Pasha was arrested here during a demonstration against the Nazis six days ago," said Erich. "That is Karl Liebknecht House, the headquarters of the German Communist Party." Dmitri looked across the square at the irregular-shaped building, the ground-floor windows of which were smashed, and the walls graffitied with the words *rote untermenschen*.

"*Untermenschen?*" asked Dmitri. He only had a limited grasp of German.

"Sub-humans," muttered Erich, ashamed to even say the translation. "After the parade last night to celebrate Herr Hitler becoming chancellor, his followers came here for their after-party."

"Didn't the police stop them?" Dmitri was in disbelief that such large-scale public defacement would be allowed in one of Western Europe's capital cities. It reminded him of the Bolshevik vandalism he'd witnessed in Petrograd fifteen years before.

"Mitya, the police joined in."

In the snow that had been piled up next to the buildings to clear a path for pedestrians, Erich pointed to the lingering red stains.

"Blood?" asked Dmitri, fearful of the answer. Erich nodded.

"We shouldn't stay here too long," advised Erich.

A patrol of brown-shirted Nazi stormtroopers entered the square opposite them.

"I see your point." Dmitri noticed that the stormtroopers were stopping anyone leaving or entering the Communist Party building.

"About the shouting earlier, I feel I must explain," said Erich, as the two men reached busy Alexander Platz.

"There's really no need to." His father's Anglophilism had given Dmitri a British sense of privacy in certain matters.

"But I want to, Mitya." Erich walked on a few steps with his head bowed. Dmitri had never seen his friend so disconsolate before; he was like a defeated boxer after a bout, one perhaps deliberately lost. "Germany has not just become difficult for Communists."

"Jews?" asked Dmitri. He'd read the news coverage in the foreign press of the Nazi Party's philosophy. In fact, having seen in Kitzbühel that a telegram had arrived from Erich, Dmitri had thought it was his tutor who needed help rather than Pasha, whom Dmitri had assumed to be living the life of a feted Russian émigré.

"The Institute told me today that I was no longer welcome to teach there. It's no coincidence this comes the day after Hitler's ascension. And I wasn't the only Jew to be let go."

"I'm sure there are other places for you to teach, Erich," consoled Dmitri; there was little else he could say to a man who already seemed broken. "Or you could go back to composing."

"My dear friend, I've assisted Furtwängler at the Berlin Philharmonic, and before that I taught music to most of the royal families of Europe. Yet today, I was dismissed from a school where I was teaching teenagers to play basic scales on recorders. There is no new opportunity for me in this Germany."

"I'm sorry, Erich." Dmitri, with the life experience of a man used to tragedy since the Russian revolutions, knew that sometimes people share sorrow without wanting, or needing, the listener to find a solution for them. Simply saying out loud what filled their thoughts opened a valve and released the pressure of anxiety.

"The Nazis call it *Gleichschaltung*. It means bringing things into line." Erich's pace slowed almost to a shuffle as he spoke. He walked with his hands held behind his back, a habit learnt over the years of pacing across a school room listening to pupils fumble with their musical instruments. His usually straight back was now hunched under the weight of his worries. "Socialists, Jews, anyone who won't raise their hand in salute to the Nazis are being forced out of their public jobs as teachers, doctors, lawyers."

As they reached the bridge over the river Spree, about to join up with the Unter den Linden, they noticed a large group of Nazis. Forming up into organised groups, Ernst Röhm's brown-shirted Sturmabteilung streetfighters were mixing with Himmler's black-uniformed Schutzstaffel elite protection squads. On the red and black flags being unfurled, a phoenix was depicted clutching a wreath and swastika in its talons.

"If a phoenix is rising from the flames of Germany's humiliation, then it is an evil bird indeed," said Erich under his breath, checking over his shoulder for anyone who might overhear.

"Another parade?" asked Dmitri.

"Not another," replied Erich, "the same one. Doctor Goebbels wants an exact re-enactment of what took place last night, only this time for the cameras."

"Impressive," said Dmitri, without thinking. The sight of so many uniformed men, forming themselves into columns reminded him of the Imperial Guard at Tsarskoe Selo, which he'd watched in wonder as a young child as the great body of men moved as one solid unit, united, strong.

"Just the latest of many frauds," said Erich. "I don't need to see this vulgar farce. Let's call on Pasha."

THE *MIETSKASERNE* were barrack buildings of five stories arranged in blocks around a series of courtyards, the size of which was determined by the need for a horse-drawn fire truck to make a turn in. These had been built quickly in the working-class districts to cope with Berlin's expansion during the late nineteenth century. Erich led Dmitri into one such complex on Wallstrasse in the Fischerinsel district.

"Don't be fooled by the building's façade," warned Erich as they passed through a tunnel under the elaborate stuccoed and corniced street entrance. The music teacher had been right, the inner design was like a slum dwelling, with mixed tones of smog and dirt covered walls, rubbish piled up putrefying under its own weight, and the odour of urine permeated the courtyards. Residents looked suspiciously through cracked windowpanes at the well-dressed visitors whose footsteps echoed up the gloomy quads.

They found Pasha sitting on a dirty mattress in the corridor outside his own two-roomed apartment. The hallway was in half light, but Dmitri could still see that Pasha's eyes had the sunken darkness, and his skin the unhealthy pallor, of poverty. His angular face had always given him an aristocratic appearance; he had been Valentino to Dmitri's Fairbanks. But that same bone structure of the romantic poet, now gaunt with hunger, cast Pasha firmly amongst the city's underclass. He was embarrassed, rather than pleased, to see Dmitri. He stood up in clothes which hung off his emaciated frame.

"Mitya?" he asked, hoping to be mistaken.

"Hello, Pasha, my dear friend." Dmitri extended a hand in greeting. Pasha wiped his palm quickly across his threadbare jacket before clasping the hand of his friend.

An old man in factory overalls emerged sleepily from the apartment, surprised to find three men waiting in the hallway. He looked suspiciously from person to person.

"It's fine, Walther," said Pasha, "these are just some old friends of mine." This reassurance didn't seem to settle the nervous old man.

"Same time tomorrow?" he asked. Pasha nodded, and tried to hurry Walther past his friends, but not before Dmitri and Erich saw the old man give Pasha a few marks, which the Russian quickly pocketed.

"Poor old chap," said Pasha, letting his friends into the apartment. "I let him sleep here during the day as he works the night shift at the paper factory and has nowhere in the city to stay." Erich knew that, far from being an act of charity, having day lodgers was a frequent practice to make extra money from a bed that was otherwise not in use during the daytime. Pasha straightened out the unwashed linen on the bed. "Sorry the place is such a mess," he said. Pasha moved broken dirty items of furniture from one place to another to disguise the extent of the reduced circumstances that he was embarrassed to have someone such as Dmitri witness.

"Pasha." Dmitri stepped forward and took hold of his friends thin, trembling arms. "I came here to see you." Pasha raised his dark-ringed eyes to meet those of his friend. Dmitri added, "I don't care about all this." He cast a glance across the bedroom-cum-living room, which was being kept in a state of rancid squalor. Men and women's clothes were hanging on a string across the room to dry the sweat, and air the filth on them, rather than because they had been washed clean. The smell of the fetid clothes had combined with the dank indoor climate to make the room claustrophobic in its unpleasantness. But Dmitri was being honest, he cared only for his friend, not the surroundings.

"Erich tells me you've been in trouble," said Dmitri.

Pasha looked across at Erich with an expression of anger at a confidence betrayed. This expression quickly changed to one which almost brought him to tears; he wanted desperately to let his emotions break free and confide in a trusted friend such as Dmitri, someone who might be able to help. Then pride blocked the tears from coming, he straightened his back and smiled broadly. This cycle of emotions took no more than a second or two.

"These are troubling times for us all," said Pasha, with an air of insouciance that the other two men did not believe.

Someone jangled a key in the door lock.

"Let's go into the kitchen. I'll put the kettle on," suggested Pasha. He ushered his guests forward and pulled a curtain across the doorway that divided the two spaces.

Men's voices could be heard whispering in the other room as Pasha fussed around the grimy kitchen trying to find enough clean items to make his visitors tea. He deliberately clanked chipped crockery and dirty pans to cover up the conversation the men next door were having. Erich and Dmitri sat at the small table and exchanged a look of concern.

"I came because Erich said you'd been arrested," said Dmitri.

"Oh, that was nothing." Pasha struck damp matches trying to light the stove for the kettle. Dmitri stepped forward and used his lighter; there were only a few pieces of half-burnt coal in the burner. "Bloody German matches," joked Pasha, tossing the matchbook onto a pile of garbage in the corner of the room. He inspected the damp tea leaves in the pot to decide whether he could reuse them.

"Your girlfriend, Jakoba, got in touch with me. She was very worried," said Erich, trying to encourage Pasha to tell the truth about his difficulties.

"She overreacts," said Pasha. He tried to find three cups and saucers that matched and were of a sufficiently clean standard to be used. "What she lacks in height she makes up for in an inflated sense of drama."

The discussion from the other side of the curtain had stopped, but was replaced by a series of groans, and creaking sounds from the wooden bed that were becoming so explicit as to be amusing.

The kettle was taking an age to boil.

"I say, shall we get out of here?" suggested Pasha, fearing the noises from behind the curtain were only going to get worse.

"I think we passed a respectable looking tavern on the way in," said Dmitri.

Pasha held the curtain aside and tried to block from being seen what was going on in the bed as he ushered his guests out of the door, but Pasha's slim frame was insufficient to the task of being a shield.

Dmitri was horrified at seeing the two men on Pasha's bed without the slightest sense of discretion. The fat old man groaning in pleasure was still wearing socks held up by knee suspenders that indicated he was not a working-class resident of the housing block; the business suit neatly folded on top of a dusty dresser supported this deduction. The young man performing the sex act with the businessman had the dirty face of someone recently come from a factory; his expression was one of neither pleasure nor pain, he could have been watching a movie, oblivious to what the lower half of his body was engaged in.

"More night-shift workers?" asked Dmitri once they were clear of the explicit scene.

"That's Oskar," said Pasha with embarrassment. "He works on the coal barges and stays with me and Jakoba." He gave no explanation how three adults could live in a two-roomed apartment which had only one bed. "He does that for extra money."

Pasha had always attracted people. His romantic features, dandified, and with a touch of femininity, had made him catnip to both men and women when he and Dmitri were teenagers in Petrograd. Pasha was two years younger than Dmitri and, while both had a sense of mischievous fun about them, Pasha had a vulnerability to his character that drew people towards him. These people wanted to love Pasha in a different way to that which Dmitri found people attracted to him as the teenage boys grew into their early adulthood.

Whereas Dmitri was a heroic figure that some rivals jealously wanted to see fail, Pasha was someone who seemed to be fighting against his destiny of heroism, deliberately sabotaging that which was waiting for him. This only made people, both young and old, male and female, want to help Pasha achieve the purpose which fate seemed to have willed for him, but which he was reluctant to seek out for himself.

Pasha's child-like insecurity and refusal to help himself could become exasperating to those trying to assist him, and he was someone who made and lost friends frequently. A few stayed loyal to their task of seeing him achieve what he himself seemed so determined to let pass him by; Dmitri was one of those.

The indecent circumstances of Pasha's current condition encouraged Dmitri to redouble his efforts. He was glad his father made him come to Berlin to help his friend.

Erich put a handkerchief to his nose as they passed the communal toilet by the stairwell.

"Scandalous," said Erich. "They charge rent at forty marks a month when unemployment benefit is only seven, and residents don't even have a toilet of their own." He was no communist, not even a socialist, but had been a positive voice over the last ten years supporting housing reformers in the city, this was when his name as an accomplished musician of some fame meant more to Berlin society than it did now.

They made a peculiar trio sitting in the window of a small tavern crowded with workers from the nearby factories: the unemployed Jewish musician, the destitute Communist, and their friend, a playboy Russian émigré prince.

"Well, someone may as well say it," said Erich, raising his tin cup for a toast, "it's a far cry from when I taught piano to both of you in the amber room at the Catherine Palace, but here's to us. *Za zdorovje!*"

"*Za zdorovje!*" echoed Pasha and Dmitri with a smile. The absurdity of their current situation was something no one could have predicted all those years before in the luxurious surroundings of the Russian Court where they'd first met.

"We can leave tonight," said Dmitri. "Come to Paris with me, both of you." Erich and Pasha each gave a smile of thanks to their generous friend, but Dmitri could tell this was not a gesture of acceptance. "Why not?" he asked.

"I have a life here," said Erich, "such that it is."

"I've run away before," added Pasha, "and I ran here. I have things to do in Berlin, important things."

"With the Communists." This was an accusation from Dmitri, not a question.

"I wouldn't expect you to understand," replied Pasha. He took another slurp of beer.

"Don't patronise me, Pavel Borisovich," snapped back Dmitri, "you're not the only one who's suffered since we were in Russia."

Pasha rubbed his dirty fingers on the lapel of Dmitri's bespoke suit jacket and said, "It feels like a real struggle."

"Boys," interrupted Erich, leaning forwards, "not here." He indicated that others were listening to their raised voices. Pasha finished his drink, slammed the tankard down, and walked out of the tavern. Erich rolled his eyes; he was used to the young man's mood swings.

"He has his father's foolish stubbornness," said Dmitri, remembering again the story of Vice-Admiral Darensky leaving his son parentless so he could enrol as a private, and fight the Germans in the war.

"And look how that ended," said Erich. "Come on, we'd better catch up with him."

They found Pasha walking along the Spreekanal. He was with a female who was considerably shorter than five feet in height, and whom Dmitri had assumed to be a child. When she turned around, he saw the unlovable face of a woman several years older than his thirty-year-old friend. They were holding hands.

She recognised Erich but was glacial in response to Pasha's introduction of Dmitri.

"Jakoba is a contributing writer to *Die Rote Fahne*," explained Pasha. Dmitri knew the newspaper to be the official journal in Germany of the Communist Party, and therefore the mouthpiece of the Bolsheviks in Moscow. Neither the diminutive Communist activist, nor the Russian prince felt encouraged to develop their acquaintance further.

"Please give up this folly, Pasha," implored Dmitri, "and come to Paris with me."

"This folly!" exclaimed Jakoba. "This is no folly, Your Highness." She spat the noble title out as an insult.

"All right, this madness, then," replied Dmitri.

"Madness, it is," she interrupted. "It is a madness which has seen one of our friends hanged without trial today. They'll be coming for the rest of us in Red Orchestra. Running away won't protect us. We must fight."

"Don't you see, Mitya, the Nazis are trying to take over the thoughts and feelings of good people under the veneer of legality which Hitler's appointment as chancellor gives them." Pasha glanced at Jakoba for a sign that his words met with her approval.

"Surely you can do more to rally international support from Paris than you can from Berlin, especially now," replied Dmitri.

"Moscow is sending someone to help; they call him the phantom. He's part of the Communist International, and will organise our resistance," interjected Jakoba. Pasha often let her answer for him. "You can help too, help your friend. Our newspaper needs funds." Like all good revolutionaries, Jakoba didn't let her opposition to what Dmitri's ancestry represented stop her from asking for money.

"Yes, Mitya," said Pasha, "join us. Fund us and fight with us." His hopeful expression had no recognition that what he was asking: for Dmitri to help those who'd destroyed his own family.

Erich tugged at Dmitri's sleeve as two Nazi brownshirts came into view on the canal path up ahead.

"We're attacking the Nazi pubs in Prenzlauer Berg tonight, join us," suggested Pasha in a whisper, as he was led off by Jakoba away from the approaching stormtroopers.

"Come with Erich and me, Pasha." replied Dmitri to his friend. "We can leave tonight."

Erich encouraged Dmitri to walk on before Pasha could reply.

As Dmitri and Pasha were pulled away by their respective companions Dmitri saw a flicker of regret in his friend's hollow eyes.

"WHAT THESE Communists accuse the Nazis of is no different to what their own leaders in Moscow have done to Russians like me," said Dmitri. He was angry that he'd failed to rescue Pasha from danger.

He'd waited to continue the conversation until they were back in Winterfeldstrasse; even in the few hours he'd spent in Hitler's Berlin, he'd realised how dangerous it was to discuss political matters within the hearing of others. Dmitri had even started to develop Erich's habit, something referred to as *der deutsche blick*, the German look, requiring you to check over your shoulder before speaking, just in case you could be overheard.

"I know," replied Erich. He opened the front door to his townhouse. "I've had the same conversations with him, but Jakoba and Oskar always bring him back to their way of thinking."

"What *is* going on there?" asked Dmitri.

"An unholy ménage-a-trois." Erich double locked the door behind himself. "Oskar sells himself to men and women, and Jakoba uses the money he makes to fund her political activities."

"That's not just bohemian," suggested Dmitri, "it's obscene."

"I agree. And I'm not sure how Pasha fits into it all, but things must get cosy with all three of them sharing the one bed."

"And all that bunkum about someone called the phantom coming from Moscow to help their resistance efforts; it's fantasy, Erich, the stuff of fairy tales."

"The Left miscalculated, and know things look bad for them now. The Nazis got power through back-room deals, while the Communists here couldn't keep track of Moscow's changing whims."

"I wish you'd let me know about this sooner." Dmitri's tone was one of support for Erich, not a rebuke; he was glad to be able to share the burden of Pasha now.

"Did Frau Renfeldt not give you a room earlier?" Erich asked, seeing Dmitri's two suitcases still in the hallway.

"I can stay at a hotel," said Dmitri. He glanced at the sign in the window offering rooms for rent. "Or I can pay."

"Don't insult me," replied Erich, "although, you'll have to fall in with Frau Renfeldt's strict regime for the paying tenants."

"Even so, if you need the room for others, just say so."

"Let's see if there are any dinner scraps left over for us," suggested Erich, leading the way through to the kitchen. Dmitri doubted he could stomach more lung soup, but he followed Erich anyway.

"I will persuade Pasha to leave Germany, I promise," said Dmitri. Erich laid out some bread, cheese and wine. "You must come too."

"No, Mitya," replied Erich. "Hitler can't fix the mess Germany's become. He'll fail and be discredited. His followers are farmers, students, businessmen; he can't satisfy them all. I can wait for this storm to pass."

"You're beginning to sound as deluded as Jakoba," said Dmitri, helping to pour the wine. "It seems people keep underestimating Herr Hitler."

The two men sat down to eat, and Erich turned on a second lamp, but this did little to brighten the gloom.

"The people are seduced by Hitler," mused Erich. "The power of seduction fades with familiarity."

"Don't leave it too late to escape, as we Russians did back in 'seventeen, Erich."

"I have the measure of Herr Hitler," said Erich.

"Don't underestimate the Nazis as we did the Bolsheviks," warned Dmitri. "You know the story of the Chinese executioner?" he asked. Erich looked back quizzically. "There was an executioner of such great accomplishment that an audience gathered to witness his skill. He waved the sword in front of the crowd and the condemned man with several elaborate strokes to show how easily he could control the heavy weapon. No one was impressed, not even the prisoner who, frustrated by the ostentatious delay to his own death, taunted the swordsman. 'Get on with it, you fool!' the prisoner shouted to cheers from the crowd, who were beginning to side with the criminal. In response, the executioner laid his sword down on the scaffold and said to the cocky prisoner, 'Kindly nod, please'."

VII

DMITRI HAD slept longer than intended. The small room was chilly, and he was reluctant to put more than an arm above the covers. He mused on the challenge ahead of him.

With a little more persuasion, Erich could be convinced to leave Berlin, thought Dmitri. Erich had spent his youth and early adulthood as a nomad teaching music across Europe. To move once more, escaping persecution, wouldn't be too much of a change for him.

Pasha, however, was a different matter. Being in Germany, under the authority of a nation that killed his father, held a special significance for him that couldn't be replaced elsewhere. In the Communists, Pasha had found a cause. As the Nazis continued to consolidate power, the political motivation to stay and fight would only get stronger.

As abhorrent as financing the German Communists would be to Dmitri, if he could convince Jakoba that it was a ransom for his friend, she might be persuaded to release Pasha from her control and from his adopted political cause. Dmitri was much more comfortable with a straight fight. Saving Pasha might require the kind of tactical manoeuvring more suited to the father of his youth: Grand Duke Andrei, the cavalry tactician.

He washed in ice-cold water, noticing from a sign on the bathroom door that hot water for tenants was only available between seven and eight in the morning, and one hour again in the evening.

Arriving back in his bedroom, shivering in his vest, Dmitri noticed the envelope that had been slid under the door. Inside was a card, on one side of which was the familiar triangle symbol of Tao Chen's Triad gang. On the reverse was an address for a nearby café and a rendezvous time, which gave him only fifteen minutes to get there.

Without having time to find Frau Renfeldt or Erich to question them about the delivery of the message, he dressed quickly in warm clothes, and hurried out into the street to hail a taxi.

"HOW DID you find me??" asked Dmitri. The wizened figure of Tao Chen seated himself at the table on the café terrace overlooking the river Spree from Wilhelmstrasse.

"The Hongmen are likes rats, Mitya, one is never far away from you." The Chinaman had foregone his usual traditional dress and was wearing a double-breasted suit and trilby hat. The masculine clothes looked peculiar on someone with his feminine face, and made more incongruous by the high-pitched voice all eunuchs were cursed with. Nevertheless, his onyx eyes hadn't lost any of their defiant intensity since Dmitri had last seen him in Paris several months before.

Tao rested the knobbly walking stick, which helped support his crumbling spine, against the vacant third chair. He waved his hand and the young German couple sitting at an adjacent table, and a middle-aged woman with several shopping bags at another, left their tables to give Tao Chen and Dmitri some privacy. The waiter didn't come to clear their tables, as would normally be the practice. This was no ordinary café scene, but a stage that had been set by Tao.

"Your presence in Berlin at this time is fortuitous, Mitya."

"I'm here to help a friend."

"Indeed." Tao Chen took his time to sip the coffee he'd brought with him from inside the café. "A noble endeavour, Mitya." He dabbed his lips dry with a handkerchief from his top pocket. "But we have something more virtuous for you, not least to say more sporting also."

"Well, I do enjoy my sport," joked Dmitri. "But my friends are in need of my help, Tao."

"The Hongmen have been cooperating with the German Weimar government in their relations with China for several years. It seems Herr Hitler is keen to continue that relationship."

"What kind of cooperation?" asked Dmitri. He was displeased to hear that Tao's organisation was considering allying itself with Hitler's new regime.

"The Versailles Treaty restricts German military production and troops, but their engineers have expertise that China needs, especially since the Imperial Japanese Army invaded Manchuria two years ago." A loudspeaker recently mounted on a post near the café was playing Nazi announcements on a loop, and the repetition of phrases such as 'Germany is Awake!' was becoming distracting.

"And Germany gets what?" asked Dmitri. He was trying to tune out the propaganda blaring above him.

"Raw materials for her growing industry, Mitya." Tao took hold of Dmitri's hand to emphasise his point. "And we need that to continue. We cannot let the Nazis ally themselves with Japan."

"And you have something that only I can do, I suppose?" asked Dmitri. He finished his coffee.

"A German general supportive of the National Socialists will soon have in his possession some compromising documents about Herr Hitler. We want them, as an insurance policy."

"But how am I supposed to infiltrate the Nazis? I rather think they'd be suspicious of unsolicited overtures from an exiled Russian prince who has no connection with Germany."

"They need people, respected voices, to take their message back across the borders of Europe. Someone with the authority of a royal title would be a great unofficial ambassador for the new regime. And they might be happy to show a friend of theirs just how transformed the new Germany under Herr Hitler is."

"Friend?" asked Dmitri. "I have no Nazi friends." He whispered this, even though no one was in earshot.

"I believe Sable Nash is acquainted with a German industrialist who finances the National Socialists."

"You mean Heinz?" asked Dmitri, laughing at the suggestion. "He's just one of the men Sable likes to accept occasional gifts from. Anyway, she's in Paris."

"No, she isn't," said Tao. "I understand Miss Nash arrived in Berlin two days ago." Tao slid across the table a small photograph taken of Sable and Heinz crossing Potsdamer Platz by the traffic light tower that made it so distinctive. "She and Herr Langer have just announced their engagement. This rather gives us an opportunity, wouldn't you say?"

"I suppose it does," replied Dmitri. He was in disbelief that Sable would take such a step, and that he had no inkling of it. He and Anna had lunched with Sable before leaving for Kitzbühel the previous week; Heinz had not even been raised as a passing comment. "Am I being asked, or told to do this?" He was reluctant to help Tao support the Nazis, and determined not to put Sable in any harm.

"Everything is a choice, Mitya. I chose to save you from the Siberian labour camp. I chose not to tell you it was your sister I was sending you to Yalta to rescue last summer. We all make choices, you see?" Tao understood it is always better to guide a man through a door than to push him. "If you help us, Mitya, we can make sure your friend Pavel Darensky is safe."

"It's not just Pasha," said Dmitri.

"Sable is in far more risk now without you next to her than if you do this." Tao could tell his friend was genuinely worried. "I don't care for the Nazis, Mitya, I'm doing this for China, to stop the Chinese Red Army or the Japanese toppling the new Nationalist government."

Dmitri was considering the risk in accepting the job, not to himself, but to others; it wasn't clear cut.

"I thought this kind of sport was just your thing?" asked Tao.

A couple of teenagers emerged from inside the café shaking a collection box. They were dressed in black shorts and tan-brown shirts, with black neckerchiefs and leather woggles to fasten them. What set these boys apart from being scouts collecting for their jamboree, were the swastika armbands marking them out as Hitler Youth. Those café patrons who were reluctant to contribute soon changed their minds after the older of the young blond uniformed youths placed a hand on their shoulder.

The teenagers approached Dmitri and Tao Chen. Ignoring the Chinaman, the wooden box was thrust Dmitri's way. He paused, unwilling to fund the totalitarian cause, and prepared to resist the threats of two brain-washed children. Tao Chen's stick was thrust against his shin under the table. From the old man's expression, Dmitri knew there was a greater cause being put at risk by his insignificant gesture of defiance. He opened his wallet and took out a substantial collection of marks; this show of an apology satisfied the stormtroopers-in-training.

"A Russian prince can hardly be renting rooms in Winterfeldstrasse if he's to be taken seriously by the Nazis," advised Tao Chen, making no further comment about Dmitri's recklessness in risking their plan before it had even begun. "Has Herr Arnheim registered you with the police yet?"

"I don't think so," said Dmitri.

"Good. You'll need to re-stage your arrival into Berlin."

"This is beginning to sound like one of Doctor Goebbels' productions," replied Dmitri sarcastically.

"Will you help us, Mitya?"

Dmitri knew how valuable an ally such as the Hongmen could be, and he was worried about what Sable had gotten herself mixed up in.

"You knew I would when you sent for me, Tao."

IN LINE with Tao Chen's instructions, Dmitri collected his luggage from Erich's, and explained that he had something important to do, but would reveal more about it later. 'Whatever you hear about me, don't trust it' he'd said, and Erich had accepted that assurance, promising that Frau Renfeldt would also forget about their visitor if anyone should ask.

Dmitri caught a train out of Berlin to Leipzig, where he crossed platforms and boarded a train back to the capital. A message had been sent by Tao Chen's organisation, alerting the rail company of Dmitri's arrival.

Not more than twenty-four hours after disembarking at Anhalter Bahnhof, Dmitri found himself on a train pulling into the same station.

In contrast to the day before, a red carpet was rolled out to meet the first-class carriage. A brass band struck up the first chords to the Horst Wessel Nazi anthem as the carriage door was opened by a man wearing white gloves.

Stepping down onto the concourse, Dmitri was presented with flowers, and introduced to some senior train company officials. An official photograph was taken with the assembled dignitaries. Heinrich Sahm, the mayor of Berlin, stepped forward to greet the Romanov prince, followed by Dr Julius Lippert, Nazi reichscommissioner for Berlin, and the real decision maker in the city. All extended their right hands in a Nazi salute, but Dmitri couldn't bring himself to reciprocate.

"Good afternoon, gentleman," said Dmitri.

"It is an unexpected pleasure, Your Highness," replied Lippert. "Is this your first time in Berlin?" Dmitri wondered if this was a test, perhaps the Nazis already knew about his sham re-arrival, but he kept his composure.

"No, Herr Doctor," he replied. He watched to see if the Nazi's expression flickered with a reaction. Noticing none, Dmitri finished his sentence, "I was here three years ago, for the premier of Fraulein Dietrich's film, 'The Blue Angel'."

"Ah, yes, the story of a great man's downfall." Lippert's comment had a tone that seemed to hint he knew the truth about Dmitri being in Berlin and was warning the prince of the consequences to be anticipated. However, Lippert was the first Nazi Dmitri had met, so he entertained the possibility that they all had a certain mistrust of anyone who didn't automatically extend an arm as an expression of fealty to the Nazi Party.

"Do you already have a hotel reservation here in Berlin, Your Highness? Or perhaps you intend to stay with a friend?" The reichscommissioner's manners were impeccable, but the Nazi's eyes had the cold light of a fanatic.

"I always stay at the Adlon, Herr Doctor."

"Of course." Lippert waved for a porter to take charge of Dmitri's luggage. "I fear the international press may have already received notice of your visit, so there may be some newspaper men and photographers to contend with outside the station."

"I'm used to it," replied Dmitri. He realised that, in agreeing to Tao Chen's plan, he had just made it extremely easy for the Kitzbühel Bolshevik spies to catch up with him, assuming Jakoba had not already relayed his presence in Berlin to Moscow. Trapped between the Nazis and Communists, Berlin was soon to become quite tight he thought, as he waved at the flashing camera bulbs.

The mayor's Mercedes limousine was driven forward to convey his city's regal guest to the hotel only a short distance further along Wilhelmstrasse.

The Adlon had been designed twenty-five years before as a European rival to the Paris Ritz, built at the astronomical cost of twenty million gold marks. Behind its austere façade, there was a huge lobby, with a filigree-banister staircase and elaborate marble columns; it had the hushed silence that luxury could command and control. Unlike Erich's dingy townhouse, the Adlon was an explosion of light from the high-voltage bulbs supplied with energy from the hotel's own power plant. Whilst all of this commended the hotel, its opulence was not the reason for Dmitri's choice; Sable Nash was staying there, in a suite reserved for her by Heinz Langer, a man who had recently become her fiancé.

Dmitri had to befriend Heinz, infiltrate the Nazis, and rescue Sable. Tao certainly did ask a lot of his indebted Russian prince, thought Dmitri.

VIII

DMITRI WAS shaving in the en-suite bathroom, pleased to have enjoyed a hot bath at last, when he heard a muffled noise in the bedroom. He wrapped a towel around his waist. He instincts were now alert to danger.

There was no other door from which to escape, and the window was of no use, being too small and three floors up. He swirled another towel into a rope and wrapped his hands in either end for protection against a knife. If quick enough, he could get this towel around his attacker's neck, cross the ends over, and tighten in a choke. If he couldn't get close enough, even the simplest manoeuvre of throwing this towel in the assailant's face would provide enough of a distraction to get past him, assuming there was only one trespasser in his suite.

The door handle turned slowly.

Dmitri prepared himself for a fight.

Once the latch-bolt was clear of the door frame, the hinges creaked open.

"Mitya?" asked Sable, her voice whispering through the crack of the opening doorway.

"You almost got this contrivance firmly in the face, Sable." He unfurled the towel. "Why are you creeping around like that?"

"Well, that's a fine welcome!" She crossed her arms. "I wasn't sure if this was the right room."

"You got my message then?" Dmitri swung the towel around her neck and pulled her closer to him. She put both hands to his bare chest to stop him. "I forgot, you're a fiancée now." He let go of the towel.

"I'm sorry you had to read that." Sable leant her shoulder against the door frame and clutched the towel around her neck like a scarf. Dmitri returned to the sink to rinse off the remaining shaving suds. He looked at Sable in the mirror as he did so.

"I had intended to tell you," she said, "but Heinz surprised me, then brought me here to Berlin, and went straight to the press with it. I think his new National Socialist friends had something to do with the suddenness of things."

"You've changed your hair," he said. The platinum dye had been replaced with a sensible shade of brown, and the short hair fluffed to give it some bounce, where previously Sable had worn it close to her head slicked into a fashionable wave design that looked like snake tracks in sand.

"Heinz now says he prefers it like this."

"I don't," replied Dmitri. She threw the towel at him and retreated to the bedroom of Dmitri's suite.

"You're always rotten to me," she called back, whilst selecting a crisp white shirt from the wardrobe. When he emerged from the bathroom, she held it up to him by the shoulders.

"I'm never rotten to you," said Dmitri, turning his back to her and sliding his arms into the sleeves as she held on to the fabric. "I'm always truthful. You look lovely, but I preferred your Paris style, that's all."

"Why are you suddenly here instead of skiing?" she asked. "You're supposed to be in Kitzbühel until next week."

Dmitri turned and, with a serious expression, said, "I came to rescue you from making a huge mistake of course." She threw the trousers of his dinner suit at him.

"I love Heinz." She was too slow in saying this to make it sound as convincing as a new fiancée should be able to do.

"No, you don't," replied Dmitri.

"Because I can only love you, I suppose?" She raised an eyebrow in disapproval. "You're conceited, Mitya." Dmitri shrugged at the accusation.

"I'm not the one in a hotel room with a half-naked man," he said. He released the towel from around his waist and let it drop to the floor. He was now wearing just an unbuttoned dress-shirt.

"*That* doesn't work on me anymore, Mitya." She emphasised the first word of the sentence. He smiled and finished getting dressed.

"I imagine your father has something to do with this engagement," said Dmitri. The bellboy had done his unpacking, so he had to open several drawers to find everything required.

"Daddy's been putting pressure on me for a while, you know that. His financial situation in the States isn't getting any better."

"This is prostitution, Sable, and I'd happily tell your father that."

"I know you would." She poured herself a drink and brought another over to the dressing table. She took hold of Dmitri's shirt sleeve and helped with the platinum and sapphire cufflink. "But it's not like that, I really do love Heinz, he's serious and dependable."

"So's a dog, but I wouldn't approve of you marrying a miniature schnauzer either."

"The barking alone would drive me mad," she joked.

"Are we still talking about Heinz?" He took the cuff from Sable to fasten it more easily himself.

"Another?" asked Sable picking up both empty glasses. Dmitri nodded. "Anyway, I don't need your approval. And I don't need rescuing either."

"Actually, both of our fathers are responsible for us being in Berlin," said Dmitri.

"How is the grand duke, and Annochka?" Sable paused, considered the amount of whiskey already poured into the glass, then continued with a more generous measure.

"They're fine. Well, hopefully. But that's a story for later. An old friend from Petrograd is in trouble here, and Papa reminded me of my princely responsibilities." He fixed the collar stud in place.

"Perhaps Heinz can help?" Sable put Dmitri's drink on the dressing table as she looked at her reflection in the mirror, without the usual self-appreciation. "He's a man of influence."

"I know," replied Dmitri, "particularly so now."

"What does that mean?"

"Nothing. Just don't mention anything about my friend to him, please Sable. Trust me, Heinz' new associates would not help my old chum." He smiled to himself at seeing the three-fingers of whiskey in the tumbler.

"You mean because he's now a National Socialist?" she asked.

"When am I going to meet this fiancé of yours, then?" Dmitri ignored her question.

"He's waiting for me in the restaurant, you can join us if you promise to behave yourself."

"I never promise that, as you well know, my darling." She helped him into his dinner jacket. He sat down on the edge of the bed to put his socks and shoes on. "Shall I join you once you've changed for dinner."

"I am changed," she replied.

Dmitri regretted his careless remark, but the Sable he was used to always made sure her choice of gown and accessories for dinner was something truly extraordinary. She was only twenty years of age, and in Paris she'd always shown the carefree bravery of youth through her flamboyant outfits; Dmitri admired her greatly for such audacity.

But now her imposingly tall, slim, shapely figure was being hidden under a sensible and shapeless olive-green dress. Only her hands and an inch or so of décolletage were exposed. Even her fingernails were unpainted, and the make-up on her face muted; she was usually more elegant than this even when going swimming, he thought. The Jean Harlow-esque glamour girl had transformed herself into a German housewife.

"And less of the 'my darlings' around Heinz please," said Sable. "He'll soon be my husband, not you." Her rebuke was loaded with disappointment.

"BOTTOMS UP!" said Dmitri. He raised his snifter of cognac as a toast.

"May your soufflés always rise," replied Sable, also raising her glass. Dmitri was pleased to see that she still had some of her former jaunty assuredness, even if it had taken several glasses of champagne during the meal to coax it back out of her.

"Prost!" said Heinz seriously; he rarely found his fiancée's witticisms amusing.

Heinz was only just thirty years old but acted considerably younger. This adolescent behaviour was in

79

opposition to his prematurely middle-aged physical appearance. He had a handsome face, but his dark hair was already showing flecks of grey, and his stomach had the hint of a paunch. He flirted clumsily, like a teenager, with the waitresses, whilst showing Sable almost no attention.

The German kept the dinner conversation focussed on eliciting from Dmitri titbits about his former life as a Russian prince and asking him to confirm salacious details about his more recent playboy exploits that had been reported in the press. Heinz giggled excitedly to himself when Dmitri confirmed that most of what had been retold was true.

Dmitri tried to navigate the conversation to more political topics. He hoped to show such an interest in the new German movement that Heinz was financing as to elicit the support of Heinz in securing an invitation to General von Beckendorff's hunting party that weekend. However, Heinz stubbornly recalled more spicy gossip about Dmitri that he wanted confirmed as true. It seemed as if, knowing his fiancée was friends with the prince, Heinz had been preparing a list of questions in anticipation of such a meeting as this.

"Mitya, you must allow me to show you Berlin at night." Heinz had allowed himself to use Dmitri's nickname without asking permission. This was just one more thing about the young industrialist that Dmitri had taken a disliking to during the two-hour meal in the Adlon's extravagant restaurant. Dmitri could think of nothing worse than spending more time with Heinz that night having to talk about his own past dalliances, especially if, as seemed to be the suggestion, Sable was to remain behind.

"That's very kind, Heinz, but —"

"Let me stop you there," interjected the host. "Several of my friends in the Party are planning a belated celebration of Herr Hitler's chancellorship tonight, and I can't think of any better surprise than the inclusion of a world-famous playboy in our ranks." Dmitri remembered the purpose of his second arrival into Berlin; he had to do anything to make progress on Tao Chen's mission.

"As long as you don't introduce me to your friends quite like that, then I accept," he said.

Sable gave Dmitri a smile of thanks, mistaking his acceptance of the offer as an attempt by her friend to build a relationship with her soon-to-be-husband. Dmitri felt guilty at the deception but reflected that there had been some truth in him saying he was here to rescue her, even if she'd taken that earlier comment as a joke.

"They're gathering at the Kaiserhof Hotel, so we should make a move," suggested Heinz. Dmitri drained his glass of another large cognac; he would need many more to get through the evening.

THE MERCEDES limousines were queuing bumper-to-bumper along a street near the eastern section of Bismarckstrasse in the western Charlottenburg district. Dmitri knew the reputation of the club called 'Cuc-Koo', and had wanted to visit, although preferably not in the company of Heinz and two of his Nazi friends. All four of them were in the back of the chauffeur driven car, their faces squashed against the window waiting for the spectacle to begin.

The entrance to the club was an elaborate diorama of a traditional Alpine setting, complete with water wheel, chalet-style cabin frontage, and a patch of meadow with a real cow munching on the grass.

At ten o'clock the large hand on the clock dial clicked onto the hour mark, triggering a series of mechanical manoeuvres. Air being pushed through pipes and bellows resulted in the familiar sound of a cuckoo's repeated call.

The water wheel began to turn, and real water splashed over its paddles. Barn doors swung open, and pairs of young men and women in lederhosen and peasant skirts emerged to dance in the meadow around the disinterested cow.

There were hints that this pleasant pastoral spectacle hid something considerably more risqué inside the club. The dancing boys lifted the peasant skirts of their partners to reveal bare buttocks, and the girls slapped the tanned thighs of the young men in a suggestive fashion.

A collection of Berlin's high society emerged excitedly from their limousines and formed an orderly queue along the cobbled street. A door opened, above which a mechanical cuckoo emerged to flap its wings in tune with the distinctive bird calls. The patrons hurried through the door into the club, Dmitri and Heinz among them. At the tenth chime, the doors closed, the cuckoo retreated, the water wheel stopped turning, and the dancers swirled back into the barn. Only the cow was left, grazing in the now-quiet meadow, utterly indifferent to the commotion that had interrupted its routine.

The traditional German mountain scene of the club's exterior disguised a funhouse for hedonists inside, an excess completely in contrast to the bucolic depiction outside. The vast club, already full of patrons admitted at earlier cuckoo calls, was thumping with jazz music provided by a full band led by Zoot, a black band leader.

Each table had an illuminated number and telephone for anonymous table-to-table calling. In the space above the dancefloor miniature aeroplanes could be hired by guests to fly them around on wires. Along one wall, behind the buffet, a giant fish tank was occupied by two topless women wearing mermaid tails, swimming back and forth, able to hold their breath for an unnaturally long time. There was also a shooting gallery, acrobats, jugglers, and fire-eaters dotted around the venue.

"This is my favourite feature," said Heinz, pulling Dmitri by the sleeve of his dinner jacket over to a giant white sheet of fabric.

Starting at one end, a blindfolded Heinz rolled himself along the sheet, on the other side of which were naked men and women, their silhouettes backlit by bright lighting. They reached out to catch him, and Heinz giggled as the multitude of anonymous hands groped at him, propelling his body along the sheet. Heinz reached indiscriminately back against the sheet at whatever body parts his clasping hands found.

It was both childish and obscene, but something Dmitri couldn't avoid if he was to win the trust of Heinz and, with it, an invitation to that coming weekend's hunting party, where he would have access to the dossier Tao Chen needed.

Dmitri reluctantly stepped forwards onto the platform. He handed his jacket to an attendant, took a deep breath, tied the black silk scarf around his eyes, and then pushed himself against the sheet. At first it felt as if was he was going to fall straight through the barrier but, seeing the sheet give way, the naked men and women on the other side grasped at Dmitri's body, taking hold of him from his ankles to the crown of his head. He only had to keep his feet steady as the bony tendrils of human limbs swirled him. The force of their grasping propelled Dmitri along the sheet.

The effect was surprisingly powerful; a full body massage from dozens of unknown hands, some gripping firmly at his body parts, others lightly stroking him. It was a shameful public indecency, but also sensual and erotic. He let his own hands slide along the sheet, feeling a mixture of bony and fleshly lumps and bumps, some of which he could identify, others just human parts that could belong to man or woman. He was both assaulter and assaulted.

Cast out by grasping hands at the other end of the sheet, the removal of touch was as powerful as its application. Dmitri felt as if a promised orgasm had been brought to a climax and then left unfulfilled. He wanted to rush back to the start and go again. He took the silk blindfold off and blinked back into full, sober, consciousness.

"Fun?" asked Heinz; he had a mischievous grin on his face, as if he'd knowingly just corrupted Dmitri which, in a way he had. "You want to go again, yes?" Dmitri didn't trust himself to open his mouth to answer. "It's better if you don't," continued Heinz, "more powerful to leave yourself on the edge." He pated Dmitri on the shoulder.

"I need a drink," said Dmitri.

"Werner and Gustav are at table number forty-three, let's go." Heinz pressed a button on a console. Seconds later a miniature train arrived, being driven by a midget in a train driver's striped cap.

Feeling somewhat ridiculous sitting in the small train carriage, Dmitri was driven speedily around the obstacles of fully occupied tables. Heinz was enjoying himself, as an adult cast back into his childhood might. To Dmitri, Sable's fiancé was both juvenile and serious, but in the wrong ways. His sense of fun was childish and the humour too obvious, whilst the seriousness of his politics was dangerous, and his treatment of Sable parochial.

Both Dmitri and Sable were the opposite of Heinz. They shared a dry wit, a sense of frivolity applied to how they lived their lives, but backed by a serious commitment to friends, family, and individual freedom.

The men and women of the 'Cuc Koo Club' mingled at ease in their evening dress, knowing they were amongst equals. Berlin's high society was served by an eclectic mix of scantily dressed waiters and waitresses, some of whom were on stilts, others riding unicycles, and yet more walking on their hands, carrying trays of drinks on their feet without spilling a drop, managing to keep their customers supplied with over-priced alcohol. It was a captivating circus of pleasure-seeking.

Dmitri and Heinz disembarked from the mini train and joined their two companions at a table on the edge of the heaving dancefloor. One bottle of champagne was already turned upside down in the ice bucket to signal its emptiness, and the need for a fresh bottle.

Before Dmitri could enjoy the music, a style that he loved, the thumping jazz rhythms of Zoot's Band came to an abrupt stop.

Those on the dancefloor began to part as, through the centre of the sweaty mass, four black-uniformed SS officers walked towards Dmitri's table. He looked up at the mirrored ceiling and could see the crowd closing back in around the Nazis as they progressed through, like a zip being fastened behind them.

The semi-nude kick-line of dancing girls fell out of formation. Some of the girls put an arm across their chests, which were naked apart from tassels, feeling suddenly ashamed to be on stage with neither music nor dancing to explain their exposure.

The four Nazis paced purposefully towards Dmitri. He could feel beads of sweat gather across his forehead, and a dampness spread down his back. What had betrayed him so early in the charade, he wondered, and how would he get out of this tight spot?

IX

"THREE SIEG heils for Germany's new Führer!" exclaimed the Master of Ceremonies. He'd been pushed back on stage and was still trying to refasten his collar.

A waitress cleared the table adjacent to Dmitri's. Those who were occupying it gave the table up without an argument but received no sign of thanks from the Nazis.

The SS officers remained standing to accept the honour on their leader's behalf. Werner and Gustav did the same. Realising what was expected of him, Heinz also stood. Around the club some patrons jumped up enthusiastically, others hesitatingly, but many remained seated.

Dmitri had to decide what he would do.

As the first 'sieg heil' disturbed the unnatural silence of the club, uttered by barely half of the crowd, Dmitri felt his legs twitch. He stood up. He noticed the eyes of some seated customers looking upon him with scorn.

Those taking part in the chant then followed the lead of the SS officers, projecting their right arms in salute up in the air. Dmitri's three companions shot their arms out, hoping for some acknowledgment of their fast reaction from the SS officers at the neighbouring table. Albeit hesitatingly, Dmitri found himself doing the same.

He felt nauseous, staring at his projected arm as if it no longer belonged to him. Heinz turned his head fractionally towards Dmitri and let a half-smile emerge on his jowly face.

WERNER AND Gustav gave their apologies as all four left the 'Cuc-Koo Club'; it was now just past midnight.

"Don't worry," said Heinz to Dmitri as he closed the door of the Mercedes in which his two friends now sat. "We'll take a taxi to a little place I know about. I think you'll love it." He gave Dmitri a conspiratorial wink. "The night is still young, Mitya."

Heinz bade the driver stop their taxi on Friedrichstrasse, just north of Belle-Alliance-Platz in the working-class Kreuzberg district.

"It's best to walk from here," advised Heinz, "just in case."

"In case of what?" asked Dmitri. No answer came back. Heinz was studying the street signs to check he knew where to go.

As they turned down a passage, a middle-aged man stepped out from the shadows. He opened a raincoat to expose himself. Apart from a small bib of a shirt around his neck and two sections of lower trouser legs held up just above the knees by string, in between these gestures of clothing he was completely naked. Dmitri's obvious astonishment, not just at the unexpected nudity, but the ingeniousness of its concealment, resulted in a physical reaction from the flasher that showed he'd received the satisfaction he required. Heinz giggled at his companion's shocked expression.

Bodies half in shadow offered themselves indiscriminately to Heinz and Dmitri; both male and female voices quoted tariffs for lewd services. Further progress along the passageway resulted in prices dropping. Some of the faces that moved under the occasional dim lamp looked no older than teenagers. Some were still dressed in their school uniforms.

Rich men in tailcoats and well-dressed women cavorted openly with rough sailors, seemingly proud to display their perversions to those passing by.

It felt to Dmitri as if Heinz were Virgil to his Dante, leading him through the inferno and purgatory. The alleyway was like a dark woodland of vice inhabited by beasts, an under-gloom of sin. As it was for Dante, Dmitri felt himself at risk of losing the 'straight line' and descending into a 'low place': the Berlin underworld.

His Christian soul felt horrified at seeing sin for what it really could be. He suspected that Heinz was leading him somewhere that even the activities of the passageway would make seem tame. This was surely more than Tao Chen could expect him to witness, not least participate in, to secure an invitation to the hunting lodge for the weekend gathering.

"Are you ready to do and to dare?" asked Heinz, stopping by an open doorway.

"It's certainly a world with much to amuse, although perhaps less to admire," replied Dmitri, trying not to let his expression seem too disapproving.

"Don't be a flat tyre, come on," urged Heinz. Dmitri was horrified that Sable was engaged to a man who would consider such a place to be entertaining, but he followed the industrialist through the doorway anyway; he needed that weekend invitation.

If the 'Cuc-Koo Club' had been the acceptable face of Berlin's self-indulgence, then the cavernous 'Catacomb Bar' was its indecent sibling. Entry to the dungeon was by a creaking lift.

"It used to stop police raids apparently," whispered Heinz. "It mysteriously breaks whenever the police use it, while the patrons escape out of any number of other exits, so eventually they stopped bothering."

In the first cellar room there were gestures towards normality, albeit only an intimation of such. There was a pianist, his hair and moustache both respectably worn. He had a well-cut dinner jacket, clean white shirt, and silk bow tie; however, underneath the keyboard could be seen his muscular legs attired in sheer-black stockings. The feet controlling the piano's pedals were clad in black high-heeled peep-toe shoes. The tune being played was light and jolly, but the lyrics were coarse in the extreme.

The heat from the stoves in each section of the cellar added to the claustrophobia.

Dmitri passed a lady of advancing years dressed in a long chestnut-brown skirt that rustled as she moved in her chair. Her blouse and cape of lace and velvet was complimented by a black lace hat. She could easily be auditioning for the role of Lady Bracknell in a production of Wilde's famous play. As Heinz and Dmitri walked past, she carefully replaced her teacup and saucer on the table next to her and bowed her head in greeting to the two smartly dressed young men. Dmitri responded with a nod of courtesy, unsure why a refined lady should be taking tea in such a place. As they continued past her and saw the rest of the scene she was presiding over, it became clearer.

"That's Baroness von Straub," explained Heinz in a whisper. "The poor young man being sexually abused on the chaise-lounge by the two roughs from the river barges is her nephew."

"But why …" Dmitri started to ask for a further explanation, but feared the answer, so he stopped. Heinz seemed to be enjoying his new companion's horror.

"The rumour in Berlin is that the old lady makes him do it, and he thinks it's the route to secure his inheritance."

"Seems a high price to pay," commented Dmitri, turning away from the depraved scene, only to then have a man dressed as a woman slide past him suggestively, and fondle Dmitri's crotch.

"It is an exceedingly high price. Especially as I know the family's banker. The Baroness hasn't a pfennig left to her name, only debts."

Dmitri felt like a priest looking over the monastery wall for the first time, and not feeling encouraged to do so again. He'd been a playboy of repute for some years, and thought he'd had his mind broadened by the bright young circles he frequently mingled in, but none of that sexual freedom compared to what Heinz had shown him in this eastern district of Berlin.

This was not freedom, thought Dmitri; it was greedy and self-destructive. He'd met many confident, sexual, aggressive men and women, but there was a morbidity to what Berlin was now showing him that night. This was not an acceptance of one's natural longings, but a determination to explore way beyond those biological boundaries.

The Great War had encouraged the next generation, and he counted himself amongst them, to live for the moment, and enjoy the lives which those casualties of war, among them millions of young men, had been denied. The 'Cuc-Koo Club' was a place where this post-war group could fulfil that promise to their dead friends and siblings; however, the depravity of the 'Catacomb Bar' was not about living life to its fullest, but a place for those who had no faith in the future. It wasn't sexual liberation, but sex without gender; not creativity, but depravity; not bravely challenging what society endorsed, but a precarious freedom on the brink of collapse; not admirable living, but depressing hustling.

Dmitri wanted to leave but knew he couldn't do so yet.

The last room they came to was much larger than the others. Debutantes and dignitaries were mingling freely with criminals and perverts to the sound of jazz music in a fug of thick smoke. Dmitri and Heinz were escorted to a table by a waitress wearing a monocle and smoking a large cigar. She was dressed in a tailored trouser-suit and flat-heeled shoes; her small naked bosom was threatening to reveal itself from behind the lapels of the tuxedo jacket. A luminous yellow snake was wrapped around her neck, and her hair had been cut into a textured crop like that of a delivery boy.

"It has been said that Berlin is a city with no virgins," joked Heinz, casting his wide eyes around the room.

"I can well believe it," replied Dmitri, offering his companion a cigarette. Two young women cavorted with each other at the table next to him.

"What a great place, no?"

"Great for syphilis," said Dmitri, trying to sound humorous rather than critical. "But I thought Herr Hitler was against such places, surely these can't remain open for long now?"

"Indeed he is, but closing them might be unpopular with some." He poured Dmitri a large schnapps. "Look over there, for example. The man in the tailcoat is one of the fifty, so called because his membership number in the Nazi Party shows he was one of the originals to join. He's just been appointed as a reichscommissioner."

"The fat man with the greasy young boy?" asked Dmitri, looking through the fog of the cellar.

"The boy's Ludwig. I hear the commissioner pays Ludwig in heroin or cocaine to remain unwashed for him. The commissioner made him a special gift of a silver syringe after a whole month of Ludwig not attending to his personal ablutions."

"That's all rather unusual," replied Dmitri, deliberately understating his reaction to yet another unpleasant perversion.

"You can get anything that attracts you in Berlin," said Heinz proudly.

"What about respectable girls?" asked Dmitri.

"But surely respectable girls are not attractive, Mitya?" Heinz seemed oblivious to the implication this comment had for Dmitri's friend Sable. "Isn't this why you've come to Berlin?" asked Heinz. "For such nightlife?" It now became clear to Dmitri that the whole evening had been a childish attempt on the part of his host to satisfy what he mistook to be the renowned playboy's natural urges. Dmitri, the incorrigible seducer, had been mistaken for a pervert.

"Actually, I came to Berlin to find out more about Herr Hitler."

"Like a journalist?" asked Heinz. There was a tone of suspicion in his voice.

"I couldn't be that impartial I'm afraid. No, I'm more interested in what he stands for, regarding the Communists."

"Of course, I should imagine you Russian émigrés are rather in sympathy with that."

"I live comfortably in Paris now," said Dmitri. "I certainly wouldn't want to go through another revolution if the French government fell to the Communists. We must stop them on every front."

"Do you have any influence with the French government?" asked Heinz, an idea seeming to develop in his thoughts. He was an ambitious young man, keen to make a name for himself amongst his chosen brotherhood of Nazis, not least because his membership number was ranked in the thousands rather than the more estimable hundreds.

"Not me. My reported exploits discredit my political standing somewhat." They both laughed. "But my family certainly know the right people."

"In that case, my friend, you should join me this weekend at a party. You do hunt I assume?"

"Only women and wildlife," joked Dmitri.

"Well, I can promise plenty of both at General von Beckendorff's lodge."

"That's very kind of you," replied Dmitri. He stifled the urge to seem too pleased at having received the invitation he'd waited all evening for.

"But there'll be plenty of time for politics at the weekend. For now, you want to hunt some urban wildlife hey?" Heinz winked at Dmitri. The uncomfortable evening was far from over yet.

X

HAVING NOT returned to the hotel until five o'clock in the morning, it came as no surprise to Dmitri that the clock read just past midday when he woke up. A knock at the door had stirred him awake, and he didn't expect there to be anybody still waiting as it took him an inordinately long time to get out of bed, find his dressing gown, and stumble half-drunk through the suite. A second knock showed that the visitor was persistent.

"Who is it?" asked Dmitri. He was still cautious about possible Bolshevik assassins or kidnappers, even though Berlin under the Nazis should be a safer city than most for Dmitri.

"Room service, Your Highness," came the reply.

Knowing he hadn't ordered anything, Dmitri opened the door slowly. He braced himself to resist a sudden barge; he held a heavy candlestick in his free hand as a weapon, just in case. He relaxed upon recognising the face of the man dressed as a bellboy in a short jacket and crimson pill-box hat.

"New job, Emile?" asked Dmitri once the door was closed.

"This suited me better than the maid's outfit," replied the French spy.

"How's my family?" Dmitri found it surprising that the French spy would be in Berlin. He was worried there was bad news from Paris that could only be delivered in person.

"Safe in Paris," reassured Emile-Jacques. He poured coffee for them both from the room service trolley which Dmitri hadn't ordered. "I've asked the Sûreté to post more detectives to the villa. Marc is also going to stay with them for a while longer under the pretence of being your father's nurse and physiotherapist."

"Thank you, my friend." Dmitri accepted the coffee, adding an extra heaped teaspoon of sugar to the dark liquid. He offered Emile-Jacques a cigarette. "So, you've come all this way just to serve me coffee?"

"The French government needs a favour." Emile-Jacques paused. "In exchange for its help with your family."

"Everything comes with a price," mused Dmitri. Emile looked embarrassed.

"There's a document being exchanged at a hunting party north of Berlin this weekend," said Emile. "We'd like you to find out what it says."

Dmitri smiled as Emile-Jacques started to detail the mission, unaware that the prince was already engaged on the task for the Chinese Triads. He didn't interrupt the French captain from *le Deuxiéme Bureau* as he was interested to know what details the French had, and how these stacked up against those of the Chinese. Over a second cup of coffee, and with Dmitri beginning to feel the chill of the room as he was still dressed just in a robe, Emile-Jacques concluded his briefing.

Most of the details were the same as Tao Chen's information, essentially that the object was a dossier about something from Hitler's past in Austria. The additional piece of intelligence that the French had, was the identity of the man who would be bringing the dossier to hand over to General von Beckendorff. After the general had assessed its authenticity, the documents would then be taken to Hitler personally by the general. The courier was none other than the young German industrialist, Heinz Langer. Due to Heinz's recent engagement to Sable Nash, a known friend of Dmitri's, the French government was of the view that the Russian émigré prince was fortuitously well placed to assist them by intercepting the dossier's transfer to the Führer.

"How did Heinz come by it?" asked Dmitri.

"The Austrians put it up for sale, and Heinz, being both wealthy and keen to prove himself worthy to his new masters, out-bid the other interested parties, among them the Chinese."

"Does Sable know anything about this?" asked Dmitri. Sable's proximity to these matters concerned Dmitri greatly, and he felt angry that foreign governments were playing games, whilst innocents such as his American friend were getting caught up in dangerous contests of espionage.

"That's unlikely." Emile-Jacques' assurance seemed unconvincing. "It seems the engagement to Mademoiselle Nash gave Heinz an excuse to return to Berlin from Paris. We think he secured the document somewhere en route, most likely Zurich."

"And the French didn't fancy bidding for it on the open market to avoid all these cloak-and-dagger theatrics?" asked Dmitri.

"That would be too politically damaging," said Emile. "France doesn't want totalitarianism to spread, and this dossier would give us leverage to keep the Nazis in check. But if the German's found out we'd been bidding for it, that would have caused problems for the diplomats."

"But if I get caught, then you've never met me, and my French passport will count for nothing, I suppose?"

"I'm aware it's an unwelcome request." Emile drained the coffee pot, pouring two small cups for him and Dmitri.

"It sounds more like an order than a request," said Dmitri. "And with my family now held as hostages." Emile's expression of regret confirmed that the Russian was being given little choice in the matter. The possibility of the French protection being removed from the villa on the Bois de Boulogne remained unspoken.

"They were going to ask someone from the Berlin office to come and see you, but I thought it should be me. I am sorry to put you in this position, even if the Elysée Palace doesn't share my regret."

"I appreciate you being candid, Emile."

"I can't stay in Berlin. You probably want me back in Paris anyway."

"And if I get this dossier?" Dmitri stood up, tightening the robe around himself.

"One of our people here will contact you after the weekend. He'll identify himself by the codename of Napoleon."

"You've got to be kidding?" asked Dmitri.

"Why?" asked Emile.

"Well Napoleon isn't exactly a hero to us Romanov's"

"You beat him, though,"

"I suppose so," conceded Dmitri.

Emile-Jacques extended his hand as a farewell and said, "Good luck."

"I've never believed in luck," replied Dmitri, shaking the French spy's hand.

Emile-Jacques presented Dmitri with the hotel docket from the trolley for him to sign.

"I have to pay for the coffee as well?" asked Dmitri.

"It looks less suspicious that way I'm afraid," said the Frenchman. Emile-Jacques then opened the door and wheeled the cart out into the hallway. "But this comes free with the coffee." He handed a small box to Dmitri, who placed the signed receipt back on the cart.

"No tip this time," Dmitri said with a wink. "The coffee was cold, young man." He closed the door firmly.

In the red box Emile-Jacques had given him was a small Leica II camera. The black vulcanite textured covering and nickel fittings glistened like new. Also in the box was a ring to clamp on the lens and three legs to hold the camera steady when photographing documents.

Like with a gun, Dmitri always checked his equipment. He removed the bottom plate of the camera and made sure that a film was already loaded around the spool; he fired the shutter release, wound the film, and made sure it was ready for the next shot. A price tag for twenty-two pounds sterling was still in the box, indicating this had been on quite a journey to get to him in Berlin; the French really wanted to know what was in the dossier, he thought.

THERE WAS no reply to the calls he placed to Sable's room.

Once he'd bathed and dressed, Dmitri decided to go and see Erich. His initial reason for coming to Berlin was to help Pasha. Dmitri didn't want to leave for the hunting weekend without at least discussing a plan with Erich about how they could get their mutual friend away from the dangerous Communists he'd become involved with.

He regretted being cautious and asking the taxi driver to stop two streets away from Erich's townhouse on Winterfeldstrasse, as a heavy afternoon snow began to fall in what had been reported as an unusually cold Berlin winter that year.

By the time he reached Erich's address, the brim and crown of his homburg hat had an accumulation of snow in them. Cold flakes also infiltrated down the back of his shirt when he shook the collar of his herringbone tweed double-breasted overcoat. Erich opened the door himself; he hadn't shaved, nor was he wearing a collar on his shirt, much less a tie.

"No Frau Renfeldt today?" asked Dmitri. He was shown inside by Erich, who was clearly embarrassed at his own appearance, and hadn't expected visitors.

"I've sent her out of the city." Erich hung his friend's damp jacket on the coat-peg. "I wasn't expecting visitors."

"Sorry for not calling ahead." Dmitri was surprised by his friend's hostility. "I thought it best not to."

"I read about your re-arrival in Berlin yesterday, with some surprise."

"I'm mixed up in something important, Erich."

Erich brushed some papers off one of the thread-bare armchairs in his sitting room, which now seemed to double-up as his bedroom also. He indicated for Dmitri to sit down. He poured them both a whiskey; there were still dregs of a previous drink in Erich's glass.

"I can't say much," explained Dmitri. "I've been asked to help in an enterprise that requires me to form a closeness with the new power in Germany, temporarily."

The whiskey was warming. Erich refilled Dmitri's glass, even though it still had liquid in it, but this gave the host an excuse to replenish his own, which was once again empty. It was clear to Dmitri that the loss of employment had already taken its toll on his former tutor. He wasn't even sure that Erich was paying attention to his explanation.

"But I haven't forgotten my responsibilities to you and Pasha. I'm hoping my new alliance might give me some influence with this government, but there's no point if

Pasha can't be convinced to leave the Communists, and Germany."

"Pasha's in hiding, and Jakoba's been arrested," mumbled Erich.

"What happened?" asked Dmitri.

It seemed colder in Erich's damp room than out on the street. Dmitri tried to resist the urge to rub his hands together to warm them, knowing this would offend his host.

"The two of them tried to bomb a Nazi tavern."

"Tried to?" asked Dmitri.

"Jakoba was dressed up as a young girl, and her doll had the explosive inside. Pasha, pretending to be her father, was supposed to cause such a commotion about her running off that no one would notice Jakoba leaving the doll behind, which was set to explode after a few seconds."

Dmitri was horrified to hear the extent of Pasha's complicity in murder. Having met Jakoba, neither her physical appearance nor character caused him any surprise that she would be involved in such an endeavour.

"But it didn't work?"

"No." Erich sounded disappointed. "The Nazis were waiting for them. Jakoba was arrested, and Pasha escaped, but every uniformed man in Berlin is looking for him."

"Where is he?" asked Dmitri.

"Safe, for now." Erich was reluctant to reveal more to Dmitri, especially after having seen the picture in the newspaper of him flanked by saluting Nazis at the train station the day before.

"What can I do?" Dmitri wasn't sure how Pasha could be helped now. Being a member of the Communist Party, even protesting in the streets, were unwise activities for Pasha to have engaged in during recent weeks, but assassination was madness.

"Find a sympathetic Nazi to help," suggested Erich. "If such a person exists."

"That sounds a tall order," said Dmitri. "As a Russian, Pasha will be considered a foreign spy."

"Moscow is still sending their so-called 'phantom' to coordinate the resistance here in Berlin," explained Erich. "After that, every Communist will be hanged, whether there's cause to or not. Moscow and the Party here are both too stupid to see their folly; it's all over now, for the Communists."

"I'll get you out, Erich. That I can promise."

"I'm not going anywhere, Mitya. It's Pasha that needs your help."

The slush of melting, trampled snow in the street outside muffled the sound of the boots, otherwise Erich and Dmitri would have heard the approaching stormtrooper squad before the sudden hammering on the front door that made them both jump up in immediate reaction.

Erich looked at Dmitri with an accusatorial hostility.

"*Achtung! Achtung! Diese Tür öffnen!*" The orders shouted through the locked door, and banging of several fists, were accompanied by a splinter of wood cracking away from the frame as a ram was thrust against the lock.

"I can't be found here!" insisted Dmitri. His panic reassured Erich's mind that the raid was not part of Dmitri's new enterprise with the Nazis.

"You won't be," urged Erich in a whispered tone of forgiveness. "In the attic there's a hatch on to the roof. You'll have to scale across from there."

Neither man paused to exchange parting pleasantries.

Erich had already slid the first door bolt across as Dmitri topped the first flight of stairs. His knee was still sore from Kitzbühel, but that didn't stop him sprinting two or three steps at a time to the top of the townhouse.

He could hear heavy steps following him up the stairs.

He trod carefully across the beams in the attic, not wanting to make a misstep and crash through the ceiling into one of the bedrooms below. He would be unable to explain or fight his way out of this situation if found.

Despite concern for Erich, Dmitri's priority had to be getting the dossier from the hunting lodge, only then would he have any chance of influencing matters for those in Paris and Berlin who needed his help. The roof hatch came into view in the gloom of the cold cobwebbed storage space. He realised he'd left his overcoat and hat on the peg in Erich's hallway; it would now be a chilly escape across the rooftops of Winterfeldstrasse, he thought.

As he eased the exterior hatch up, a strong hand clasped his wrist from the other side. With one heave Dmitri was through the roof opening. Another hand gripped his throat trying to crush his windpipe. Dmitri was pushed against the chimney stack. His shoes slipped on the roof tiles.

"*Hör auf, Oskar!*" ordered Pasha. He was clinging on to the other side of the chimney.

The struggle loosened several tiles that slid off the edge of the roof and crashed down in the garden below, fortunately falling to the back of the house. The young man from the coal barges released his grip, allowing Dmitri to gulp at the icy air, refilling his lungs.

Both Pasha and Oskar were barefoot and dressed just in trousers and vests.

"You'll both freeze out here," said Dmitri in a whisper. He steadied himself by dropping a leg either side of the roof ridge. Pasha and Oskar clung to either side of the chimney.

"It's better than being shot in the warmth of the bedroom," replied Pasha. "The Nazis won't stay long anyway; they're just checking on anyone who's ever met me."

"They seem pretty sure of themselves to me." Dmitri didn't believe they'd break down a door without intelligence that Pasha was inside.

"That's their usual manner," said Pasha. Oskar couldn't join the conversation as he didn't speak Russian. Instead, he kept his eyes on the roof hatch, ready for any other unwanted visitor.

"Surely now you must see sense, Pasha. You have to leave this country."

"And hand them Germany without a fight, Mitya? No." He rubbed his bony hands together, but almost lost his balance. "Evil triumphs when good men do nothing."

"And the Communists are good men, Pasha? You have a short memory. Germany is not your country." Dmitri had to sit close to Oskar so that his whispered tones would be heard by Pasha on the other side of the chimney. There was something disagreeable about the young barge worker that made Dmitri feel uneasy that his friend was involved with people like him and Jakoba.

"Moscow's sending someone, things will change then," said Pasha. "Leaflets and political meetings are no good anymore, we need action."

"And bombs in dolls are better?" asked Dmitri.

"When they explode, yes."

"Don't do anything else so stupid again. I'll find a way to help you, Pasha."

"I saw the newspaper, Mitya. I don't want your help."

"It's not what you think, it's complicated. I'm still your friend, Pasha." Dmitri thought for a moment and allowed his mind to be cast back to happier times with his childhood friend, little orphan Pasha. "Do you remember when we played hide-and-seek in the Imperial Park?" asked Dmitri. "You almost got caught by the plainclothes policemen, but I came back for you." He paused. "I'm here for you now, Pasha."

"As I remember it, you only stayed with me until the tsar's daughters arrived, then you went off to the Chinese pagoda and kissed Maria Nikolaevna."

"We were in our Corps de Cadets uniforms, you and I, Pasha," added Dmitri. "And Masha said: 'I don't kiss soldiers', so I had to prove her wrong, didn't I?"

Dmitri took out all the money he had in his wallet.

"Take this at least, for now," he said.

Pasha moved behind the chimney, so he couldn't be seen. Oskar, more accustomed to taking money from men, reached across and snatched the notes. The force of his seizing it against Dmitri's intention almost destabilised the Russian prince. He waited for Pasha to re-emerge.

"Pasha, don't be childish," urged Dmitri. "Come out and talk to me."

Pasha remained hidden.

"Well, suit yourself then," said Dmitri as he swung his legs around so that he was facing in the opposite direction. He looked back, but could see only Oskar, who was greedily counting the money.

Dmitri edged carefully along the roof ridge sliding on his bottom. He used his legs and hands to maintain his balance across the width of the tiling and tried to limit the amount of snow he dislodged. He navigated around the next chimney, then crawled out along the ridge of a gable to reach the eaves, from where he could drop to the balcony of a neighbour's bedroom.

He was still not safe. If the occupier discovered him and raised an alarm, it wouldn't take long for a police officer to implicate Dmitri in the stormtroopers' raid at Erich Arnheim's house next door.

The downpipe from the guttering looked in need of significant repair, but it was the only piece of building furniture that Dmitri could use to scale down to ground level. He perched himself on the outside of the iron-work balcony and extended his foot across to the cast iron bracket fastening the downpipe to the wall.

The leather sole of his heavily scuffed toe-cap Oxfords slipped off the metal.

With an extra stretch Dmitri's foot took hold and he transferred some of his weight to that leg. The bracket immediately gave way. The rusted bolts disengaged from the wall. The grinding of iron seemed loud enough to raise an alarm. Dmitri froze with one leg on the loose bracket and the other still on the balcony.

No one came to investigate the unusual sound.

With one kick, he then brought both feet back to the balcony. The pipe would not hold his weight, so he would have to go inside the property. The bedroom was in darkness, and fortunately the French windows were unlocked.

Every careful step across the bedroom seemed to produce a new and deafening noise in the old house. The creaks and yawns echoed tauntingly, as Dmitri moved as stealthily as his jewellery thievery over recent years had trained him to do. There was a light on in the hall on the ground floor, but Dmitri was able to dart from shadow to shadow as he descended the three floors to the exit. The house was as cold as Erich's, but the walls of this property were still cluttered with framed pictures, and the hallway furniture seemed to be in positions the objects had occupied for many years.

The front door was locked.

In semi-darkness, Dmitri lightly fingered the objects on the nearest table to find a key. It was tempting to hurry due to the fear of sudden detection, but he kept his nerve and cautiously handled each object and checked inside each box or drawer. There was no key. This heartened him to the idea that perhaps the householder was not home.

The front sitting room was in darkness, but he dared not risk leaving the door open to benefit from the hallway light. Once behind the closed door, Dmitri inched his feet forward in the dark. His toes and legs felt for objects, and his hands were loosely held out ready to catch anything he accidentally dislodged. It took an age to traverse barely fifteen feet, but he made it to the window. He hid himself behind the heavy curtains in case someone should decide to enter the sitting room.

The street outside was busy with pedestrians. Two cars were parked outside Erich's address, and one man dressed in the black outfit of the SS was leaning against an open car door smoking a cigarette held in a lacquer holder. Dmitri couldn't leave until the Nazis had finished searching Erich's house, and when the street had less pedestrians paying attention to the terrace of townhouses.

The SS man waiting by the car had the demeanour of someone in charge. He clearly enjoyed being seen. His peaked black cap was worn forward on his head. His eyes peered out from underneath, wondering whether any pedestrian would dare to make eye contact with him; none did. The officer was middle-aged, and he had the stomach to prove it; the belt of his long black military-style overcoat held the bulge in place. Dmitri imagined the man would look much less intimidating out of his costume.

There was a sound from next door, and then Erich was roughly dragged down the steps. The stormtroopers on either arm didn't let his feet find their footing. His face had trails of blood streaked across it. Dmitri reached for the latch on the window and swung it back.

The SS officer stepped forward from the car and ordered that Erich be held upright. Unlike the pedestrians, Erich met the SS officer's gaze. The Nazi continued to puff on the cigarette holder. The SS officer curled his lip in a smile of malicious pleasure.

Erich spat a mouthful of blood at him. The fluid landed on the oak leaf insignia of the collar of the Nazi's overcoat. It dripped down onto the black leather shoulder belt that connected with his strained waist belt.

The small gesture of defiance was unexpected and took the SS officer by surprise. He stared at the trickle of bloody saliva and was without immediate reply to the insult. The guards dragged Erich to the car and threw him in the back seat. The SS officer was still in shock. The ash of his cigarette formed into a heavy column ready to break free. Erich was driven away.

Dmitri hadn't opened the window. His hand was still on the unlocked catch. Could he have helped, he wondered, feeling shameful for not having done anything.

The officer was called inside Erich's house.

With the street clear of Nazis, Dmitri realised this was his chance. He eased up the window and waited for two pedestrians to pass by on the street outside. When the moment came, he quickly fed his legs and body through the gap and dropped down into the street.

"*Polizei! Polizei!*" someone shouted.

Dmitri burst into a sprint away from the sound of the woman calling for help.

Not knowing where he was going, and looking conspicuous without an overcoat or hat in such wintery weather, Dmitri followed every narrow alleyway he found, keeping away from the main streets. He couldn't risk running at full speed, both his sore knee and the icy pavement risked him slipping, which would make his capture even more likely.

He collided with a young woman wearing a housemaid's uniform. They both remained on their feet, and Dmitri picked up the brown paper parcels tied with string that he'd made the woman drop. He apologised, stupidly doing so in French rather than German, and resumed his running pace.

He had a few coins left in his trouser pocket, the only money not given to Oskar and Pasha, but he couldn't risk hailing a taxi, as the driver would surely take special notice due to him being inappropriately dressed for the weather. He slowed to a fast walk, and found the canal, from where he could get his bearings. It would take too long to walk back to the hotel, and the first police or Nazi patrol he came across would undoubtedly stop him and take his details as he was so conspicuous, no longer being adequately dressed for the weather.

At Potsdamer Strasse a crowded tram heading north was just about to leave. Dmitri dashed out from the unlit side-street and boarded the trolley. When squashed amongst other passengers, his lack of an overcoat and hat made him less noticeable. He leant down to check through the window whether any uniformed men were following, but none had emerged from where he'd come, as the tram groaned into motion.

Dmitri made a promise to himself on the tram that he would do something for Erich when back at the hotel.

He entered the hotel by a side door into the interior garden. In the lobby, pretending he'd just come from his room, he asked the concierge if the correspondent for Le Figaro newspaper was in the hotel.

"I haven't seen Monsieur de Chautemps this evening, sir."

"Would you let me know as soon as he arrives please?" asked Dmitri.

"Where have you been?" interrupted Sable, having emerged from the lift.

"I was sightseeing," lied Dmitri.

"You'll dine with me tonight won't you, Mitya?" she asked. "Heinz has flown to Zurich on business."

"Does he often go to Zurich?" asked Dmitri. He remembered the details of Emile-Jacques' briefing from earlier.

"I suppose many people go to Zurich, don't they darling? Why?"

"I thought he was attending a hunting party this weekend." Dmitri was worried that Heinz' invitation had been disingenuous, or perhaps forgotten in the hours of drinking which followed it being offered.

"He's only in Zurich for tonight. You're joining us for the hunt, aren't you, Mitya?"

"Heinz mentioned that?"

"Oh yes, I heard him talking to some others about it before he left for Switzerland. He was pleased you agreed. Thank you, Mitya, I knew you'd like him."

"Your fiancée is certainly a man of many unusual qualities, Sable," replied Dmitri, being as diplomatic as he could. "Let me freshen up, and I'll join you in the bar." Erich had been arrested. It was almost inevitable that Pasha would soon be too. Dmitri was keen to ensure that at least Sable was safe.

XI

SABLE WAS waiting in a corner booth of the hotel bar. It took Dmitri a full lap of the room to find her. He'd never known Sable Nash not to sit at the very centre of every room she was in.

"Whatever are you doing skulking in the corner?" he asked.

"Shh," she hissed. She pulled at his jacket sleeve to bring him downwards into the booth. She slid across the seat so that his body hid hers. "Magda Goebbels is here, and Ilse Hess."

"So?" he asked.

"They're simply too awful, Mitya!" She hunkered down in the leather seat. "One's the wife of that little club-footed man that seems to be everywhere, and the other insists on being called 'Madam Reich Minister'. I much prefer Eva, but I'm not supposed to know about her."

"Don't you think we should say hello? Afterall, you'll soon be one of them." His comment was critical. The anger over what had happened to Erich encouraged him to redouble his efforts to bring Sable out of her association with Heinz and the Nazis.

"Heinz doesn't believe half their nonsense. He just joined the Party because he could see where things were going."

"What about you?" asked Dmitri, taking the opportunity to probe a little more, and discover just how far Sable had got herself involved.

"Herr Hitler's all right I suppose." She peeked around Dmitri's shoulder to check whether Magda and her entourage of Nazi ladies were still in the bar.

"You've met him?"

"Once or twice," she said nonchalantly. "He covers his mouth when he laughs, just like a sweet little girl. Don't you find that odd, Mitya?"

"It's not the strangest thing I've heard about him."

"What do you mean?" she asked. She moved Dmitri over in his seat to provide a better screen behind which she could conceal herself.

"It's some of his politics that make me more concerned than his mannerisms."

"Did you know he's a vegetarian? Isn't that peculiar?" she asked.

"I'm told he doesn't drink either."

"Well, that does it!" she exclaimed. "He must be a heel." She peeked out again from around Dmitri's shoulder. "I'll be so glad to have you at the hunting party, Mitya. Heinz is always leaving me with his German friends, and these Nazis are so humourless, don't you think?"

"They're comical, but perhaps not in the way you're thinking," replied Dmitri. "I need to talk to you about the hunting party, Sable."

"Shh, Mitya, I think they're going." Sable ducked back behind Dmitri and prodded his elbow for him to turn around and check for her.

Once the Nazi women had left, Dmitri was sent on ahead to the hotel's restaurant to make sure they hadn't moved in there, which they hadn't.

"Are you happy here?" asked Dmitri, hoping a softer approach might persuade Sable to listen to his advice. They'd been seated in the centre of the Palm Court restaurant in full view and hearing of the other diners. He had to steer the conversation back to the hunting weekend again.

"I think I'll get used to it," she replied, scanning the room in between glances at the menu.

"You'll live in Berlin once you're married?"

"Gosh no!" she exclaimed, horrified by the idea. "Heinz has a property near Essen, and from there I'll be closer to Amsterdam than here."

"Planning your escape route already?"

"And Heinz has agreed to keep the flat in Paris, so you won't be rid of me, Mitya."

"Damn," he curled his mouth and shook his head. "And I specifically asked Heinz to ensure that I would be shot of you!"

"Annochka said I should tell her every time you're beastly to me, so watch it. And you still haven't told me why you left Kitzbühel so quickly. Do I have to write and ask *her*?"

"The Bolsheviks found us there. Papa was attacked."

"Jeepers! I had no idea, Mitya." She threw her menu down. "How is he?"

"Fine. In fact, he surprised us all with his resolve. The French are protecting them back in Paris, where they're safe."

"I shall write a long letter to Annochka tonight." She opened the menu again. "I've no appetite now. Your poor father."

"We live in dangerous times, Sable."

"Is that why you're in Berlin?" She still hadn't received a satisfactory explanation from Dmitri about his presence in the German city. "Because of the Communists?"

"Broadly." He never lied to Sable, but she didn't need to know the details. "But I can't say much more."

"You're very brave. An incorrigible brute to girls like me, but brave with it." She poured him a fresh glass of champagne.

"I need you to be brave also, Sable. You're not going to like what I'm about to ask you to do." He took the bottle from her and finished serving them both. She looked up at him with wide expectant eyes, ready to obey. He took hold of her hand, which had turned suddenly cool.

"What do you need me to do?" she asked.

"Don't come with us to Schorfheide this weekend." He could see she was about to protest. "Tell Heinz you're unwell, and stay here in Berlin, please," he added quickly.

"But darling, you don't need to worry about the Bolsheviks getting to you there, they wouldn't dare. Just tell Heinz about it, and he'll make sure there is even more security. That's what's so marvellous about Herr Hitler, he hates communism too."

"You mustn't tell Heinz, or anyone, my darling. Please."

"That's silly, Mitya, I have to go. Heinz is expecting me." She pulled her hand away from Dmitri's. "He's going to be my husband; you can't keep me away from him."

"I know that, and there's more I can't tell you, but you must trust me, Sable."

"Is Heinz involved somehow?" she asked. From her tone it was unclear whether she was hopeful or fearful of Dmitri confirming a serious misgiving about the man who had so unexpectedly proposed to her, after having sought her father's permission, and with it an inability for Sable to refuse his offer.

"No. But nor do I want him to be."

"Then don't you go either, Mitya. Whatever it is, make an excuse and stay here in Berlin."

"I must go," he insisted, "but you cannot, Sable. Please promise me."

"I can't." She ran her hands up and down her upper arms. "All this is giving me the heebie-jeebies. I don't like it, Mitya."

"I know, and I am sorry, darling. But I must have your promise." He took hold of both of her hands; she seemed so fragile, and far from the throw-of-the-head flirty jauntiness he'd become used to from the young American he knew in Paris. "Please, darling."

"Your Highness?" They were interrupted by a straight-backed blonde-haired young man.

Dmitri turned around and dropped Sable's hands into her lap when he saw the black SS uniform of the man who'd approached their table and spoken to him. Draped over the SS guard's arm was a tweed overcoat identical to the one Dmitri had accidentally left at Erich's house.

"Yes?" Dmitri tried not to sound too cautious or guilty.

"SS-brigadeführer Vogel would like to see you, sir." The young, uniformed guard stood to attention waiting for Dmitri to stand up. Dmitri paused to reply, having been caught by surprise. He tried not to stare at the overcoat but couldn't help it. He tried to find some feature that marked it out as not being his. The officer held a hand out to his side towards the exit of the restaurant.

"He wants to see me right now?" Dmitri tried to sound imperious rather than humbled by the ill-omen the guard was carrying.

"I'm afraid so, sir. Kamerade Vogel has an important matter he wishes to discuss."

"But my guest and I were just about to eat." Dmitri was reluctant to have anything more to do with the National Socialists until the following day when he would leave for the weekend hunting party. He hoped they wouldn't want to make a scene in public if he insisted on staying where he was.

"My apologies, Your Highness. But the brigadeführer is waiting in the hotel director's office. I must insist."

"Oh, very well, then." Dmitri stood up, feigning irritation. He took his time to button up his dinner jacket.

"You are also to join us please, Fraulein Nash."

Sable was startled that the SS guard knew who she was. She looked as worried as Dmitri at the arrival of the tall SS officer, and the unusual interruption of their dinner.

She wondered if her having dinner alone with a man other than her betrothed had caused disapproval. Since being brought unexpectedly to Berlin by her new fiancé, she had already been reproached by him for her use of make-up, her flamboyant wardrobe, and even the height of her heels and colour of her hair. These had been things which seemed to attract Heinz in Paris, but in Berlin had become unacceptable to the ambitious National Socialist convert. When she asked him about this, Heinz simply added smoking in public to the list of banned habits, so she was reluctant to press the point further in case the prohibition list grew.

Dmitri wanted to hold Sable's hand to reassure her. He could see she was worried, but he thought it wiser not to. They followed the SS guard through the restaurant.

If he was about to be arrested, Dmitri was sure there was nothing to implicate Sable, as it was well known by Heinz that the two had been friends in Paris.

Other diners tried to catch quick glances. The foreign correspondents began scribbling notes in their pocketbooks; the sight of an émigré Russian prince and American socialite being escorted out of the restaurant of Berlin's best hotel by an SS guard made for an interesting headline.

"Your Highness, I apologise for interrupting your dinner. I'm Wolfrick Vogel." Dmitri recognised the SS officer from the raid at Erich's house earlier. He saluted Dmitri when the Russian entered the office that was usually occupied by the hotel's manager. Having no option to refuse, Dmitri responded with the same Nazi salute, which Sable also presented, albeit with little enthusiasm. Vogel reached for Sable's hand to kiss it. "And it's a pleasure to meet you at last, Fraulein Nash."

"The young gentleman said there was a matter of some urgency you wished to discuss with me," said Dmitri. He took out the tortoiseshell cigarette case and offered the cigarettes to the SS leader. Vogel slid one out of the retaining band and snapped the heels of his high boots together to signal his thanks. He fixed the cigarette in the lacquer holder. Sable waved Dmitri's offer of a cigarette away. Dmitri hoped his show of aristocratic hospitality might cast doubt on any suspicions the Nazis had of his real reason for being in Berlin and for visiting Erich's townhouse.

"Herr Langer called at my office on Potsdamer Strasse earlier today," said Vogel. "I understand the two of you enjoyed a night out in Berlin?"

"And much of the morning," replied Dmitri. He began to wonder what Heinz had to report that seemed so urgent as to have interrupted his trip to Zurich with a visit to the SS headquarters. Had Dmitri said something that led them to Erich's house?

"Quite so," replied Vogel. He leant forward to accept a light for his cigarette. His flabby jowls formed into rolls of fat as he inclined his chin downwards to the flame. "Herr Langer was keen to tell me about the generous offer of financial support you made for the Party."

Sable's shoulders released their tension, and she allowed herself a smile of relief. Dmitri vaguely remembered having made such an offer once he and Heinz had returned to the Adlon in the early hours of the morning. He'd wanted to make sure Heinz remembered the invitation to the hunting party and thought a financial donation would demonstrate his seriousness as a potential ally for the Party. It seemed he had been right, even though no cheque had yet been written, nor would it.

"I'm against communism, Herr Brigadeführer," replied Dmitri. He was hoping his concerns about the overcoat had been misjudged.

"Then, in the National Socialists, you have found a strong ally, Your Highness. The red pest will be crushed." Vogel formed his black-gloved right hand into a tight fist. "Germany is awake, Prince Dmitri."

"As I'm beginning to learn," said Dmitri.

"I have just come from a series of house raids in which we rounded up more of the vermin." Vogel puffed excitedly on the cigarette. Dmitri held his breath, waiting for an accusation from the SS commander. "I met with the Führer earlier this evening and informed him of your donation." The Nazi smiled. "The Führer has authorised me to bestow upon you the title of 'Protector of the SS' with his gratitude."

The tall SS guard who'd escorted Dmitri from the restaurant stepped forward with a diploma, on the top of which was written *'Meine Ehre heist Trueu'*.

Vogel saw Dmitri trying to read the German dedication and translated it for him, "It says: 'my honour is my loyalty', Your Highness, and I am pleased to present it to you."

The guard handed an SS pin to the brigadeführer, which Vogel attached to the lapel of Dmitri's dinner jacket.

"I'm honoured to receive this." Dmitri tried not to sound sarcastic. The diploma and badge seemed to him nothing other than an acknowledgment of having agreed to pay protection money, as one might to a local gangster who threatened to smash your shop window unless you contributed. As the SS leader shook Dmitri's hand, he swung the prince around and a photographer, who'd been standing behind them, stepped forward. The flash of the bulb blinded Dmitri. That was not a photo he wanted framed for posterity.

Dmitri considered whether this might present an opportunity to help Erich, somehow to explain that he'd been unable to reach his friend, who he was worried about. Perhaps, he thought, the SS officer would consider that helping a high-profile new ally was worth more than another prisoner in their cells at Spandau. It was a gamble that relied on the SS officer being a rational, reasonable man. Nothing so far indicated to Dmitri that was the case with Brigadeführer Wolfrick Vogel. If Dmitri's gamble didn't pay off, and if Pasha and Oskar had also been found at Erich's house, then he'd be under a level of suspicion that could sabotage him successfully getting the leverage he needed at the hunting party.

Dmitri posed for a second photo. He did nothing to help Erich, for the second time that night.

"I shall be joining you at the hunting party," said Vogel.

As the guard held open the tweed overcoat, for Vogel to slip his arms in, Dmitri saw his own initials monogrammed on the inside pocket. Fortunately, his tailor in Paris used the Cyrillic alphabet.

"We can talk some more then," added Vogel.

The sleeves of Dmitri's coat were too long, and the waistline too tight, for its new owner.

"I look forward to it," replied Dmitri. He pretended to read the text on the diploma scroll, and not stare at the monogram.

After exchanging the extended arm salutes that were becoming no less uncomfortable for Dmitri, the SS men left Dmitri and Sable alone with the photographer. The photographer placed his camera on the desk and went to the door of the office to check the SS had left. Dmitri saw his opportunity and emptied a glass of water that was resting next to its decanter on the desk over the camera, dropping the empty glass next to the ruined device, as if his arm had accidentally knocked it over. This had the added advantage of ruining the SS diploma that was also on the desk.

"I'm most terribly sorry," said Dmitri. Seeing the water dripping off his camera, the photographer was horrified. For good measure, Dmitri picked up the damp camera to hand it back to its owner and snapped open the back-cover to prematurely expose the film inside. "I fear my clumsiness may have accidentally ruined your camera. Please make sure you charge the cost of a replacement to my room, suite two zero six."

Dmitri pushed the damp diploma in the bin, and hurriedly led Sable out of the office by her elbow.

"Mitya, you did that deliberately," she murmured quietly. Her feet struggled to keep in contact with the marble floor as Dmitri accelerated towards the restaurant, keeping a tight grip of her arm.

"Let's finish our supper," he replied. "I suddenly find myself with a very bad taste in my mouth."

XII
Schorfheide, Germany.

DMITRI HAD hardly slept the night before, but he tried to remain awake on the drive to the hunting lodge.

Each time he closed his eyes, he saw a flash of his Cyrillic monogram inside the coat now confiscated by the SS commander. He then worried about the danger Erich and Pasha might be in and was reminded how close he also was to being discovered as a spy.

The correspondent for Le Figaro didn't visit the Adlon the night before, and a fitful night's sleep had settled Dmitri's mind that having Erich's arrest reported in the foreign press might be more of a hinderance than help anyway.

The dossier was now of greater importance than just helping the Chinese. The information contained in the file Heinz had would ensure the continued French protection of his family from the Bolsheviks in Paris. If Dmitri were to rescue Pasha and Erich from the Nazis he could only hope to do so with significant leverage, something the rumours of the dossier's contents seemed to imply it contained. He would be hunting earnestly this weekend, but not for wildlife.

His thoughts were preoccupied by the overcoat. Someone would eventually translate the Russian initials, and it wouldn't take long for the 'DAR' to lead back to Dmitri. He could claim it was a gift to his former tutor from some years ago, but if Erich didn't say the same under interrogation, then the discrepancy would condemn them both. Much worse to consider was the possibility that either Erich or Pasha had already implicated Dmitri under interrogation, and the shadow of suspicion was even now hanging over him.

As Heinz's chauffeur, leant to Dmitri for the long weekend, weaved the smooth eight-cylinder Mercedes limousine through the outskirts of Berlin, Dmitri, seated in the back, wondered if he was en route to a Nazi trap.

The huge city began to thin out as they drove through its outer limits. The grimy buildings, neon lights, and smog-laden air were replaced by a village of temporary shelters made of packing cases. These accommodated some of the half a million unemployed Berliners who'd been moved out of the tenement buildings, those which Pasha now lived in with those Berliners able to pay the rent through factory work.

Rag-dressed children begged by the side of the road. An elderly veteran from the Great War picked through the mounds of city waste dumped here. Crutches supported his only remaining leg. On the old man's left sleeve was a red armband with a black swastika motif.

Isaak, Heinz' chauffeur, seemed to deliberately slow the limousine as if he wanted his well-dressed passenger, who was being driven to a hunting party with high-ranking Nazi officials, to witness the destitution which those foreign visitors who only ever stayed in the hotels along the Unter den Linden rarely saw.

Dmitri sat forwards in the soft leather seat to show Isaak that he was not shying away from the reality outside the window.

From the chauffeur's name, Dmitri guessed him to have Jewish heritage, and wondered how Isaak had remained in the employ of Heinz Langer, a man seeking to raise his profile in a political movement that included a divisive racial policy. Dmitri considered telling the driver that he was just a guest, not a supporter, of the National Socialists. Then he looked down at the SS badge awarded the day before that he'd now pinned to the lapel of the replacement overcoat. He eased himself back in the seat and turned his face away from the window.

The arrival of the Brandenburg countryside was most welcome. The wintery forests of oak and pine reminded Dmitri of Grimm's fairy tales. The occasional wooden lodge along the road, and a castle turret spied through the skeleton forest, conjured up images of wicked witches, men with long-bows, and dwarves. This was the ancient Prussian hunting ground, preserved for German aristocrats, a preservation that it would seem the new nobility of National Socialists were keen to continue. The ice age had left a landscape of small hills and lakes surrounded by heathland, untouched woodland, meadows and moors. This protected beauty was just thirty miles from the grime of the city.

When the long coachwork of the Grosser-Pullman Mercedes-Benz limousine turned off the country road and swung through entrance gates, Dmitri was surprised to find that the hunting lodge was actually a grand castle of gable-fronted fieldstone with a staircase tower and gothic parapets. Flanking the main castle were a cavalier house for staff, and stables.

"*Wilkommen im Jagdschloss Albrecht.*" Dmitri's hostess greeted him. She had been waiting for him in the great hall, a room decorated with hunting trophies, examples of ancient weaponry, and sturdy wooden furniture. "I'm Hedda von Beckendorff," she added.

"Prince Dmitri Andreevich Romanov."

"I know who you are," she replied. Her tone hinted at flirtation. She bobbed in a shallow curtsey.

His hostess was in her mid-forties, with pencil-drawn eyebrows set slightly too high, giving her an unnatural fixed expression of severe surprise. He'd expected someone older, and with a touch more of the comely Brun-Hilda about her, rather than the light-eyed, slender-bodied vixen who presided over the airy castle. He would have guessed her to be Scandinavian rather than German. She had a cool force of regal authority to her. You could conquer a country with a woman such as Hedda von Beckendorff, thought Dmitri.

"My reputation often precedes me, Frau von Beckendorff." He kissed her hand in greeting. "But I am quite well house-trained."

"That is a shame, Your Highness. All the ladies will be most disappointed."

"I find that I'm growing into my pedigree," he said.

"Whereas I have a fondness for strays, Prince Dmitri." A housemaid appeared at the foot of the grand staircase. "The general will be receiving his guests before dinner in the sitting room. Lutzia will show you to your room, and your luggage will follow presently."

"Thank you for your hospitality," said Dmitri. "I'm aware of being a late addition to your plans."

"I always embrace change," she said, quickly adding, "Particularly when it's for the better."

AFTER AN extravagant dinner, the men were smoking cigars and drinking cognac in the drawing room.

The muttering of male voices was broken by the sound of a jazz record from the gramophone as the ladies filtered through from the dining room. The general's eighteen-year-old daughter, Trude, started to wiggle to the

124

beat of the record she'd chosen to play, a selection made deliberately to offend her parents' conservative guests.

"I put an advertisement in the Volkischer Beobachter to try and find one," said Dr Julius Sauber, the rotund middle-aged doctor who had been seated next to Dmitri at dinner, and who'd followed the Russian prince through to the drawing room afterwards.

"An advertisement?" asked Dmitri. He was trying to keep up with the tedious doctor's conversation.

"Yes, an advertisement, for a wife."

"Oh, I see. Yes, that sounds a good idea."

"I shall read it to you." The doctor took out a pair of small round glasses and looped them over his fleshy ears. Dmitri was more interested in finding out where Heinz was, as Sable's fiancé had yet to arrive at the castle, than listening to Dr Sauber. "Here: 'Fifty-year-old doctor. Male children wanted with young healthy Aryan virgin. She should be undemanding, thrifty, used to heavy housework, broad-hipped, with flat heels and no earrings.' What do you think, Prince Dmitri?"

"I have seen many such girls in Berlin, Herr Doctor," said Dmitri.

"Then send them my way, sir!" The doctor laughed uproariously at his own joke.

Trude von Beckendorff began moving towards where Dmitri was sitting. Her steps matched the beat of the music. She was the opposite to that described in Sauber's advert. There was a feline, seductive danger to the general's daughter, albeit that of a kitten who hadn't yet grown into a cat. She'd stared at Dmitri during dinner with an unrepentant petulance, making her annoyance at being seated so far away from him quite clear to everyone there. Whilst her Delilah-esque beauty meant Dmitri would be nervous about letting her cut his hair, she was a welcome escape from the wearisome doctor.

"I'll freshen our drinks, doctor." Dmitri took the two glasses over to the table where a selection of decanters had been lined up. His manoeuvre took him away from Trude. He was amused to see her change direction to join him at the drinks table; it was a mistake that a seductress more experienced in the game would not have made.

"Are you ignoring me, Prince Dmitri?" Trude asked.

"I doubt any man's ever ignored you, Fraulein."

"Is one of those for me?" She leant back against the table, her body close to Dmitri's, as he poured two fresh glasses of brandy.

"No." He softened the reply with a smile, then crossed back to Dr Sauber, and handed the German his drink.

Dmitri didn't retake his seat but rested his drink on a bookcase shelf and took out his cigarette case. Trude sidled along past the bookcase, running her finger gently over the spines of the books. Dmitri held the cigarette case open for her.

"I don't think I shall," she said, turning her back on Dmitri. She picked up the glass of brandy he'd put down and took a sip. The strength of it caught in her throat, but she tried to disguise the shock. She turned back around and said, "But I should like to dance." She removed the cigarette from his lips and placed it in an ashtray, but the music then stopped as the stylus had reached the end of the record.

"What a shame," said Dmitri. He swallowed what remained of his drink and reclaimed his cigarette.

Trude dashed to the gramophone to flip the record over, but her mother reached it first, and the older woman closed the lid, snapping shut the catch.

"Good!" thundered the general from his seat, where he had been deep in serious conversation with Brigadeführer Vogel. "I've heard quite enough of that negroid decadence." Vogel raised his glass as a toast to Hedda for her decision to stop the jazz music.

"I believe we have an accomplished pianist with us," said Hedda, addressing the room.

Panicked guests looked from one to the other, fearful that the hostess had been misinformed about one of them and their musical abilities.

"It's been reported that Prince Dmitri knows his way around a piano," said Hedda, adding, "Amongst other things."

The hostess was wearing a floor-length two-toned gown, the black skirt of which swished across the thick carpet as she approached the piano. The low-cut upper half of the dress was in ice-white fabric, with two straps across her back that showed off the decade's new erogenous zone; Hedda von Beckendorff had clearly chosen to ignore the conservative fashion protocols of her husband's new affiliates. Her auburn hair was brushed back from her forehead and styled high with hair lacquer, giving her tall body even more height.

She lifted the keyboard cover of the walnut-veneer Louis XV style Steinway, and rested an arm on the scalloped edge, waiting for Dmitri to accept the invitation.

"I know a ditty or two," said Dmitri. He took his invited place on the padded bench in front of the ivory keys. He tested the piano's sound with one or two notes, then adjusted himself comfortably on the seat.

His hands found the keys as he began to play the adagietto from Mahler's fifth symphony. It was a melancholic, almost funereal piece. Dmitri had chosen it for that reason, as a subtle reflection of his true feelings about being a guest at the hunting party. The loneliness, struggle, and yearning of the composer was powerfully heard, especially when played with the rich tones of the solo piano.

As the piece progressed, the music bringing all guests into its power, the remaining mumblings of conversation in the drawing room stopped. All attention was on the pianist and his instrument.

Dmitri was just quick enough to snap his hands back as Brigadeführer Vogel approached the piano and slammed the cover down on the keyboard, bringing the spell of the haunting music to an abrupt end.

"Mahler was a Jew!" bellowed Vogel.

Dmitri had to check himself, and not fling up the cover to commence a frenetic rendition of a Mendelssohn symphony, demonstrating the beautiful legacy these men had left their German ancestors, philistines who now sought to prevent such music being played. But he could not react, other than to feign apologetic remorse.

"The new Reich will not permit such inferior music to be played anymore," continued Vogel. "German nationalism will no longer be undermined by Jewish culture."

From across the room Dr Sauber clapped in agreement. Several of the ladies tapped their rings against their brandy glasses or coffee cups to show their conformity with Vogel's view.

Dmitri lifted the keyboard cover and commenced a rendition of the most frivolous, comic folk tune he could recall, the sound of which intentionally, if subtly, mocked the group's barbaric ignorance. He then feigned modesty and refused the calls from Hedda for him to continue the entertainment once he'd stepped away from the instrument; he would not play the piano under censorship.

General Terrill von Beckendorff navigated his way over to Dmitri, who'd chosen to isolate himself by browsing along the stacks of the general's bookshelves, and with his back to the group. At seventy-two-years of age, he was the image one would expect of Prussian military authority. He wore his dinner suit like a uniform. His grey hair was kept cropped and his moustache intimidatingly formidable with its elaborate handle-bar curves. His back was still straight enough to intimidate any foreign army commander seeing him through field-glasses across a battlefield.

"You've noticed the picture?" said the general, in a tone which made any question sound like a statement. Dmitri was staring at a depiction in oil of soldiers in the trenches of France during the Great War, a piece that didn't seem to fit with the Italian Masters hanging on the other walls.

"It's certainly unusual," said Dmitri politely.

"A Rubens was there before." The general looked at the amateurish painting illustrating the recent war, as if bringing forth the memory of what it had replaced. "This was a gift from Herr Hitler. He painted it himself." The general gave out a low growl. "This was the only frame that fitted it."

"You must be honoured to have the new chancellor of Germany's art on your wall, general?"

"I'm surprised my wife hasn't shown it to you already," he said. "She usually wastes no time in doing so with new visitors."

"Perhaps she'll show me around later."

"I'm glad you're here, Dmitri Andreevich." The general's use of Dmitri's patronymic showed his familiarity with Russia. The omission of Dmitri's royal title revealed the general's intolerance for such pomp. "Did you know that I was in the Crimea when it was a German protectorate in nineteen-eighteen."

"That was a long time ago, general." Dmitri despised the Bolsheviks, but the Germans were close runners-up in his dislike. It had served Berlin's purpose to support the revolution and bring down the Romanov dynasty to force Russia's exit from the war. Once that had been achieved, the Kaiser judged his interest best aided by a restoration of the monarchy in Russia that he'd help depose, but under a German puppet of their choosing this time.

"I remember your parents well," reflected Beckendorff. "Were you also in the Crimea?"

"Only to dig a grave." Dmitri knew he had to remain on friendly terms with the German host for the sake of the mission, but his right fist was clenched, ready to throw a punch at the man who shared blame for what had happened to his mother.

"It's shameful that so many members of your family died." The general was still staring unappreciatively at Hitler's painting.

"Murdered, you mean General," said Dmitri in a tone of reproach.

A loud noise in the sky above the castle ended, thankfully, the conversation that Dmitri knew he could not continue with his German host if he was to keep his temper in check.

"Light the beacons!" bellowed the general. Guests started to rush outside to investigate the disturbance.

Dmitri remained behind and fixed himself a fresh drink. The mention of the Crimea had been an unwelcome jolt to his memories, and the complicity of Germany in his family's tragedy stoked his hostility to them.

He'd been told by other émigrés in Paris about those months of the German protectorate in the Crimea. The Bolsheviks in Moscow feared a German attempt to restore the monarchy, so Dmitri's godparents, the tsar and tsarina, were executed with their children.

The tsar's brother, Germany's primary choice as new monarch, had already been murdered in Siberia; and, in Alapaevsk the day after the tsar was killed, a grand duke and duchess, as well as five princes of Russia, who were Dmitri's contemporaries, were buried alive in a mine shaft. That could so easily have been the fate of Dmitri and his whole immediate family. Reports from the locals in Alapaevsk, relayed to the White Army that soon arrived, said that most of the Alapaevsk Romanovs were merely injured by being thrown down the mine shaft. They could be heard singing hymns as the assassins filled in the grave.

Dmitri blamed the Bolsheviks and the Germans.

None of these details had yet been discussed with his father in the months since the grand duke's mental recovery. Anna had asked, but Dmitri told her it was best she didn't know. Nor had Dmitri spoken to his father about witnessing his mother's assassination and having to bury her with his bare hands by the side of the road in Yalta. The grand duke had fallen into his thirteen-year catatonia when he was told the news of his wife's death, so everyone in Paris had judged him not yet strong enough to know any more details, and Dmitri's father had not yet asked for any.

When Dmitri did join the other guests on the steps of the castle, he saw the servants hurriedly lighting two lines of fire beacons along the hedge-lined formal strip of lawn. Above them in the night sky the guests could hear the engine hum of a Deutsche Luft Hansa Junkers.

The small mono-wing aircraft came in for a low pass, then the hum of the engine roared as the plane climbed and turned to line up for its landing.

Everyone except the general clapped as the landing gear of the corrugated metal duralumin plane touched the ground. It bounced back up then re-joined the snow-dusted grass, the rear-skid eventually also making contact with the ground. It came to a halt just meters away from the terrace, it's single propeller gradually coming out of its rotation, and the engine spluttering to a stop.

"That's ruined my lawn," grumbled the general. He returned inside now that he was satisfied the landing he'd been told to expect hadn't caused any further damage to his family's estate.

Heinz emerged from the cabin, but there was no ladder for him, so he had to jump down. He lost his footing. A member of the house staff picked up the dropped briefcase, which Heinz immediately snatched back. Dmitri knew why Sable's fiancé was so keen not to be parted from the document holder.

He was glad Heinz had now arrived, even thought that meant Dmitri had to take the risk of getting access to the dossier Heinz was guarding so closely.

"How was the journey?" asked Dmitri, once everyone had reconvened in the drawing room.

"Intolerable." Heinz took a glass of brandy in one gulp. "It's the mail plane, so we had to stop at Stuttgart, Erfut and Halle. My bones are all broken." Dmitri refilled his glass, noticing Heinz had brought the briefcase with him into the drawing room. Heinz had propped it against the piano, keeping it in view. "At least you're here anyway, Mitya."

"It's a shame about poor Sable," said Dmitri. "She was terribly unwell when I left earlier today. I wondered whether I shouldn't stay there with her." Dmitri was glad of providing Sable with an alibi to her make-believe illness that he'd forced her to lie about.

"A suite at the Adlon makes for a fine hospital. You and I have much to achieve this weekend anyway." Heinz seemed little concerned by his fiancée's absence.

"Have we?" asked Dmitri.

Heinz was called away by Hedda before Dmitri could clarify the statement; he took his briefcase with him.

Dmitri waited for Heinz to return, as the other guests went off to bed.

When he was the last person left, the arrival of the staff to clear up indicated it was also time for him to retire. He would have to come up with a plan to view the dossier the next day before it was sent on the onward journey to the Führer.

XIII

DMITRI WAS an excellent hunter, but the new clothes
he'd had to buy in Berlin the day before, as he'd packed
for skiing not hunting, gave the impression of his being
an amateur. The chamois gun pad stitched to the right
shoulder of his tweed shooting jacket to protect the cloth
from recoil damage was pristine. His riding breeches and
knee-high field boots were similarly unscuffed. His
collarless plaid shirt, cravat, and shepherd's checked flat
cap were the only used items of his ensemble, but they
weren't enough to set him amongst the seasoned hunters
in the group.

The ladies, who weren't hunting, passed around trays
of schnapps to the men dressed in field-coats with
pockets large enough for cartridge shells. The general was
wearing a Tyrol style felt hat, attached to which was a
large brush of wild boar hair pinned to the cord hat band.

Heinz arrived late. He was dressed in tweed with a
grouse helmet that was reminiscent of the Scottish hunts
Dmitri had participated in.

Hedda intercepted her daughter to reach Dmitri first
and offer him a schnapps. She was dressed in a muskrat
fur coat with a suede belt that showed off her narrow

waist. A bright cockade was attached to the chenille brim of the hat covering her auburn hair. Trude huffed from a distance in disappointment.

"*Waidmannsheil!*" bellowed the general in traditional hunt greeting.

"*Waidmannsdank!*" replied the guests in thanks.

One of the gamekeepers brought Dmitri the gun that he was being given to use for the day's boar hunt, along with a bag of bullets and pair of field-glasses. Unfastening the crocodile skin gun-slip, Dmitri was surprised to find that he'd been lent a very fine Merkel rifle with classic arabesque engraving on the side plates, under carriage, and trigger guard. The weapon had a high lustred wooden stock of oak with exquisite graining. The ornamentation and craftsmanship suggested this was a display rifle rather than hunting weapon, perhaps a decision taken after seeing Dmitri's new clothes; the general clearly expected the Russian prince to find himself part of the theatrics, rather than the action, of the hunt.

Trude was given the honour of blowing the horn to signal the commencement of the hunt. In reply to her call, 'Horrido!' the men replied with, 'Joho!'. After three repetitions, everyone roared a mighty, 'Hussassa!', and the group headed towards the forest, leaving the women behind to prepare the castle for the post-hunt meal.

The snow-dusted ground was hard underfoot, which meant the boar would be even faster in the chase. The keepers divided the group up and directed them to different positions amongst the forest of leaf-less oak and pine trees.

Dmitri was paired with Dr Sauber.

"The treibjagd are very good here. They'll drive plenty of game our way," said Sauber. The German had a Rigby Mauser rifle slung over his shoulder. He offered Dmitri a flask of whiskey.

"Do you hunt here often?" asked Dmitri.

"Frau von Beckendorff is an old friend, and a generous host. Are you a keen hunter, Your Highness?"

"I have some experience with deer, but not boar." It was Dmitri's habit to insist people call him by his first name. However, with the Nazis he decided not to give that encouragement.

"Then do you mind if I take the first shot?"

"Be my guest," replied Dmitri. "I doubt we'll run out."

The distant noise of the beaters prompted Sauber to aim his rifle towards a small clearing between two clusters of trees. The beaters fell silent, and there was a peculiar quiet in the forest, before a rumble could be heard.

A sounder of boars dashed between the trees running right to left across Sauber's path. The German was taking too long, thought Dmitri. Sauber brought one pig into his sights, then followed it across the clearing. He took the shot too late, hitting a tree rather than the animal he'd been aiming for. It was then too late to find a new target.

"*Sohn einer Hündin!*" swore the doctor.

"To be correct, Herr Doctor, I think it was probably the son of a sow, not a bitch," joked Dmitri, taking some small pleasure in the Nazi supporter's failure.

They heard the second call of the treibjad beating the game in their direction. Sauber didn't stand down but checked his rifle as if preparing to try a shot again.

"Your turn, Prince Dmitri," said the German as he relaxed the gun in his hand and stood back. He'd deliberately waited until the rumble of the boar could be heard, to handicap Dmitri with no preparation time. But the Russian didn't need any.

As the first brown-coated boar appeared to his right, Dmitri swung the ornate rifle up to his shoulder. The sounder looked to be of sows and their young. They were running in a panic through the forest.

Instead of finding one pig and following it, Dmitri could read the game and foresee their reactions to the landscape.

The first shot hit one of the small twenty-kilogram frischlingen; the bullet striking in the upper front third of the piglet's body. The animal rolled over in the snow on the spot, whereas a heart or lung shot would let it run on a short distance before collapse, which would affect the path of the others behind it.

Dmitri found a new target, a large bache, and fired. He felt the hot metal shell case being ejected by the bolt action as it hit his hand.

The Russian prince repeated the fluid motion of his weapon and body working as one, without pausing to acknowledge his second clean kill.

Aim, fire, swing, reload, aim. All in one movement.

By the time the huffing and screeching pigs had run out of range, four animals lay fallen in the forest in front of Dmitri, some with their legs still twitching as the bodies succumbed to death.

There was no more talking between Dmitri and Sauber.

The German, completely focussed on his surroundings now, took his place for a second attempt. He only managed to kill one animal.

For Dmitri's second turn, the Russian sent three more of the bulky animals crashing through the snow of the forest which had been the medieval fighting ground for Germanic tribes over hundreds of years but was now the scene of his victory.

The final shot of the hunt was reserved for a four-hundred-pound boar. The protruding canines on its plow-like head signalled the majesty of this king of the swine in the Brandenburg forest. The impressive boar was running at full speed through the trees. It took two bullets to bring it down, but the second of Dmitri's shots sent the mighty beast flipping over, a spray of blood following its body through the air. It regained its legs, stumbled a few more steps, then fell down dead.

As Dmitri and Sauber caught their breath, watching the field of battle to see if any of the fallen pigs regained their footing, a bullet was shot from behind them. It smashed into the trunk of an oak tree barely an inch away from where Dmitri was leaning.

Sauber dropped his rifle and fell to the floor on his face, his podgy little hands clasped over his head for protection.

Dmitri quickly crouched behind the trunk. With his rifle raised and ready he brought his breathing under control. He watched unblinking for any sign of approaching danger.

Once the beaters arrived to collect up the carcasses, Dmitri reasoned the danger had passed. Only then, as Sauber tried to disguise his show of cowardice with concern for Dmitri, did they notice the blood on Dmitri's upper sleeve. A fragment of bark shrapnel from the tree had lodged itself in his arm. Dmitri pulled the wooden shard out of his bicep without flinching and made his way back to the castle where the general was waiting.

"I can't think how this might have happened," said the general.

The other guests emerged from the forest to join them. Steins of beer were being handed out, and the dead animals lined up ranked according to each guest's tally.

"I really don't want a fuss made," replied Dmitri. "I'm sure whoever accidentally let their gun go off will be horrified with themselves. I don't care to make that any worse." He suspected the shot had been no accident, but it didn't serve his purpose in getting access to the dossier to initiate an investigation which might reveal his true motives for being at the gathering. "I'm happy to keep this between us, do you both agree?" The two men nodded. Dmitri wrapped a clean handkerchief given to him by Sauber around his wound. "I'll say I fell, and if the culprit wishes to apologise to me privately later, then so be it."

"Such chivalry does honour to your noble lineage, Your Highness," said Sauber.

"The great-grandson of a tsar!" exclaimed the general in agreement.

As Dmitri had killed the most, he was presented with a hunting dagger by Hedda von Beckendorff. The twenty-inch weapon had a stag-horn grip, top filial of oak leaves, and a cross-guard of a hunting motif. He also had the honour of acknowledging the end of the shoot by performing the ritual known as the last bite. Choosing the large boar that he finished his shoot with, Dmitri snapped a branch in two. He placed one half of the branch in its mouth to signify the beast's last meal, and the other he kept for himself, sharing that meal with his kill. Another branch was lain across its coarse-haired body. A brush of hair was clipped from the carcass, and the end tied with twine, for Dmitri to wear in his hat.

When back in his room, washing and changing for the celebration dinner, he heard a quiet knock on his door. Hedda von Beckendorff was waiting in the hallway.

"I'm a terrible nurse," she said. "But ..." She held up a collection of medical supplies and shrugged her shoulders.

"Then it's lucky I'm not mortally wounded." Dmitri opened the door wide. He was just wearing his riding breeches. He showed her the gash on his arm, which he'd just tried to clean, and which was trickling blood from the re-opened wound. Hedda pushed her way into his room and closed the door behind her.

"But I do need to improve my bedside manner," she whispered.

"Then we could both do with the practice." Dmitri slid the ruffled taffeta collar of Hedda's evening gown over her powdered shoulder.

XIV

THE GENERAL'S wife attended to her hair in the mirror. She was naked. Dmitri, still lying on top of the crumpled sheets, rummaged through the medical supplies which had been discarded earlier when he'd pushed her back on the bed.

"You've made a shocking mess of my hair," said Hedda. She stepped into her dress. "Come and zip me up."

Dmitri padded casually over to her. She watched him in the mirror. He slowly eased the zip of her gown up, then kissed her neck.

"Don't," she said, pulling away from him. Dmitri always enjoyed seeing the flirtatious lust turn so quickly to guilt, once the married or engaged woman realised they had to return to their husbands or fiancés. He worried about the day when that guilt didn't arrive, because then he knew there was a lingering responsibility. But Hedda was just like the others, the release on the bed had also released him from any further obligation.

He applied a double bandage to his arm, ensuring no dabs of blood would stain his evening shirt, then dressed, and made his way down to dinner.

He didn't see, as Hedda also hadn't, that Trude was hiding in an alcove along the hallway. She'd been watching the Russian's room for nearly forty-five minutes. Since seeing her mother enter, and not quickly leave the young prince's room, Trude had been crying.

The celebration dinner was a more formal affair than the welcome meal had been the previous evening. Some of the men were in evening tails with silk lapels, and all the women were bejewelled.

Dmitri wondered whether any of the glistening ornaments had once belonged to his family. He'd heard stories of tsarist diamonds sewn into the hems of the suits worn by German businessmen returning from trips to Moscow and wishing to keep the purchases away from the customs officials of the Weimar Republic. In between polite conversation with the elderly wife of a Polish count, who'd been seated to his left, Dmitri started to memorise what pieces were worn by which lady, just in case a future escapade to Germany might prove necessary after consultation with the grand duchess back in Paris about which pieces needed rehoming.

Once the staff had made sure all guests had a full glass, Trude stood up at receiving a signal to do so from her father. The general tapped his wine glass with a knife to bring the room to silence, then his daughter delivered the grace. However, it was unlike any such grace Dmitri had heard before.

"Führer, my Führer, sent to me by God. Protect and preserve me all my life. You have rescued Germany in our hour of need. I thank you for my daily bread. Stay with me, never leave me. Führer, my Führer, my faith and my light." As the eighteen-year-old progressed through this rendition, her voice became more fervent. By its conclusion, her chin was held high with pride and deluded belief. It sent a shudder through Dmitri, realising such a girl had been indoctrinated so easily.

Many of the guests, unfamiliar with such a grace, were unsure how to follow the verse. Hedda stood quickly, as did Brigadeführer Wolfrick Vogel. They both extended their right arms in salute, which the other guests then stood to copy.

"Sieg Heil!" called Frau von Beckendorff. Only her husband didn't participate; he stood to attention but said nothing.

The dinner had been a chilling inauspicious start to an evening that only got worse for Dmitri.

The men withdrew for cigars and brandy. Vogel was drunk, and full of self-pride at the demonstration of solidarity with the creed he'd supported for so many years, but which had, until recently, been a small movement in Bavaria led by a comical former army corporal from Austria.

"He's a failed teacher," explained Heinz, managing to sit with Dmitri after a day being separated. He gestured towards Vogel, who was declaiming on Nazi philosophy for his assembled audience. "Sacked from multiple institutions until the National Socialists took him in and gave him a job."

"That explains his keenness to educate *us*," replied Dmitri, trying not to sound too cynical, as he hadn't yet got the measure of the depth of Heinz' loyalty to the new governing party in Germany. Sable had indicated Heinz's conversion from a traditional monarchist party to the National Socialists had been opportunistic rather than ideological. This had been supported by some of the comments made during their long drinking session together after escaping the moral fleshpots of the Catacomb Bar, but Dmitri was still cautious.

"Blood and soil!" exclaimed Vogel to his audience. "Germany was like Sodom on the eve of destruction until Herr Hitler came to power. The Germans of Bismarck can never become docile sheep. Hitler will wipe away the shame of Versailles and foreign occupation, we must exert our force on the world once again. The death-knell has sounded for those who oppose us. We shall beat the red front to a pulp!"

"The National Socialists recently built their first school," whispered Heinz to Dmitri. "Would you believe it doesn't even have a library?"

"Violence! Strength!" cried Vogel, continuing his monologue of slogans. "Racial superiority, and obedience are what Germany needs. Am I not correct, General?" He looked to their host for support, but the general just held out his glass for a servant to refill. Mistaking this gesture for a salute, Vogel felt emboldened to continue. "One People. One Reich, One Führer!" He too raised his glass.

"He's right about Sodom, though," suggested Dmitri to his companion.

"Vogel's right about a lot of things," replied Heinz, "but not everything." He took Dmitri's empty glass. "Another?"

"Herr Langer, do you agree with me?" Vogel stopped Heinz just as the young businessman tried to sidle past to reach the drinks table. He immediately wished he'd stayed on the sofa and waited for a servant to refresh the glasses.

"Yes, Kamerade Brigadeführer." Heinz stepped quickly around Vogel, but the failed teacher grabbed the industrialist's forearm and brought him back into the centre of the room.

"And yet you employ a driver who is a Jew?" Vogel's tone changed from rallying leader to that of a prosecuting barrister.

146

"Isaak is only seventeen years old. His father was chauffeur to my own father," replied Heinz in a feeble-voiced justification.

"Have you no other defence?" demanded Vogel.

"I wasn't aware I was on trial, Brigadeführer."

"We are all on trial, Herr Langer." Vogel released Heinz's arm. Almost immediately he changed his mind and decided the matter was not settled. "In fact, let's have a trial. You —" He pointed towards one of the staff. "Bring the driver here, to us."

"Really, Herr Vogel, let's not ruin a good day's hunting," said Dmitri, unsettled at how the evening was going.

"You, Prince Dmitri, recently became a protector of the SS!" Vogel was so drunk as to have lost all sense of restraint, but he was a high-ranking National Socialist, and knew this made people fear him. "We are all soldiers." The general shifted uncomfortably in his chair, but he offered no argument against the Nazi now holding court in the drawing room.

Minutes later, the houseguests were assembled on the terrace; the women had joined them. In front of them was Heinz's young driver, the seventeen-year-old Isaak. He'd been brought from his bed in the staff quarters. He was dressed in a collarless shirt, trousers held up by braces, and had slipped unlaced boots on for the walk across from the old cavalier house. The general, complaining of illness, had remained inside the castle. Dmitri, having been rebuked by Vogel when calling for restraint, placed himself at the back of the group; he couldn't speak up again, as the attention drawn to him would risk his mission.

"My name is Isaak," replied the young man when asked by Vogel to identify himself.

"Your full name, Jew!" demanded the SS officer.

Realising this was an interrogation, Isaak paused before answering. He had to decide whether to humble himself before the Nazi officer or show defiance to the insult.

"My name is Yitzhak Aaron Meyer, and I am Jewish." He chose boldness.

"Hah!" Vogel turned to address his audience. "Langer has been employing a Jew, allowing these foreign tenants in Germany to take good jobs away from our own German race, while their racial comrades abroad agitate against us." Some of the group shook their heads disapprovingly at Heinz, who had been pushed forwards to stand in judgement with his driver; others in the group dropped their heads in shame at not stopping the unpleasant drunken spectacle.

Dmitri remembered what Heinz had told him about Vogel losing several teaching jobs, this explained the SS officer's hatred of a Jew like Isaak occupying a well-paid job as chauffeur to a wealthy industrialist. He had no interest in witnessing the young man's humiliation, and realised this would be a good opportunity to sneak back into the castle and rummage for the dossier. As he turned to leave, Trude looped her arm through his. She pushed her body against his, keeping her thigh pressed against him. He was trapped.

"We must clean up our territory without mercy!" declared Vogel, waiting for dissention. None came. Heinz stood with his head bowed and his shoulders slumped. Isaak held his head high. Despite the cold, and being dressed only in shirtsleeves, the young chauffeur didn't shake.

"The Jews deserve what's coming to them," said Hedda von Beckendorff. She stepped forward to stand with Vogel as judge of the Jewish chauffeur. "We are doing mankind, tortured by Jewry for thousands of years, an inestimable service."

"One cannot afford sentimentality in a situation such as this," added Dr Sauber in a quivering voice, wanting to be sure Vogel heard his support, but nervous about speaking up.

"The Führer is the untiring pioneer and spokesperson for the radical solution the situation demands," said Vogel. "We must rid ourselves of this destructive plague in the body of our nation!"

"I'm going to bed, Herr Langer," said Isaak, having heard quite enough of the house guests' offensive racial abuse. He now felt himself released from any duty of obedience or servility his lowly rank in Heinz Langer's household gave him. Heinz nodded his agreement, wanting to bring the unpleasantness to a swift conclusion, but not feeling strong enough to do so himself.

"You see how the Jew thinks himself master of the German?" bellowed Vogel to the group.

"I am also German, sir," replied Isaak. "I was born here."

"You see how the existence of our blood and our soil is at stake!" Vogel dragged Isaak back by the arm, as the young man started to walk away.

Outraged by the chauffeur's show of insolence, Vogel produced a small-calibre gun from the pocket of his dinner jacket. A murmur of surprise was gasped amongst the group. Dmitri unhooked Trude's arm from his, and stepped forward to see more clearly, feeling he now had to intervene, but knowing to do so would expose him. He thought of his family back in Paris in danger if the French withdrew their protection, and of Erich in Nazi custody. He stopped himself.

"Party comrades!" called Hedda, turning to face her guests. "We must disregard sentimentality. Herr Doctor Sauber is correct." The middle-aged doctor dropped his shoulders and tried to creep backwards into the group of guests.

"Herr Langer." Vogel threw the small gun out to Heinz so that he could keep a firm grip on Isaak; however, the driver was now standing defiantly still, facing his accusers, he would not run away. Heinz stared at the gun lying on the damp grass. "You are the bearer of the will and the honour of the Party, of this political order, an instrument of the Führer. Pick up the gun."

Heinz didn't move.

Dmitri tensed. Memories of his mother's execution in front of him years before overwhelmed his rational thoughts; he knew he had to do something but, as with the Red Army thirteen years before, he felt incapable of stopping the inevitable. His body shivered. This was not his fight. Heinz, the man who would marry Sable, had to end this madness himself. He was a millionaire industrialist who he had the ability and financial influence to stop the National Socialists, not just tonight, but thereafter.

"Are you too weak?" asked Hedda "You swore an oath." She bent down, picked up the gun, and pressed it into Heinz' hand. He refused to take it from her but didn't resist her curling his fingers around the weapon; she held them in place and raised the pistol to Isaak's neck.

"We have a duty to the Führer," said Vogel, "with whom our nation has been blessed only once in two thousand years, not to shrink back from our duty."

Heinz couldn't look at Isaak, but the young man stared at his employer, unblinking and unafraid.

"Party comrades!" Vogel raised his voice to be heard by the whole group. "You see how dreadfully narrow the way between Scylla and Charybdis is, between what's right and wrong." The guests were silent and unmoving, frozen in fear and anticipation.

"The Jews will destroy us if we don't defend ourselves!" called Hedda. She looped Heinz's forefinger onto the trigger.

"Obey your orders, Langer!" barked Vogel. "Obey your Führer!"

Heinz screwed his eyes closed.

Dmitri, jolting himself out of the inertia that memories of his mother's death had brought on, pushed himself forwards through the guests, but his path was blocked.

Heinz twitched his finger.

The gun clicked but didn't fire.

Heinz opened his eyes and looked at the faulty weapon. He'd made the awful commitment, but nothing had happened. He pressed the gun against Isaak's neck and pulled the trigger again.

The gun clicked a second time without firing.

Heinz pulled the trigger rapidly repeatedly, hearing nothing but small clicks, pushing the weapon into Isaak's neck.

"Hah! Well done, comrade!" laughed Vogel. He reached into his other pocket, took out a handful of bullets, and threw them in the air like confetti. "You honour the Führer." The guests followed Vogel's lead in a hesitant round of applause.

The guests quickly retreated inside to warm themselves with brandy and coffee.

"Take the car, and leave for Berlin now," whispered Dmitri to Isaak, pushing him towards the staff building. The young driver hadn't yet come out of his defiant trance-like state. "Go now, tonight." urged Dmitri.

Heinz was leaning with his eyes closed against the stone balustrade of the terrace, unable to look upon the world which would now be forever changed for him.

Coming to his senses, Isaak's expression acknowledged what Dmitri had told him. He looked around to make sure there was no one else lurking in the half-light from the castle's drawing room and hurried off into the safety of the darkness beyond.

Dmitri walked up the steps, not stopping to console Heinz.

XV

FORTUNATELY FOR Dmitri the guests all went to their rooms for an early night, unsettled by what they'd witnessed. They were also unwilling to remain in the company of Brigadeführer Vogel and Frau von Beckendorff, in case they should be called upon to prove *their* loyalty to the Führer.

Also to Dmitri's advantage, Heinz remained in the drawing room drinking, allowing Dmitri the opportunity to search his bedroom.

He found the briefcase, but no dossier.

It was possible that the general, upon hearing what had happened on his own terrace, might bring the hunting party to an early close the following morning, and with it Dmitri's access to the dossier, which the general presumably now had taken possession of.

He had to find the dossier before the morning.

Dmitri waited in his room for two hours until he was sure no guest would still be awake. He left his shoes behind and crept to the general's study on the ground floor of the castle. The moonlight shining through the un-curtained windows in the grand hall helped him to find his way in the dark.

The study was full of memorabilia from the general's past military campaigns. Dmitri switched on the small torch that had served him well on the many past escapades to steal back the Romanov family jewels sold by the Bolsheviks to foreign aristocracy. But he was not in the study to find jewellery. If caught, he would have no moral defence for this theft. Having brought the camera and document tripod Emile-Jacques had given him, there would also be little plausible excuse he could give for being in the study with such equipment in the middle of the night.

This was not thievery, thought Dmitri, it was espionage. And the punishment wouldn't be arrest, it would be execution. The terrace outside had been cheated of a death earlier, but it might yet have a blood sacrifice if Dmitri was discovered.

He found what he was looking for in the top drawer of the general's ornate wooden desk.

Dmitri squashed sofa cushions along the gap at the bottom of the door to the hallway and checked that the heavy curtains were fully closed. Only then did he risk switching on the main lights in the study, which would be needed for photographing the documents.

He skimmed through the first page of the papers in the brown file, just enough to prove to himself this was from Austria, and that it related to Adolf Hitler's past. The general had even attached to the inside cover a scribbled pencil draft of a letter summarising the contents of the file; who had seen it, namely Heinz Langer; and the price paid to the Austrian spies to secure it. One hundred thousand gold marks was enough to produce an entire play at Berlin's best theatre, but it was a price Heinz could easily afford if it secured him favour with the new chancellor of Germany, reasoned Dmitri.

Dmitri fixed the three legs to the lens and attached the camera to this. He clicked shots of each page. When he'd finished, he took a second set just in case.

He put his ear to the door to check whether any noise could be heard in the hallway. Hearing none, he felt safe enough to be even more thorough. The final page of the dossier had a list of witnesses in Austria who had contributed evidence for the compilation of the file. Dmitri wrote these details on a slip of paper, reasoning that, if the camera film should have to be discarded, the French and Chinese could at least make their own enquiries about the file with those who'd provided its contents.

Feeling emboldened by the ease of the task so far, he allowed himself a few moments to skim through the rest of the paperwork. The information was so valuable as to warrant not just the price paid, but the tight chain of communication from Heinz, to the general, to the Führer himself, circumventing all other Nazi Party officials.

The revelation it contained was worth the price.

Dmitri quietly closed the door behind himself. In semi-darkness of the hallway he paused, checking around and listening for any noises. Having come from the light of the study a few seconds earlier, to the darkness of the hallway, his eyes hadn't adjusted properly to the blackness otherwise he might have seen the shadow of someone else in a doorway further along the corridor.

Feeling pleased with his success, Dmitri crept silently along the hallway. Only when at the grand staircase, where he could believably claim to be restless from a lack of sleep to explain his presence out of his room, did he relax his body. He relaxed his shoulders and lengthened his stride into a more comfortable walk.

Behind him, still in the darkness, the flame of a cigarette lighter momentarily lit up the face of the person who'd watched Dmitri tiptoe shoeless out of the study.

The lighter flame was extinguished, leaving behind it the orange glow of a burning cigarette.

DMITRI WAS late for breakfast, deliberately so. He hoped to avoid polite conversation with the uncivilised houseguests. He'd also taken an extra precaution of hiding the roll of film from the camera where discovery would be unlikely to incriminate him. The French and Chinese had been right to ask him to carry out this mission, thought Dmitri, feeling proud of his success.

The morning schedule included a dove shoot, after which Dmitri would make up an excuse to leave for Berlin. The afternoon and evening had been left deliberately free, and he suspected this was to discuss political matters. Heinz had said upon his arrival in the airplane that there was much to do that weekend, and it hadn't seemed as though he was referring to the shooting of game. The final day promised riding to hounds and a farewell lunch. If Dmitri could leave after the morning's shoot, he would spare himself a further twenty-four hours in the company of such people.

He already had what he'd come for.

But there was an additional reason for him wanting to get back to Berlin early. Sable could not be allowed to marry Heinz Langer. Dmitri would not see his friend align herself to a man, not least to a political movement, that humiliated people, as had happened the night before, because of their religion. The Romanov family knew what persecution felt like, and Kitzbühel had shown that such intimidation continued to blight his family. He could not allow Sable to be corrupted. Arriving back in Berlin before Heinz would give Dmitri a day's advantage to influence Sable and get her back to the safety of Paris.

He strolled across the park to join the guests, the gamekeepers, and their dogs standing in a line, awaiting the beaters to disturb the doves from their hiding places. He made for the general to give his apologies for his lateness, and to explain that he'd been called back to Berlin a day earlier than planned. He'd asked a member of the general's staff to place a call to Berlin as an alibi, and had remained on the telephone talking to nobody, long after the receptionist at the Adlon had confirmed his instruction to have a room ready a day earlier than expected.

"I'll have one of the staff drive you back," said the general, offering surprisingly little resistance to Dmitri's announcement. He assumed the old soldier had perhaps been informed of the events from the evening before, and accepted Dmitri's explanation as the false excuse he knew it to be, understanding the Russian's distaste at witnessing a summary execution, albeit a false one, when so many of the Romanovs had faced a similar fate.

However, thought Dmitri, if the general took exception to such Nazi stunts as what had happened to Isaak, why had he been selected as the intermediary between the purchaser and subject of the highly sensitive dossier. Dmitri's scan of the file the night before had revealed it to contain original documentation proving Hitler's own Jewish heritage. Such information, if released, would destroy not only the new German chancellor's reputation, but that of the political movement he had constructed. To be entrusted with that documentation, to the exclusion of all other senior Party members, set both Heinz Langer and Terrill von Beckendorff in an exclusive category of those who had the Führer's trust. To such men, the torture of Isaak the night before should seem unworthy of disrupting the higher purpose of their political cause.

The lack of protest to his early departure made Dmitri feel more, rather than less, anxious.

"In the meantime, Dmitri Andreevich, take my gun and enjoy the shoot." The general passed his shotgun to Dmitri. "I have matters to attend to at the house anyway." The general marched off, waving for his valet to remain and assist Dmitri. The general's haste in returning to the castle after hearing that Dmitri would be leaving the estate early unsettled the Russian prince even further. This anxiety was to the benefit of the doves as Dmitri's aim was unsteady.

"Not so good with birds!" called Vogel, seeing Dmitri miss several easy shots.

"I wouldn't say that," murmured Hedda von Beckendorff with a wink. She'd joined the men for the dove shoot. She was standing a few paces away from Dmitri in the line.

"Perhaps I should sit this one out," said Dmitri. He handed the shotgun to a valet and made his way back to the castle. He wanted to get back to Berlin as soon as possible. He had Sable, Erich, and Pasha to get free from this poisonous country; if the Chinese and French wanted the roll of film, then they'd have to help Dmitri's friends as a condition of the exchange.

Dmitri was packing his luggage when the general entered his room without knocking, his expression was one which alerted Dmitri to danger.

"You must go now," urged the general.

"If the car is ready, General, I shall finish packing and say goodbye to your wife."

"No, I mean right now." The general looked back in the hallway, as if waiting to see someone else following him to Dmitri's room. "I saw the look Vogel gave when you announced your early departure."

"A look?" queried Dmitri.

"You're not safe here. I'll have your luggage sent on to the Adlon. But you must go now, there's a motorbike behind the stables." The general stepped out into the hallway to leave. He poked his head back into the room. "I was glad to hear Mahler played here," he added. "I don't know when I shall hear it again, Dmitri Andreevich. Give my regards to your father." He was then gone, not wanting to be discovered warning the Russian of imminent danger.

Dmitri wondered if the general could be setting a trap in collusion with Vogel, encouraging the Russian to incriminate himself somehow by seeming to run away. But the old man had been the only one during the last two days to give Dmitri any sense of rationality.

He decided to trust the old soldier. But there was one quick task before he left.

In Heinz's room, Dmitri went to collect the roll of film he'd hidden in the industrialist's luggage while Heinz had been at breakfast. This had been a precaution, letting Heinz unwittingly carry the evidence back to Berlin, Heinz being the only one not under suspicion of anything as he'd had the original file in his possession.

He unfolded the used shirt Heinz had worn the previous day, and which wouldn't be touched until back in Berlin by the laundress at the hotel. The roll of film Dmitri had wrapped inside earlier that morning was not there. He shook the shirt, checked the floor where he'd done so, and then emptied the rest of the clothes from this particular suitcase.

There was no film.

The general had been right, Dmitri was in danger. Someone knew what he'd really joined the hunting party for.

He walked casually through the castle so as not to raise any suspicion in case he met other guests. It was difficult resisting the urge to run.

He went to the study. If he couldn't have the film, and his deception had already been uncovered, then he'd take the original dossier instead.

Once out of the side door next to the new kitchens, and with the sheaf of documents folded and shoved into the side pocket of his belted shooting jacket, he sprinted for the stables, checking behind that no one was watching or following him.

He did a full lap of the building, but there was no bike. What he found instead horrified him.

Isaak's body was lying on its side. The bullet hole in his neck was a dark spot against the ghost-like whiteness of his frozen face. His unresponsive eyes were locked in an expression of surprise.

The young man's shirt had been torn off, and a star of David carved on his chest with the point of a knife-blade. The frozen streams of blood across his stomach showed this torture had been inflicted whilst he was still alive. There was a spray of blood against the fieldstone wall of the stables. Had Isaak also been told to run for a motorbike but had found himself without the promised transport, and in a trap, thought Dmitri.

If this was an ambush, then Dmitri wanted to ensure he wouldn't be found unarmed. Sliding open the door of the stable to find something to use as a weapon, he saw an object covered in a tarpaulin. Underneath was a ten-year old BMW R32 motorcycle.

"Leaving us so soon?" The German's voice was heavy with confidence. "Turn around very slowly please, Your Highness, I have a gun."

Dmitri held his hands out to his sides, and slowly turned to face Vogel. Luckily, the German was alone, but he had a two-barrel shotgun pointing at Dmitri from a distance too great to give the Russian any hope of intercepting him, but close enough to ensure a fatal hit.

"Well, the party has rather gone off the boil, don't you think, Brigadeführer?" joked Dmitri.

"Not at all." The Nazi adjusted his stance to ensure he was stable if he was required to shoot. "There's still much on offer to keep us amused."

"Isaak doesn't look terribly entertained."

"Alas, the recreation on offer isn't to everyone's taste." Vogel tightened his grip on the weapon and moved his finger into position over the trigger to show he was a serious threat. "Let me return this." With his free hand he slid the herringbone overcoat left at Erich's from around his shoulders and threw it onto the cobbled floor of the stable. It landed with Dmitri's Russian monogram showing.

"I have a better trade," said Dmitri. He had one last chance to survive this confrontation. "The Führer would be interested in what I have to offer."

"I'll allow you to beg for mercy if you'd like," said Vogel. "I'm sure you and your family became used to doing so when the Bolsheviks defeated you, with so much ease I might add." He removed his finger from the trigger. "But a deposed Russian prince, and a very minor one at that, has nothing to offer the new Reich chancellor."

"But a *Jewish* Reich chancellor might be intrigued," said Dmitri.

"Hah! Those are old rumours. Fairy-tales, Your Highness. Nothing more."

"This one has a happy ending, but perhaps not for you. I have proof."

"And I'm supposed to allow your return to Berlin to get it?"

"No, I have it here." Dmitri reached slowly into the side pocket of his jacket and brought out the folded sheaf of documents. Vogel had brought the shotgun up to shoulder height, ready to shoot if Dmitri had a weapon of his own.

"Fake, no doubt," said Vogel, seeing the papers. "And I still have the advantage. When I arrest or kill you, I can check them anyway."

Dmitri made two quick steps to a burning brazier that provided heat for the stables. He held the documents inches from the flames.

"Stalemate now perhaps, Herr Vogel?"

The men were trying to determine each other's intentions. The German had missed his chance to shoot when Dmitri moved to the brazier, this meant he thought the documents might be genuine, or that he had orders to bring Dmitri back to Berlin alive for interrogation. That gave Dmitri at least a fighting chance.

"Put the gun down, Vogel. I'll remove my hand from the flame, then we both step away, and I'll hand you the documents."

"Why would I care if you burn them?" laughed Vogel.

"I thought you might be interested in the list of witnesses it contains," replied Dmitri. "People with big mouths it seems."

Vogel's smile was replaced by a thoughtful frown. He'd been made to feel stupid, something he thought would not happen once his chosen Party had come to power; it reminded him of a past where people like Dmitri humiliated him. Shooting the Russian aristocrat would be a pleasure. But the file was valuable and could elevate him in the ranks of the Nazis. Dmitri fanned the flames of the brazier with the file, taunting the German.

The SS officer kept his eyes on Dmitri as he crouched down. He left the shotgun on the floor.

Dmitri moved the documents away from the fire.

Slowly, they each then took a step away from the objects of danger, then another, and another, until both were far enough away.

"Now, place the documents on the floor," instructed Vogel, adapting the plan Dmitri had suggested. "And then step back several large paces."

"You can have one page to start with, to check it's genuine." Dmitri laid a piece of paper on the ground and stepped back. Vogel took the bait, moving even further away from the shotgun. As he crouched down to pick the first document up, he took his eyes off Dmitri. This was a mistake the Russian had been hoping for.

Dmitri scrunched together the remaining pieces of paper that proved Hitler's Jewish ancestry, including the list of witnesses, and threw them towards the brazier.

Vogel lost his footing as he hurled his body forwards to intercept the documents. As the crumpled papers crackled into the flame, Vogel's arm tipped the brazier over. Half of his face and upper body was covered by the flames and burning coals.

The Nazi's screaming echoed chillingly around the double-height stable. It made the horses in their stalls whinny with panic and kick the wooden doors of their boxes. Dmitri could smell burning hair and flesh.

Dmitri picked up the shotgun and peeked through the stable door to check whether the noise had attracted anyone else's attention. In the distance he could hear the shots from the dove shoot which was continuing on the other side of the castle.

He went back to the crying, writhing body in the stable. He aimed the shotgun at the brigadeführer's half-scorched face.

"Please, God, help me!" cried Vogel. Dmitri was unsure whether Vogel wanted to be spared or put out of his misery with a quick death. The noise he was making decided Dmitri's mind. He waited until the man's eyes, one of which was unrecognisable as such, were looking at him.

Dmitri aimed the shotgun at Vogel's head, but his target then lost consciousness and there seemed little need in risking the sound of gunfire from the stable being heard.

He scooped up the discarded overcoat and dusted off the dirt.

With the leather riding cap buckled under his chin, and the goggles in place, both of which had been looped over the handlebars, Dmitri straddled the BMW motorbike. He jumped down on the kick-start lever with all his weight. The engine spluttered but didn't take. He was being too forceful. He relaxed his legs and tried again, using a smoother motion from the weight of his body rather than leg muscles, and with a full follow through. The engine rumbled into action, began to falter, then recovered and eased into rhythm. He adjusted the fuel and air control levers on the handlebars and sat down on the padded seat as the bike eased forward.

The Isle of Man TT race in nineteen-twenty-eight was the last time Dmitri had ridden a motorbike. Back then, he'd been on a three-speed single-cylinder 500cc Moto Guzzi racer, propelling the Italian-made bike to break the lap record of the Snaefell mountain course. He'd overtaken the Sunbeam to put himself in the lead, but the appalling weather conditions of heavy rain and thick mist, coming after a period of drought, punished his bravery. Outside the Quarter Bridge Hotel, he fell heavily, buckling the Moto's front wheel and breaking his left leg. He hadn't been back on a bike since then.

But this was no time for caution or fear.

He pushed the BMW up to its top speed of fifty-nine miles-per-hour before he'd even exited the Jagdschloss Albrecht estate.

He adjusted the handlebar mounted controls to keep the eight-and-a-half horse-powered engine running smoothly, and he settled himself on the springed seat. He didn't know how to get back to the city, nor whether anyone would be following in close pursuit.

The bike took the curves well at top speed, and this gave Dmitri confidence in his riding skills, despite his lack of recent practice, and in the bike's ability to keep up a fast pace. The brake block on the fixed rear wheel was inadequate to the task of stopping suddenly, so Dmitri had to trust in fate, and hope the cruel luck of the Isle of Man five years before didn't strike again.

XVI
Berlin

ONCE THE road signs started showing directions for
Berlin, Dmitri followed a deliberately circuitous route.
Now the Nazis knew what his real reason for being in
Germany was, he couldn't return to the hotel.

He headed for Erich's house. He wanted to check
whether his former tutor had been released from custody,
and, if so, to get him, Pasha and Sable together and force
them to join him in an escape from Germany. That was
the best plan he'd thought of on the long ride back to the
city. If his friends were still in custody, then he would get
himself and Sable out of the country as a priority, and
rethink how best to help the men he'd grown up with.

The bright winter sun that accompanied his ride
through the Brandenburg countryside had begun to set as
he arrived on Winterfeldstrasse in the south of the city.
He made two circuits past Erich's house to ensure no
police or SS were waiting in any of the parked cars or
keeping watch from the cafes opposite.

He parked the motorcycle nearby, and walked back to
the townhouse, combing a hand through his swept-back
dark blonde hair that was damp with sweat from the

leather riding helmet. He smoothed out his pencil-thin moustache and flipped up the lapels and collar of his overcoat to hide the hunting tweeds worn underneath. No one seemed to be paying any undue attention as Dmitri walked up the front steps to Erich's door.

The curtains in the sitting room window twitched. After a long wait the door was unlocked and opened.

"Get in," said Oskar. He closed the door quickly behind Dmitri, after dragging the Russian inside by the sleeve of his overcoat. Dmitri was surprised it was the eighteen-year-old factory worker, Pasha's lover, who had been the one to admit him.

"Herr Arnheim?" asked Dmitri. Oskar had gone back to the front window to peer from behind the curtain, nervously watching the street outside for any suspicious change Dmitri's arrival prompted.

"Under arrest," said Oskar.

"Pasha? Frau Renfeldt?" asked Dmitri. He noticed the state of disorganisation the room had fallen into.

"Both gone." Oskar went to the other side of the window and pulled back a fraction of the curtain to check from that angle as well. "It's just me here."

"Why?" asked Dmitri.

Oskar looked at Dmitri as if he didn't understand the question, then replied, "Because the police haven't caught me yet."

"You're not safe here," said Dmitri. "Where has Pasha gone?"

"Here's as good as any place." Oskar returned to his surveillance of the street. "Where else should I go?"

"Come away from the window, Oskar."

"I must keep looking."

"Don't worry. I wasn't followed." Dmitri touched Oskar lightly on the shoulder, trying to reassure the young man that there was no immediate danger in the street. "Tell me what's been happening, then I can help."

Dmitri switched on a table lamp to brighten the gloom, but Oskar immediately turned it off again. In the half-light Dmitri could see the young man, barely more than a boy, was petrified. He led the German away from the window and indicated for him to sit on the threadbare sofa.

Most of the bottles from Erich's drinks cabinet were empty, some had been left littering the floor around the dresser. Dmitri kicked these out of the way and poured what remained from one bottle into a glass.

"It's not quite a Gin Rickey, but you take what you can get." He handed the glass to Oskar, who took a tentative sip. "You need more medicine than that," suggested Dmitri, guiding the glass back up to Oskar's mouth.

On the two previous occasions that he'd met the young German, the labourer from the coal barges had elicited Dmitri's disgust. But his staying behind, keeping guard of Erich's house while the music tutor was in prison, had a heroic element to it, even if the house also provided Oskar with a hiding place.

"Why have you stayed?" asked Dmitri.

"I've been waiting for you," said Oskar; he now appeared somewhat revived by the alcohol.

"For me?" asked Dmitri.

"You have something for me?" asked Oskar.

"I haven't got anything for you." Dmitri looked quizzically at Oskar, wondering what the young man could mean.

"I'm Napoleon."

Oskar handed the glass back to Dmitri, who drained it of the remaining liquor. The bitterness helping him recover from the surprise of Oskar's revelation that he was the contact Emile-Jacques had mentioned.

"I don't have the film," said Dmitri regretfully.

"What about the document itself?" asked Oskar.

"Neither the documents, nor the photographs." Dmitri looked around for another drink. "You're Napoleon?" he asked.

"What happened?" enquired Oskar, not answering Dmitri's question.

"I hid the film," said Dmitri. "But when I went to retrieve it before leaving, the damn thing was missing."

"And the file?"

"That was destroyed." Dmitri thought it prudent to not divulge the full circumstances of how the paperwork had been irretrievably lost.

"But you saw its contents?" asked the young German.

"I saw enough to know why the French want it. You've been working for them all this time? Did Pasha know?"

"The French got in touch after I met Pasha. They take an interest in Russian émigrés here in Berlin. Pasha doesn't know."

"And where is he?" asked Dmitri again. There were too many questions Dmitri had for Oskar about how he came to be recruited by the French, but his priority had to be the friends who still needed Dmitri's help. He could ask Emile-Jacques about Oskar another time to satisfy his curiosity about the tactics of the *Deuxiéme Bureau*.

"In hiding, but I don't know where," replied Oskar. "We decided it best that way."

"I need to get back to the Adlon," said Dmitri, standing up. "I must get to Sable; she's in danger."

"Sable?" Oskar seemed unsure about who this was. Oskar's confusion made Dmitri question how much the French might have told this young man about his task as Napoleon, the messenger. "Does she know about the file, about why you went to Schorfheide?"

"No, nothing." Dmitri went to look out of the window himself now, to make sure the street was clear for him to leave. "But I must tell her the truth now." As

Dmitri paced towards the door, Oskar closed it. Dmitri tried to push the muscled young man out of the way.

"Don't be foolish!" exclaimed Dmitri.

Oskar didn't move.

"Get in touch with the French while I'm gone," suggested Dmitri. "I'll come back for you, then we'll work out a plan."

Oskar pushed Dmitri, who fell backwards onto the sofa. As the Russian prince stood, Oskar flipped back the lapel of his jacket to reveal a small SS pin, just like that awarded to Dmitri by Vogel several days before. The German's previous expression of fear, and the jittery body language was immediately replaced by a grin of satisfaction.

Dmitri made a dash for the window, but Oskar tackled him to the floor. The two men struggled, but Oskar's boxer-like arms were suffocating Dmitri in a bear hug. His legs were looped around the Russian's as a wrestler might subdue his opponent in a tournament. Oskar was a trained fighter. Dmitri's restrained body writhed, but his exertions were useless.

A beam of light crept across the carpet as the door opened.

Framed in the light of the doorway were two men.

Both were dressed in the black uniforms of the SS.

XVII

SPANDAU PRISON was in the west of the city. Dmitri spent the journey wondering how the Nazi's had known the codename of his French contact. Wild thoughts began to question the motives of the French government. Were they in collusion with the Nazis, or perhaps just the loyalty of Emile-Jacques was now in doubt?

Once at Spandau, Dmitri was strip-searched, and his expensive clothes ripped apart. But there was no camera film.

"Don't be too disappointed," said Dmitri with a smile.

"We already have enough evidence to hang you," replied one of the SS guards. He noticed the seven-point orthodox Slavonic cross Dmitri wore on a chain around his neck. "Take it off."

"You'll have to fight me for it," said Dmitri. If the Bolshevik guards in Siberia hadn't managed to confiscate the religious symbol given to him when he came of age by the tsar and tsarina, his godparents, then a Nazi street thug in a uniform was certainly going to have to work harder to get it than just asking Dmitri to remove it.

"You might try to hang yourself with it. Take it off or I'll hurt you," threatened the guard. He stepped close enough to Dmitri that their noses were almost touching.

"Your breath alone might even kill me," quipped Dmitri. The blow to his gut had been expected so he'd tensed his muscles to absorb the impact. "Do they not teach dental hygiene at street thug school?" asked Dmitri, provoking a second strike, this time from the guard's cosh.

"Enough!" barked a senior officer wearing the uniform of the regular Prussian police rather than the SS. This man slid a knife under the neck chain to cut the metal. He kept the broken chain but handed the crucifix back to Dmitri. "He's a Christian, and a foreigner," advised the senior police officer to the SS guard. "That means different treatment."

The guard took the cross out of Dmitri's hand and inspected it. He then slipped the metal object inside the bandage on Dmitri's arm which was still covering the hunting injury. The guard wrapped a hand around Dmitri's upper arm and squeezed where the cross now was. He only released his grip when the blood was showing through the fabric.

One of the other prisoners issued Dmitri with a set of prison clothes; a label with the number 1016 had been roughly stitched to the sleeve. Once dressed in the ill-fitting grey rags, Dmitri was told to hold his arms out, onto which was stacked a putrid mattress, two blankets, a cover for the mattress, a bed sheet, a towel, dish cloth, chipped enamel bowl, mug and tin basin. The gun-toting guard pressed a revolver into Dmitri's back to push him into the cellblock corridor.

At the door marked number 33, Dmitri was once again pushed forwards. The room was no more than ten feet in either direction. In addition to a metal-framed bed with broken springs, Dmitri's new accommodation was furnished with a table, chair, toilet bucket, wash bucket, broom, and water pitcher. The cell door was slammed and locked behind him.

"You missed dinner," said the guard. "And I'm afraid room service is closed for the night, Your Highness." He slid the wicket shut, and Dmitri could hear him laughing, as the echoes of his steps grew quieter.

By moving the chair next to the wall, and standing on the back of the wooden seat, Dmitri was able to peer through the small barred window at the top of the exterior cell wall.

He could see the mediaevalesque turrets of the entrance gate where his captors had brought him into the prison complex. There was a garden and surrounding that a brick wall fifteen feet in height topped with rolls of barbed wire. This was just the inner wall, there being another a short distance beyond as an outside perimeter. Towers had uniformed armed guards inside, and searchlights mounted on them.

Everything suggested to Dmitri that he was going to be a guest at Spandau for some time, rather than an overnight visitor. He worried about Sable, knowing he was now incapable of helping her. Even if she didn't come under suspicion due to her close association with Dmitri, Heinz would be sure to accelerate the marriage to prove both his and Sable's loyalty to their new German masters. Dmitri was confident he could have encouraged Sable to break an engagement, but a marriage was more final.

The cell lights were turned off at what Dmitri estimated to be ten o'clock.

He could feel every broken spring digging into his back under the paper-thin stench-releasing mattress. For many other political prisoners in the same situation as Dmitri, that first night would be spent in wakeful fear. But Dmitri had spent two years in Siberian labour camps after the Revolution. It had taken him months of restless nights in Siberia, but eventually Dmitri had learned techniques to clear his mind no matter what the conditions. He focused on his breathing to defy his conscious, anxious brain, and to get some sleep.

Every fifteen minutes during the night the guards at Spandau opened the wicket of his cell door and shone a bright torch onto him, but this was also something he'd experienced previously. After several hours of being awoken by the disturbance, Dmitri had settled himself back into the mindset of Siberia. He knew how to survive.

The cell lights were switched on in the early morning. Dmitri jumped out of bed immediately, not wanting to give the guard doing his rounds any excuse to punish him. Survival meant finding an intelligent balance between obedience and defiance. Following routines for sleep, work, ablutions, and feeding made sense. These basics were needed, so resisting them only made inmates too weak to withstand the pressure when it really counted.

The cell door was opened, and Dmitri presented himself ready for the day. He'd already washed in the freezing water provided, swept his cell, dampened down his hair, and run a finger around his teeth. He followed with his mug and bowl, as the line of prisoners was led to the canteen.

As with Siberia, Dmitri saw the ill-placed defiance of some prisoners being punished with enjoyment by the guards, as men were dragged from their cells, beaten with clubs and fists. These prisoners shouted: "Red Front!" to provoke an even more violent reaction from the guards. They had soiled their own clothes, and their faces were unwashed, both decisions which they mistakenly thought inconvenienced their captors, but just hindered their own chances of survival.

Breakfast was watery coffee and stale bread. No prisoner was permitted to talk to another, but Dmitri scanned the room to check whether he could see either Erich or Pasha. He did recognise one face, sitting three benches away, but it wasn't one he'd hoped to ever see again.

Gennady Bunin glowered back at Dmitri, as if he'd been waiting for some time for the Russian prince to look across; his shaved head was wrinkled in a scowl. The former family chauffeur, now a Red Army revolutionary, conveyed through his large dark eyes all the hate Dmitri had seen when Gennady was holding Anna hostage in Yalta the summer before.

There seemed nothing left of the man who had checked on a young Dmitri when the boy-prince had been unwell. The broad shoulders Dmitri had ridden safely on as Gennady carried him around the imperial estate at Tsarskoe Selo, were now hunched to his ears. The Communist leant on his elbows, the unshaven chin resting on hands which had once held books of fairy-tales in them, and from which he'd read animatedly to the giggling son of his employer.

Gennady had once been like an older brother to the Russian prince, but that had counted for nothing when revolution came. Dmitri remembered the sadism of Gennady and his wife towards Anna whilst she was their prisoner. He shuddered at the memory of Anna being abducted in Istanbul after her rescue last summer; it had been on Gennady's order that his sister be kidnapped. He clenched his fist thinking how close his father had come to being killed in Kitzbühel at the hands of Gennady's Bolshevik spy, just the week before.

They knew each other better than any two men in Spandau, yet no other two prisoners could be such enemies as he and Gennady had become.

"Prisoner ten-sixteen." A prod to the shoulder from a wooden club reminded Dmitri this was his identification number. He stood up. "This prisoner will take you to the laundry, that's where you'll be working today." A skinny boy, who couldn't have been any older than fourteen, was standing next to the guard, with his head bowed; the number on his sleeve was 906, indicating he'd been in Spandau for some time. The boy walked off, and Dmitri followed, remembering to take his meal things with him. Dmitri glanced back, and saw Gennady still glaring at him. Dmitri winked at his enemy.

"I'm Mitya," whispered Dmitri, touching the teenager on the shoulder to get his attention. The boy shrugged off Dmitri's hand, and didn't reply.

The prison laundry was humid with steam, but the heat was a welcome change from the freezing cold of the cell and canteen. A civilian laundress, an unhealthily large woman with a face of deep crevasses and folds of fat, oversaw the operation. She barked orders and used a wooden spoon as a weapon to encourage quick obedience. Two guards with holstered revolvers and unholstered clubs stood watch at either end of the room.

As he scrubbed the sheets, his hands becoming red and numb in the too-hot tubs of water, Dmitri took quick glances to check either for Erich or Pasha. He wrung out the sodden sheets and fed them through the heavy rollers of a large mangle, before looping them over lines to dry, and then repeating the cycle with a fresh batch of dirty sheets.

Another habit he'd learnt in the Siberian camp, and one which he was pleased came quickly back to him as instinct, was to constantly carry out surveillance on his surroundings. As he worked Dmitri made a mental note of routines, security features, and potential intelligence which could aid an escape. Sometimes a sudden opportunity presented itself, and the prisoner had to be ready to exploit that to get free; otherwise, every small detail of how a prison ran had to be committed to memory and a long-term plan formed to exploit any weaknesses identified.

Dmitri's ability at both short and long-term escapology had seen him moved from camp to camp, and further east, across Siberia. It had been such a movement, taking him closer to the territory of the Chinese, that had facilitated his liberation by Tao Chen's Hongmen crime gang. It had taken Dmitri two years of captivity to gain his freedom, it had taken his sister over a dozen, but neither had given up hope during their imprisonment in Russia. In Germany, the Nazis had only been in power for a week; the regime was still on uncertain foundations. His situation in Spandau was favourable to a positive mindset.

"Ten-sixteen and nine-zero-six, take those sheets to the reception room!" The frau-laundress accompanied her order with a whack from her wooden spoon to the thigh of the teenager whom Dmitri had been paired with for the day. Collecting a stack of folded blankets and sheets, Dmitri followed the boy and one of the guards across the cellblock to the same room where he'd been inducted into prison life the day before.

Dmitri and prisoner 906 were kept at the back of the room as three new prisoners were led in, still dressed in their own clothes, and looking dazed, scared, and tired. The two younger men looked like factory workers, but the middle-aged man had the girth of someone used to good dining, and a set of clothes that showed he lived in one of Berlin's better neighbourhoods.

A jug of castor oil was passed down the line.

"Drink!" ordered the same guard who'd tried to take Dmitri's crucifix.

All refused to drink.

After a beating, each man tilted the jug to their lips and drank.

Once stripped, their clothes searched and confiscated, a guard surveyed the new prisoners in turn, from head to toe.

"Religion?" he asked of each man, paying attention to their genitals, and smirking at the two who were obviously Jewish.

None answered his question, prompting a fresh round of fist-blows.

A man entered the room. He was dressed in a smart suit. He remained in the shadows by the door, and casually smoked a cigarette, but the atmosphere in the room changed markedly with his arrival. The uniformed guards and Prussian police stopped the beatings, and handed the prisoners their new inmate uniforms, each with a number stitched on the sleeve; these were 1017, 1018, and 1019.

The men were asked a series of questions about other Marxists, the locations of secret printing presses, and weapons capabilities of the Berlin rebels.

"The first man to answer the questions will be released immediately, and the remaining two interred indefinitely here in Spandau," promised one of the guards.

After a period of time, and with no man having answered the guard's questions, the figure in the shadows by the door crushed his cigarette on the floor, as if signalling for the questions to stop. He stepped out of the shadows but was looking at Dmitri rather than the three newest prisoners. He was a man similar in age to Dmitri, and almost as handsome; however, scars on both sides of his face gave the German's strikingly good looks a sinister quality. His black hair was swept back in the same style as Dmitri's and smoothed down with hair cream. He nodded to the guards and left the reception room through the door he'd entered fifteen minutes before.

No sooner had the civilian with the scars closed the door, than the guards abandoned their restraint and resumed their abuse.

The three inmates were beaten with clubs until blood soaked through the clothes from where the skin had broken. Eventually the castor oil the men had been forced earlier to drink took on its laxative effect, and each prisoner soiled themselves, to the amusement of the guards. This stopped the beatings.

Dmitri and prisoner 906 were told to hand out the same inventory of items Dmitri had been supplied with the evening before. The three inmates, not being given a clean set of clothes, were ushered out towards the cell block.

"I'm Viktor," whispered prisoner 906 in the few seconds that he and Dmitri were left alone. He looked horrified at what had just been witnessed.

"Pleased to meet —" Dmitri didn't finish his sentence, as a guard returned to escort them back to the laundry.

Dinner consisted of soup, being little more than a bowl of lukewarm water with a few chunks of uncooked vegetables floating in it, and a part-boiled potato. Dmitri had arrived at the canteen earlier than most, so he'd finished his meagre meal when a senior guard ordered all prisoners to stand.

The more experienced prisoners didn't need prompting for what was required next, and they raised their right arms in a Nazi salute. A mumble of voices repeated the senior guard's mantra: "To our beloved chancellor, Adolf Hitler, a mighty Sieg Heil, Sieg Heil!" Those who refused to comply had their soup bowls upturned and their potatoes stamped into mush on the floor by the patrolling guards; they received swipes with a club across their backs and legs until their arms were raised to the requisite height, and the chant repeated loud enough as to be considered acceptable. Some prisoners replaced their 'Sieg Heils' with a whisper of 'Red Front' and, where this was heard, the culprit was dragged out of the canteen.

Dmitri had raised his arm and chanted the Nazi slogan several times in the last few days as part of his mission to get the dossier, so he saw no reason not to do so now as a continuation of that façade. He was no National Socialist, but neither was he a Communist. His resistance, when it did come, had to make clear his allegiance to a creed of freedom that neither of those political ideologies represented. Instead of mumbling, he sang the chant with gusto, adding a music-hall comedy to it, enough to show he was joking, but not so much as to warrant a beating. The guards and fellow prisoners were confused by his performance, which was what he wanted.

No sooner had the cell light been extinguished, and Dmitri settled himself on the insufficient bed, than his cell door was opened again.

"Get up!" ordered the guard. Dmitri was not surprised by the disturbance; in fact, he was more astounded that it had taken this long for him to be summoned for interrogation.

He was led to an office.

"I'm Rudolf Diels," said the man from earlier with the scars across his face. "Please take a seat." He didn't offer his hand in greeting. This showed he was experienced enough at interrogations so as not to give the interrogatee a false sense of power by refusing to shake the hand offered. Nevertheless, his manner was civil, albeit not friendly, and he had stood up to acknowledge Dmitri's entry into the office.

The guard closed the door, with himself on the other side. Rudolf studied a file laying open on the desk in front of him, paying no attention to Dmitri, nor showing any fear of being attacked by the prisoner. Dmitri relaxed back in the chair and pretended to flick some dust off his well-worn inmate trousers, as if they were a pair of tailored flannels; he wanted to show his interrogator that he was not nervous about what was to follow.

"You sang very well at dinner," said Diels, looking up from the file. He continued to smoke his cigarette, without offering one to Dmitri. This was another indication that he knew what he was doing. The offer of a cigarette was, in Dmitri's opinion, an unoriginal tactic to establish rapport and trust as a lead-in to the serious questioning. It was also something else the obstinate prisoner could refuse, bolstering their sense of rebellion. Dmitri considered himself to be a higher class of inmate, worthy of Diels' subtler approach. "Such a show of enthusiasm when singing confuses the guards," added Diels.

"I've always enjoyed the theatre," replied Dmitri with a smile. "And comic farce is my particular favourite, so I was happy to join in." Rudolf stared at Dmitri for a second or two, then smiled. "I'll even lead the choir tomorrow evening, if you'd like," added Dmitri. "Some prisoners probably need a good old sing-song to cheer them up a bit."

"It's a duelling injury," said Diels. He noticed that Dmitri was looking at the scars on his face.

"I hope she was worth it." said Dmitri.

"It was a dispute over Hegel." Diels returned to the file on the desk.

"He seems your type," said Dmitri. "I much prefer the physical to metaphysics."

"Like Terrill von Beckendorff's wife?" Rudolf asked the question without looking up from the file in front of him.

"And very nearly his daughter too," joked Dmitri. "I'm sure Hegel himself would have appreciated my efforts exploring personal freedom this week."

"It's the reason behind those efforts that I want to ask you about."

"You mean I haven't been brought to Spandau to debate nineteenth century philosophy with you? That is disappointing."

"Why are you helping the Communists?" asked Diels.

"I'm not," said Dmitri. "And it should embarrass you to ask such a question, considering my family background." Dmitri had switched from a jovial to a superior manner, remonstrating Diels in both his tone and body language.

"Our agent saw you with Pavel Borisovich Darensky."

"Pasha is an old friend, why wouldn't I say hello when in Berlin?" Dmitri would cooperate to a point. If he could cast sufficient doubt over the information gathered by the SS and his motives, then it might result in him being deported as an unwelcome alien, rather than shot as a spy. He was a high-profile person, whose disappearance would raise questions of the new regime in Berlin.

"You financed the Communists," accused Diels.

"No. I gave my friend some money." Dmitri stood up and walked to the door. "You are clearly misinformed, Herr Diels. Perhaps I should come back when you've sorted the mess of your interrogation notes out?"

"It's Herr *Doctor* Diels actually."

"And I'm a *prince* of Russia, so I think I win that round as well." Dmitri tapped on the door, and the guard opened it. Diels waved him away; the interrogator was losing control of his own interview, and he was becoming frustrated.

"The laundry is an easy assignment, Prince Dmitri. I could instruct the warden to reallocate a less civilised job to you."

"Just as long as it's not teaching you how to fence properly, Herr Doctor. That would be too difficult."

"Guard!" Diels was experienced enough to know he'd lost the momentum this time.

XVIII

DMITRI AND Viktor remained working in the laundry together for the next few days. On one rare occasion when no guards were present, they were able to talk.

"How long have you been here?" asked Dmitri, wiping the sweat from his forehead with the dirty sleeve of his shirt.

Viktor checked that no guards were about to return, then he answered, "A few weeks."

"You seem quite young to be a political prisoner." Dmitri picked up the other end of the sheet Viktor was trying to fold.

"It's my mother they want," said Viktor, "but I refuse to tell them where she is."

"Your mother?"

"Marianne Lázár."

Dmitri shrugged.

"You don't recognise the name?" asked Viktor. He was confused that Dmitri, a fellow political prisoner of the Nazis, was ignorant of such a name. "You're not a communist?"

"No," said Dmitri. He put the folded sheet on top of the pile and took another one from the basket for the two of them to fold.

"Jewish?" asked the teenager.

"Wrong again," said Dmitri.

"Then -"

"You won't like me very much when I tell you my full name," said Dmitri.

Viktor stopped folding the sheet. His expression turned to one of fear.

"I am, or at least I used to be, Prince Dmitri Andreevich Romanov of Russia."

"Romanov? You mean you're one of the —"

"A fairly low ranking one," interrupted Dmitri, "But, yes, my godfather was the tsar."

"So you're not a communist."

"Far from it," said Dmitri, adding, "but nor am I a National Socialist."

"How did you end up in here?" Viktor returned to folding the sheet with Dmitri.

"The new masters of Germany took a dislike to some of my recent antics."

"Such as?" asked Viktor.

"I'll make you a deal, Viktor. I won't ask you where your mother is hiding if you don't ask me what I've been up to in Berlin. OK?"

"I suppose so," said the boy.

"But I will tell you this," added Dmitri. "You are doing remarkably well in here for someone your age. I wasn't much older than you the first time I found myself a political prisoner, in Siberia."

"How long were you there for?"

"Two years."

The mention of years, prompted Viktor to tremble. Seeing this, Dmitri dropped the sheet and put his arm round the teenager's shoulders.

"No matter how long the days in here seem, Viktor, they will end, you will be free, and you'll be pleased at the strength you've shown."

"I know it's what my mother expects of me." Viktor quickly corrected himself, "I meant to say, it's what the Party expects."

"Well, I'm not sure about the Party, but your mother will be proud of you. I'm sure she's doing everything she can to get you out of here."

The arrival of the guards prompted a return to silence between Viktor and Dmitri as they continued to fold sheets.

"WHY WERE you at Terril von Beckendorff's hunting lodge?" asked Rudolf Diels in yet another of his middle-of-the-night interrogations.

"As I've already told you, Herr Doctor, I was invited there as a last-minute guest by Heinz Langer," replied Dmitri. "We *have* covered this already. Would you like me to write that answer down, so you won't keep forgetting?"

"They'll be plenty of time for your written confession," said Diels.

"*You* say confession, *I* say recollection. Must we do this again? I enjoy long pleasant chats with friendly people as much as the next prisoner, but -"

"Perhaps a touch of harsh treatment might do you some good," interrupted Diels.

"Harsher than this? As a guest, I do have some significant complaints already," joked Dmitri. "For starters, the room service leaves something to be desired."

"Every prisoner talks eventually."

"I'm beginning to think you're only keeping me here so that you can practice your English, Herr Doctor."

"You are not a soldier, Your Highness," said Diels as he lit himself a cigarette. "As such, you are not covered by the protections of the Geneva Conventions. You are a spy. You are an uncooperative prisoner. And, to be frank, you are boring me."

"Well, I'm sorry that you find my company so dull, Herr Doctor. I see no need to maintain this acquaintance if it bores you. *I* know nothing, *you* know nothing, so this does all seem rather pointless."

"You're intelligent and inclined to talk. Eventually, you will say something I want to hear. If you won't tell me, then perhaps the heavy-fisted guards might elicit what I need." Diels stood up from his desk and walked over to the door behind Dmitri.

Without turning around, Dmitri replied, "I doubt they have the stamina."

"And then, of course, there is your *friend*." Diels leant close to Dmitri's ear. "Miss Sable Nash. I would hate for your silence to implicate her." He puffed on the cigarette and blew the smoke in Dmitri's face. "She *might* be left alone in exchange for some information from you."

"Nice try, Herr Doctor," said Dmitri coughing, "but you're fishing and I'm not going to take the bait."

"How does it feel to have the safety of Miss Nash in your grasp? It would take such little cooperation from you to ensure her continued..." Diels paused, then added, "good health. Miss Nash *is* going to be picked up by the Gestapo, so be reasonable. Why be a fool?"

"Try again, Herr Doctor."

"You're a man of experience, Your Highness. There's no need for this silly defiance on your part. I could have you transferred back to the comfortable surroundings your hotel while we investigate, under house arrest of course, but I would need you to tell me what was in that file you took at the hunting lodge."

"A file, you say? I know nothing about that." Dmitri continued to stare at a picture on the wall behind Diels' desk, rather than follow his interrogator as he walked around the room.

"Everything you've said is lies!" hollered Diels. "You will see what the new German masters can do."

"I've been thoroughly underwhelmed so far," said Dmitri.

"Or you could be shot while attempting escape!"

"Escape? I'll give it a go Herr Doctor, by all means."

"In this prison there are talkers and workers." Diels sounded as if he was preparing to make a political speech.

"And which are you?" asked Dmitri.

"Get up!" demanded Diels. "I am the one asking the questions."

Dmitri nonchalantly stood up.

"We have two possibilities here," continued Diels. He was standing with his body almost pressed against Dmitri's. Only now did he realise he was shorter than his prisoner, and it was unsettling to have to look up to speak to Dmitri. "One is that you tell me all about that file, who asked you to get it, and what was in it. I shall release you and, under guard of course, ensure you cross the border back into France."

"Just out of curiosity, what's the other possibility?"

Diels lifted up a cover, under which was a desktop wooden framed device. On one end was a leather strap and buckle, at the other was what looked like a large metal stapler.

"We call it the finger crimper," said Diels. "This metal device is clamped to each nail and very slowly pulls it away from the nail bed, eventually tearing it completely from the finger. In medieval times denailing was known to destroy people's sanity."

"I don't suppose it smooths out hard skin as well?" asked Dmitri. "Only that laundry has given me terrible calluses."

"It will also quickly cure you of this stupid attempt at humour!" barked Diels. He took a breath to calm himself. "Please sit down, Your Highness."

"No, I prefer to stand actually," said Dmitri.

"Your capture shows how clumsy you are. Nobody knows whether you're alive or dead, so you've already lost. If you talk, you'll get everything back."

"During my life, a lot has been taken from me, Herr Doctor. What makes you think I can't withstand a further loss?"

Diels took one of Dmitri's hands and stroked the fingernails. As he smiled, the scars on his face wrinkled. "Shall we find out?" he asked.

Dmitri leant forwards, leaving his hand in Diels' grasp, and whispered, "Now listen here, you annoying, disfigured policeman. Your questions are tedious, and your assumption that I have anything to tell you is false. So, once again I say, admit you've got it wrong and release me. Otherwise, stop tickling my hand like a schoolgirl and let's put that ludicrous looking contraption of yours to the test, shall we?"

"Guard!" Diels flung Dmitri's hand away and put the cover back over the torture device.

If two years in Siberian labour camps hadn't made Dmitri confess to make-believe crimes against the Russian people, nor go insane, then several days in Spandau and a series of threats wasn't going to break him.

IT WAS only after a week of incarceration that Dmitri found himself close enough to Gennady that the two could speak. When Gennady was moved to the cell next to Dmitri's, the former Russian prince recognised it for the latest intimidation tactic it so obviously was.

"You sweep like an aristocrat," grumbled Gennady, when he and Dmitri were tasked with cleaning the corridor of the cellblock together.

"And you complain like a servant," replied Dmitri. "So the world is as it should be."

"Why are you here?" asked the Red Army soldier.

"I tell you everything, and you relay that to the Nazi guards I suppose? I've fallen for that tactic once before, in Belgrade."

"I'm not a Nazi," barked Gennady. "How could I possibly be?"

"Once a traitor, always a traitor," replied Dmitri. He continued sweeping. "How's the leg?" He noticed that Gennady still had a pronounced limp from the fall when Anna pushed him out of the window.

"Strong enough to kick a Romanov."

The two men continued cleaning. Gennady broke the silence, perhaps realising that he had to earn Dmitri's trust if he expected the fellow Russian to provide any information.

"Moscow sent me to coordinate the Communists here, but I was arrested at the Polish border," he said.

"So, you're the mysterious phantom then?" asked Dmitri.

"What do you know about it?"

"The man who betrayed you is called Oskar, at least that's the name he's been using. He's the reason I'm in here too."

"I don't understand," said Gennady. "What are you?"

"Don't worry, Gennady Vladimirovich, I'm neither a Nazi nor a Communist. I'd like to see both you *and* Oskar hang, so I'm not sure what that makes me really."

"An aristocrat." Gennady smiled at his own cleverness.

Dmitri kicked the bucket of filth they'd swept up so that it fell over into Gennady's cell.

"Whoops," said Dmitri. He strolled off along the cellblock when the dinner bell rang out.

THE FOLLOWING morning, Dmitri and Gennady were once again tasked to work together, but this time the former Romanov family chauffeur didn't attempt to converse. The Russian prince, who had once considered Gennady one of his extended family, also had no interest in speaking to the Bolshevik revolutionary.

The room they were taken to was being prepared for executions.

A glance of fear crossed between Dmitri and Gennady, each thinking that they were about to die and, worse, to die together.

When four hooded prisoners were brought in, their number corresponding to the four hooks fixed to the crossbeam above them, the two Russians realised they had been brought together to witness what would happen to them if both persisted in not divulging any information about their presence and activities in Germany.

Dmitri recognised the slim body of one prisoner before the hood was lifted to confirm Dmitri's fear.

Viktor looked at Dmitri with an expression of blame. The assurance of survival given to him by the Russian prince, who'd escaped from a Siberian labour camp, was about to be proven false. But Dmitri knew he shared greater responsibility than just a false guarantee of a long life; the Nazis had most likely selected Viktor for execution precisely because the teenager had been someone Dmitri had formed a friendship with. Viktor was being hanged because he'd shown Dmitri a small measure of companionship.

"For God's sake, tell them Viktor!" shouted Dmitri. He received a rifle butt to the stomach for his outburst. On the ground, he continued his plea to the teenager, "Tell them where your mother is!" Dmitri took several kicks to his torso. "He's a boy, you monsters, just a damn boy!" He spat out globs of blood as he shouted at the Nazi guards. From a crouched position, Dmitri scurried towards Viktor, but was knocked to the floor again before he could reach the trembling young man.

Dmitri's hands were tied, and a filthy rag stuffed into his mouth. He was dragged back across the room next to Gennady to witness the executions.

A guard looped piano wire around each of the meat-hooks. One by one the first three of the condemned prisoners had their heads pushed through the wire loops as they cried and begged for mercy. Viktor was kept to one side to watch what would happen to him next.

The more the prisoners struggled and writhed, with their hands tied behind their backs and their feet lashed together with rope, the greater the amusement of the SS guards.

A civilian cameraman was filming the whole horrific scene.

"For the Führer," said the camera operator proudly, noticing Gennady watching what he was doing.

Once the first three prisoners were in position, a guard used a crank to slowly lower the platform the prisoners were standing on. The noise of the gears turning corresponded to the tightening of the wire as the ground underneath, which the prisoners' feet were kicking to find, moved beyond their reach. It didn't take long for the kicking to stop.

The cruellest torture had been reserved for the fourteen-year-old Viktor, who was pushed to the platform and had the wire looped around his neck. The guards didn't ask Viktor to divulge the whereabouts of his mother; this confirmed to Dmitri that they wanted the boy to die, and for the Russian prince to witness it. What Dmitri had yet to divulge about the mysterious file had been deemed of greater value to the Nazi interrogator than Viktor's secret.

Viktor didn't cry, nor did he scream. He was numbed by shock. The prison guard turned the crank, and the platform started to lower.

Dmitri struggled to break free. His body was soaked in sweat as he pushed against the two guards holding him. His screams were muffled by the gag. He could taste blood.

When it came Viktor's turn to meet death, and his feet were no longer able to touch the retreating floor as the wire tightened and sliced into his neck, the guards lifted him up to revive him, then lowered his body to strangle him again. It took four such repetitions, and one of the guards to faint in horror, before the teenage prisoner stopped twisting and thrashing in the agony of an excruciating death, and his body hung limply from the meat hook.

Dmitri didn't see this; he'd closed his eyes. No matter how many Nazi fists attacked him, he refused to watch. But he heard the taunts of the most sadistic of the guards, and this reminded Dmitri of his mother's execution, that he had been forced to witness, when the Red Army soldiers treated her death at the end of several bayonets as a kind of sport.

Each victim had lost control of both bowel and bladder during the last moments of life, so the SS guards would not go near the hanging bodies. Dmitri and Gennady were ordered to unhook the corpses.

Dmitri vomited after releasing Viktor's body from the hook.

A doctor confirmed each person was dead, and Dmitri and Gennady were ordered to take the bodies to a waiting truck.

Dmitri pushed Gennady aside so that he could attend to Viktor's body himself. He carried it carefully and closed the young boy's monstrously disfigured eyes. The body weighed almost nothing. He cried and didn't wipe away the tears that came freely; he wanted everyone else to see and understand what they'd done.

Mankind had shown Dmitri once again the unimaginably cruel depths it could descend to.

A second cohort of prisoners suffered the same fate as the first, with Dmitri and Gennady being called upon to repeat their undertaker duties.

As he carried the filthy bodies of men who'd been shown no humanity, Dmitri thought about his two years as a Siberian prisoner, and of the friends he seen die there. He'd witnessed enough horrific death for several lifetimes, and now poor Viktor, a child would be added to his nightmares. Dmitri was numb. He couldn't think, he couldn't fight, he couldn't resist. He'd been broken.

The two men did as they were ordered. As Dmitri and Gennady stepped over the bodies already in the truck, placing the last one on the pile, the rear doors were slammed shut, trapping them inside, and the truck sped off.

Dmitri and Gennady were thrown off-balance, falling onto the mound of corpses. A volley of gunshots pierced the rear compartment of the truck, thudding into the corpses nearest the door. The vehicle accelerated to its top speed. The sharp turns tossed the two live men in the back against each other and the dead men with them.

When the vehicle came to a stop, Gennady and Dmitri were ready to fight whoever opened the rear door.

"Comrade Bunin?" asked a man, directing his question to Dmitri.

"Who wants to know?" said Dmitri. Gennady remained towards the back of the truck and stayed silent. Both suspected a Nazi rouse.

"Moscow informed us you'd been taken to Spandau. We were instructed to —"

"You are not Gennady Bunin," interrupted a slim, aristocratic-looking woman, who stepped forward through the line of armed men to speak to Dmitri. Half a dozen revolvers now pointed at him, and Dmitri raised his hands in surrender. She turned to the other man in the truck and said, "He is."

XIX

"I'M PLEASED to see you again Comrade Lázár," said Gennady. "I recognise you from Moscow."

"Red Front!" declared Marianne Lázár, raising her right fist. All but Dmitri repeated the salutation.

As Gennady and Dmitri jumped down from the truck, Viktor's body was accidentally flipped over by their movements. Marianne Lázár stared at the boy's dead face. His eyes were coloured entirely red from the burst blood vessels, and the ripped flesh from around his neck hung in torn strips. She put a hand to her mouth to stop herself either from crying or being sick.

Marianne looked away; her eyes were glassy with tears not yet released. She blinked these away, and her face hardened its expression. There was something both terrifying and alluring about her almond-shaped eyes, dishevelled-but-attractive dark hair, and pale face. There was a sultriness and confidence to her that Dmitri recognised as attractive to him, but which he tried to ignore.

"Your son?" asked Dmitri. One of the Communists quickly covered Viktor's face with a piece of sackcloth.

"He didn't betray you," said Dmitri, adding, "You should have surrendered."

"Then we'd both have died for nothing," she said. "Who are you?" She had the gravelly voice of a heavy smoker, and the hard-edged beauty of a *femme fatale*.

"He's certainly no Communist," said Gennady. "Shoot him."

Marianne Lázár took a revolver from the hand of the man nearest to her. She raised the weapon to Dmitri's head.

"You're no better than the monsters who killed Viktor," said Dmitri. His expression continued to condemn her, not for what she was about to do, but for what she'd failed to do, resulting in her son's torture and death. "You were able to save *him*." Dmitri inclined his head towards Gennady. "But not your own child."

"Moscow only authorised the rescue of -" began Marianne. Her arm began to lower as she glanced across at her son's body.

"I've heard it all before," interrupted Dmitri.

Marianne stiffened her arm and raised the gun to Dmitri's forehead.

"Wait!" shouted Pasha, pushing his way through the line of revolutionaries to make sure the voice he'd heard really was one he recognised. "I'll vouch for him."

"This isn't a damn country club!" bellowed Gennady. "Give me a gun and I'll shoot the Romanov swine myself."

Pasha addressed Marianne. "Like it or not, comrade, this man came to Berlin to help me. And perhaps it would benefit you, indeed all of us, to know why he was also in Spandau prison being interrogated by the Nazis?"

Marianne Lázár lowered the gun once again.

"Pasha makes a good point," she said. "Why are the Nazis interested in you?"

"If you don't mind, *comrade*, I'll speak with my friend alone," said Dmitri. As he glanced back at Viktor's body he added, "It's been rather a difficult day."

"ERICH'S HERE, Mitya," said Pasha. "I'll take you to him." Pasha hurriedly escorted Dmitri away from the armed Communists. He led Dmitri into a cabaret club where the air still smelt of alcohol, cigarettes and sweat. "The Nazis shut this place down two days ago, so we're using it as a temporary headquarters."

Men and women were sleeping in the dining booths around the perimeter of the small club, others were by the bar cleaning weapons, and drinking freely from the stock they'd confiscated.

"Oskar's a Nazi, Pasha," said Dmitri.

"I know," replied Pasha. "I found out just in time." Pasha descended the spiral staircase at the rear of the stage.

"But too late for Erich?" asked Dmitri.

"The SS worked him over thoroughly, Mitya. He's not in a good way at all, but his mother's with him."

"Frau Renfeldt?" asked Dmitri.

"You're not surprised?" Pasha was about to knock on one of the former dressing rooms when Dmitri took hold of his hand.

"What's Gennady doing here, Pasha? And why have I been rescued from Spandau?" Pasha led Dmitri on a few steps away from the door he'd been about to knock on.

"We didn't know about you. One of the prison guards, a Prussian officer, is sympathetic to Moscow's cause, so he made sure Gennady was part of the executions today. We arranged to collect the bodies for burial, so Gennady could be rescued."

"Lucky me," said Dmitri.

"Maybe," replied Pasha. Dmitri understood what his friend wasn't saying; a Romanov prince was no safer with Communist revolutionaries than he was as a guest of the National Socialists in Spandau prison.

"And the boy?" asked Dmitri. "Why save Gennady but not her own son?"

"As she said, Moscow wouldn't sanction it," said Pasha.

"Really?" exclaimed Dmitri. "And these are the heartless people you've taken up with, Pasha?"

"The Nazis killed Viktor, not the Communists," said Pasha.

"If you really see it like that, Pasha, then there's no hope for you."

Pasha didn't reply.

Frau Renfeldt performed her customary curtsey when Dmitri entered the small dressing room where Erich was recuperating. Cabaret costumes and make-up littered the floor, and a smell of grease lingered in the airless room. Despite there only being muted light from the one lamp, Dmitri could see how swollen and bruised Erich's face was. Both legs were fastened into make-shift splints. He was lying on seat cushions placed on the floor.

"Mitya?" Erich tried to sit up on his elbows, but the pain was too sharp.

"Yes, It's me, Erich." Dmitri crouched down and reached for Erich's left hand. It was bandaged. Dmitri noticed that the two forefingers were missing.

"They took them," mumbled Erich indistinctly through swollen, split lips, and a mouth of missing teeth. He pulled his mutilated hand out of his friend's grip. "But they didn't take my Guarneri." He looked across at a violin, once owned by Louis XV, and which had accompanied Erich across Europe since his youth.

The pale orange varnish of the violin glowed brightly despite the half-light of the room, as if asking to be played by the man who would never be able do so again. The instrument had now become an ornament, a memory, a painful reminder, as the Nazis intended it to be. It would have to get used to remaining silent. The Nazis had cruelly removed the fingers Erich needed to play it but had let the musician live.

"I'll get you to safety," promised Dmitri. He was ashamed that he had so far failed to do just that. He doubted whether this was an assurance he could now honour. Viktor had already learnt how empty Dmitri's guarantees had become; making more promises to Erich now seemed dishonest.

"It's my fault," murmured Erich. "I'm sorry."

"You have nothing to apologise for," said Dmitri.

"The beatings…they were…I told them about you." Erich turned his face away from Dmitri, then added in a whisper, "I am Napoleon."

Frau Renfeldt attended to her son, as he drifted in and out of consciousness. This was the first time Dmitri had ever seen her without the disagreeable expression which had always seemed to be her natural temperament; it had been replaced with the gentleness of a mother whose son was broken. She was unrecognisable, and able to freely acknowledge the son she'd accompanied for many years as his housekeeper.

"He didn't betray you for several days under torture," said Pasha, once he and Dmitri had left Erich to rest. "You can see how long he held out."

"No one could resist that," said Dmitri. "I must get to Sable, Pasha. Have you any clothes I can change into?" He held out his arms to show the full awfulness of the prison uniform he was still wearing.

"Only those confiscated from the real drivers of the prison truck."

"I guess they'll have to do."

"Lázár won't let you leave, Mitya, not now you've seen where we're hiding."

"Yes, she will," said Dmitri. He took the prison shirt off and unwrapped the bandage from his arm. The seven-point crucifix dropped into his other hand, along with a piece of paper that had been kept safe between the two bandages since his escape from Schorfheide. On this was written the list of witnesses he'd copied down from the dossier; names and addresses of people who could corroborate the rumour of Hitler's Jewish ancestry.

"This is why I was in Spandau," he said. "I have something valuable to bargain with."

XX

"SABLE'S CHECKED out," said Pasha.

"Christ!" exclaimed Dmitri.

"Well, that's settled then," said Gennady.

Pasha had gone into the Adlon Hotel to give Sable the message that Dmitri was waiting for her by the Brandenburg Gate. Gennady's presence was one of the conditions allowing Dmitri to leave the temporary headquarters of Berlin's Communist resistance.

"But her correspondence is being forwarded to the Kaiserhof Hotel," added Pasha.

"Then let's hurry," said Dmitri.

"The Kaiserhof has been taken over by the National Socialists as their unofficial headquarters whilst the transition to the Reichstag is taking place," said Pasha. "Hitler even has a suite of rooms there."

"And?" Dmitri was already walking off, only to be pulled back by Gennady.

"The deal was to let you visit the Adlon," said Gennady. He thrust the barrel of a gun into Dmitri's ribs.

"No, the deal was to get in touch with Sable," said Dmitri. The hatred between the two men was made explicit in each's eyes but, for now, each needed the other. "So we go to the Kaiserhof."

Instead of top-hatted doormen, the Kaiserhof had SA brownshirts on guard at every entrance. Identity papers of guests seeking admittance were being checked. Red banners with the black swastika on a white circle were draped from the balconies. This was not somewhere any of the three men could enter freely.

"Well, without the film, you must give us the addresses," reminded Gennady.

"You quit very easily, don't you Gennady Vladimirovich?" said Dmitri. "I remember you being much more tenacious as our chauffeur; perhaps that career suited you better."

"I'm very determined to return you to Russia for trial and execution," said Gennady. "So don't get cocky. You can be sure I'll be the one pulling the trigger."

"Oh, hang the film!" said Pasha, taking on the role of moderator between the two enemies. "If Mitya says his friend from Paris is in trouble, then we have to do something to help her."

"I have little interest in the welfare of a rich American socialite." Gennady stepped back into the shade of a doorway as more SA stormtroopers arrived at the hotel entrance opposite them. "We Communists must defeat National Socialism."

"Moscow has unclear priorities," said Pasha, betraying the beginnings of a loss of faith in the cause he supported. "Russia has been telling us to defeat the Socialist Party here and ignore the Nazis. Moscow just wants hegemony over the workers, regardless of the consequences."

"Both Stalin and Hitler require fear, not faith," suggested Dmitri, keeping his eyes on the hotel from their position on the opposite side of the street. "It wouldn't surprise me if the two leaders hadn't worked out a deal together."

"A Communist Party take-over here has never been a priority for Moscow," added Pasha, "but we allowed ourselves to be betrayed trying."

"Moscow hasn't betrayed you," barked Gennady, "It has sent me."

Dmitri realised Pasha was thinking more about Oskar's betrayal, not Moscow's. He looked up and down the street at the shops with their windows broken and frontages defaced by slogans demanding, 'Jews get out!', and declaring, 'Germany awake! Death to Judah! Heil Hitler!'. Seeing such racial animosity openly tolerated reminded him of Isaak's fate; this made him more determined to find Sable, despite the obstacles.

"Have either of you got any money?" asked Dmitri, coming up with an idea. Pasha handed over a few coins, all that remained of the bundle of German marks Oskar had taken from Dmitri the previous week. "Come with me," said Dmitri. They stepped into a tobacconist's shop, the windows of which no longer had glass in them.

Minutes later Dmitri walked up the steps of the Kaiserhof hotel carrying a small parcel wrapped in brown paper and string. As he was wearing the uniform of a delivery man, which the Communists had confiscated earlier from the genuine drivers of the prison truck, he felt confident that the guards might not ask him for identification.

He walked confidently up the steps, at the top of which he approached an SA guard.

"Would you deliver this?" asked Dmitri, adopting the weary attitude of a delivery man.

"Do we look like postmen?" rebuked the guard. "Do it yourself." Dmitri had known that if he'd tried to enter the hotel he would have been stopped. However, trying not to enter resulted in the opposite reaction, as he'd hoped it would. He understood people well.

The guard didn't ask for identity papers, but checked the name on the parcel, and let Dmitri pass unhindered. Being cautious, Dmitri had written the parcel's addressee as: 'SS-Brigadeführer und Generalmajor der Waffen-SS und Polizei Wolfrick Vogel.' The rank of the parcel's intended recipient was of sufficient seniority that Dmitri assumed the SA guards would not hinder its delivery. He had been right.

The lobby of the Kaiserhof Hotel was more like an operations room for a military campaign than a luxury hotel reception area. Men were dressed in a variety of uniforms, including the brownshirts of the SA, the black tunics of the SS, and the blue uniforms of the Prussian Ministry of Justice.

"I have a delivery for Brigadeführer Vogel," announced Dmitri to the clerk.

"The Brigadeführer is away, leave it with me." Dmitri did as he was told. His worries at his German accent being easily detected as foreign were unnecessary as the clerk, disgruntled at having his hotel lobby appropriated by the National Socialists, showed little interest or diligence in his work.

"I also have a package to collect from Herr Heinz Langer," added Dmitri.

"He's out," barked the reception clerk.

"Perhaps you could try his room? Or I'll go and knock to save you the trouble."

"No need," replied the clerk. "I saw him leave with his wife."

Wife. Dmitri repeated the word in his own mind. He was too late. Sable had got married whilst he'd been in Spandau.

"Shall I wait?" asked Dmitri, maintaining his composure.

"Come back later."

"Perhaps they've only gone out briefly. I probably should wait as my instructions were to collect."

"Don't bother, they've gone to some rally," said the clerk. "Thankfully, this lot will be going there too soon." He inclined his head towards the groups of uniformed men talking noisily, disturbing the usual quiet. He slid a few pfennigs across the desk for Dmitri as compensation for the lost tip from Heinz.

"Thanks." Dmitri took the coins.

Gennady waited nervously across the street with Pasha. He couldn't accompany Dmitri into the hotel but would look ridiculous to Lázár's Berlin Communists if he lost their Romanov prisoner, especially as he had neither the camera film nor the witness addresses needed for the enquiries in Austria into Hitler's ancestry.

"There's a Nazi gathering tonight," announced Dmitri, re-joining Pasha and Gennady. "Heinz and Sable are there."

"Where?" asked Gennady, growing impatient with the prince's delays.

"Wherever *they* go," said Dmitri indicating towards the Nazi troops.

"And the film?" asked Gennady.

"That's what I need Heinz for."

"THERE'S A Communist with a gun standing behind you," said Dmitri. He'd found Heinz in the crowd gathered in Opernplatz.

Heinz looked first at Dmitri, then behind, where he saw the unfriendly eyes of Gennady, and the muzzle of a revolver almost touching him. He turned back to face the spectacle.

The large public square included the State Opera House on one side, and St. Hedwig's Cathedral on another. The quadrangle was filled with a mighty gathering of students, uniformed National Socialist Party officials, and curious Berlin residents. In the centre of the square a wooden pyre had been constructed, now with a fire roaring stoked by the repeated hurling of books to feed the hungry flames. The activity was encircled by spectators carrying lighted torches that cast curious shadows upon the ornate facades of the buildings. The crackling sound from the burning wood and volumes of books seemed trapped in the square, creating a curious vibration in the unquiet atmosphere.

Sable was standing to the other side of Heinz. She made a quick glance across at Dmitri, then turned back to face forwards, trying to disguise her surprise.

Pasha took up a position to Sable's left; the four of them stood in a line watching the book burning, with an armed Gennady positioned closely behind.

A truck pushed its way into the square through the torchlight perimeter and the agitated crowd. The driver honked the horn in celebration of bringing new kindling for the fire. Members of the German Student Union unclipped and lowered the side of the truck, from which hundreds more books cascaded onto the ground, these having been confiscated from dozens of libraries around the city.

Students rushed forwards, scooping up armfuls of books, which they then tossed into the flames of the literary pyre, chanting oaths about destroying subversive literature, and purifying their German culture against immorality. Some adults picked up those books dropped by the student fire-stokers and tossed these on the bonfire. Some had brought small children with them and encouraged these youngsters to mimic the teenage students in destroying volumes of literature deemed un-German by the new creed of literary critics taking power across Germany. Dmitri was amazed that an educated nation such as Germany could participate so willingly in a demonstration of mass barbarianism.

"Heinz told me about Isaak," said Sable. She slid herself between Dmitri and Heinz, putting herself deliberately in the line of fire from Gennady's gun. She didn't turn towards Dmitri but spoke loud enough to be heard above the music and singing of the student philistines. "We're trapped, Mitya."

Heinz slowly reached behind, and guided Gennady's weapon to his own back, away from Sable's.

"My fellow students ..." One of the Nazi leaders stood on a swastika-draped podium to address the crowd. "The era of exaggerated Jewish intellectualism is now at an end."

"You have to leave Germany, Sable," said Dmitri.

"Don't you see, Mitya, we can't," she replied.

"Heinz might not, but you can."

"He's ashamed of himself," she said, touching Dmitri's fingers with her own in a light passing connection of affection. "This isn't a club you can resign from; membership is for life."

"Your husband must let you leave with me," said Dmitri, turning to face Sable.

"We're not married, yet," she said, not turning away from the pyre of books.

The noise of chanting from the crowd was getting louder as the Nazi speaker roused them with more rhetoric about the dangers of un-German culture.

"Hurry up, or I'll kill you all," said Gennady, stepping in closer. He prodded the gun alternately in each of their spines. The increasing number of uniformed Nazis in the square was making him anxious.

"...and the future German man will not just be a man of books but also a man of character, and it is to this end that we want to educate you ..." the speech continued to blare around the square, as the students heaved more and more books onto the flames of the enormous bonfire.

"If I could have stopped what happened to Isaak, Mitya, I would —" began Heinz.

"You could have, but you didn't," interrupted Dmitri. "I saw what they did to him."

"I've told Sable everything."

"And yet you've let her remain here, in Berlin, to watch this."

"Sable is in more danger if I do anything to raise suspicions. We're trapped."

"I'm taking her with me tonight, Heinz." Dmitri leant forward and turned to face Sable's fiancé. "They're only interested in you."

"Take this as well then." Heinz passed the roll of camera film that Dmitri had previously hidden in his luggage at Schorfheide to Sable, who then gave it to Dmitri. "I watched you go into the general's study, I guessed it was for the dossier," added Heinz.

"Give me the film," instructed Gennady, having seen the exchange.

"So, you'll give it to the Communists?" asked Heinz. "I suppose that's best. But will they help Sable or your two friends?"

"They only help themselves," mumbled Dmitri, more to himself than Heinz. As he reached across to pass the film back to Gennady, he thought about Viktor. The boy's mutilated neck and face was a horrifying image he couldn't forget. The wriggling body and the piano wire were images which flashed into his mind. Viktor could have survived if his mother had tried to save him; she was the person Gennady would give the film to. He would not help the Communists.

"Sorry, *comrade*," said Dmitri to Gennady as he threw the roll of film into the fire. Gennady pushed forwards but could only watch as the film curled and melted in the flames. This brief distraction gave Dmitri the opportunity to wrench the gun out of Gennady's hand.

"Now they don't have it, and you don't have it," said Dmitri. He pocketed the gun before someone in the crowd raised an alarm.

"…that is the mission of the youth," continued the Nazi speaker, bringing his homily on the virtues of ignorance to a climax, "and you do well at this late hour to entrust to the flames the intellectual garbage of the past …"

Gennady was at a loss of what to do. With no film he had nothing to give Marianne. And with no gun, he had nothing with which to compel Dmitri to come with him or to hand over the list of names.

"I'll ensure the Communists don't let you get out of Berlin," hissed Gennady.

"And with one shout from me, I can ensure you don't leave this square," replied Dmitri.

"Not without condemning yourself."

"Then you have a decision to make, comrade, is my hatred for you and what you represent greater than my own safety?" asked Dmitri.

"I'll find you, Romanov," said Gennady.

"I'm counting on it," replied Dmitri.

Gennady scanned the crowd and walked off where there were the fewest uniformed Nazis.

"Why burn it?" asked Pasha.

"Your friends never going to help us," replied Dmitri.

The excited crowd erupted into a rendition of the Horst Wessel Nazi anthem, converging on the podium and the uniformed National Socialist banner-bearers standing around their spokesperson.

"Why are these books so dangerous?" asked Sable. The crowd around them began to disperse towards the podium.

"Knowledge makes people unpredictable," suggested Heinz.

"I don't let my friends burn," said Dmitri. He reached down and picked up a copy of 'The Sun Also Rises'. "Even if I can save only one," he added.

The people standing by him were too distracted to notice this act of defiance, one which was important as he'd spent time with Hemingway in Paris. The writer had spoken to Dmitri of his disgust at New Yorkers burning James Joyce's 'Ulysses'. Dmitri held the book at his side, waiting for someone to challenge him.

Sable smiled at her friend's gesture. Despite the risk, she stepped forwards and picked up a slightly charred copy of Heinrich Mann's 'Professor Unrat'; watching the film adaptation two years before had been one of her first cultural introductions to Germany.

Heinz crouched to the litter of books that had missed the fire, and which had not yet been scooped up by an energetic student. He took a copy of Helen Keller's 'Out of the Dark', acknowledging his own recent moral blindness. Sable took hold of his free hand, glad that her fiancé had joined her mutiny.

Pasha was less quick to ally himself with them. Heinz, a wealthy industrialist who'd financed the National Socialists, and Sable, his American socialite fiancée, were his enemies. His Communist friends had died because of the political party Heinz had helped bring to power. Burning of books was not the most supreme act of injustice he'd witnessed recently. Picking up one volume seemed an insufficient act of protest; he wanted revenge that would destroy the fascist system.

"We have to go," suggested Dmitri. "Before we're noticed."

The three book-carrying dissenters started to edge away from the fire. Dmitri looked back at Pasha, his eyes pleading with his friend to join them. He was about to lose sight of Heinz and Sable, so had to decide whether to stay with Pasha or leave with them.

Pasha, framed by the flames of the bonfire behind him, looked as if the blaze would swoop over and engulf him at the slightest change in wind direction. Dmitri remembered his father's instructions in Kitzbühel, a reminder about duty and sacrifice.

Sable had Heinz, but Pasha had no one, not even the Communists now. Dmitri, a prince of Russia, could not leave his countryman alone as Pasha's own father had done. Pasha needed Dmitri more than Sable. Dmitri returned to the bonfire.

"Do you remember how the tsar's valets used to get angry when we deliberately disarranged Uncle Nicky's monthly books that he'd carefully put in order of preference, Pasha?" asked Dmitri. "Your father was furious, but the tsar let you stay for the evening and he read to us all in his clear gentle voice."

"I haven't thought much about my childhood, much less my father," said Pasha.

"Books are important Pasha; family is important; survival is important. You and I know that more than most," said Dmitri. "That boy, in the palace study is as much you as the person you are today. Perhaps there's a way for you to be both?"

Pasha bent down and picked up a copy of Remarque's 'All Quiet on the Western Front', a piece of literature decrying the human costs of war. He fanned the pages quickly, trying to decide whether it should go on the fire or not. Pasha, the orphan, knew the price of war.

"Now they burn books, soon they will burn bodies," said Pasha. He glanced across at the people emptying the truck of books as he made this prediction. "Let's catch the others up, Mitya," he said. He kept hold of the book.

215

XXI

PASHA WAS now dressed in Isaak's chauffeur uniform and driving Heinz's Mercedes Grosser-Pullman limousine. Dmitri sat next to him wearing an overcoat that Heinz had provided, and which covered up the courier's uniform Dmitri still wore underneath.

"I told one of the SS officers at the hotel to inform their colleagues in Essen that I would be travelling there tonight," said Heinz. He leant through the window of the limousine that divided him and Sable in the back from Dmitri and Pasha in the front cab.

"And they'll let you leave Berlin?" asked Dmitri, leaning back.

"I told them my wedding was in Essen. They know that's where my estate is, so it makes sense that I'd be getting married there."

Dmitri hoped the mention of a wedding was nothing more than a rouse for the benefit of the Nazis. Even with Heinz's show of remorse, and his rejection of National Socialism, the industrialist still fell short of the standard Dmitri would accept of someone suitable to marry his American friend.

"We need to make a stop first," said Dmitri. He checked that the gun he'd taken off Gennady was loaded.

Pasha drove past the entrance to the cabaret club which the Communists were using as their temporary headquarters. The lack of people outside didn't mean the rebels had moved on, and if they had, Dmitri worried for Erich and his mother.

"I'll go in alone," suggested Pasha, having parked the limousine. He picked up the gun Dmitri had left on the seat. "I'm still one of them."

"No, I'm going with you," insisted Dmitri.

"I'll go," said Heinz. "I can pretend I'm a jazz lover looking for the cabaret club. If there's any trouble, I'll just curse my bad luck and leave." He was out of the limousine before Dmitri could offer an argument. His idea also made the most sense, so Dmitri sat back and searched the borrowed overcoat for any cigarettes.

"No one goes to the cabaret on their own," said Sable. "It looks more convincing if I'm with him." She leapt out of the car and ran across the road, holding up her skirt to jump over puddles in the blocked gutters.

"Sable, no!" exclaimed Dmitri, flinging the door open and narrowly missing a passing car. Pasha pulled him back into the vehicle.

"Leave them" urged Pasha. "Your lady friend seems perfectly capable of taking care of herself."

"Her choice of fiancé would suggest otherwise," said Dmitri, accepting Pasha's instruction to remain in the car.

"So you aren't convinced by his sudden renunciation of Herr Hitler?" asked Pasha. He offered Dmitri a cigarette.

"Regardless of that, how the deuce can Sable stand him?"

"Are you jealous, Mitya?" suggested Pasha.

Before Dmitri could answer the question, Sable emerged from the club, waving that it was safe to join her.

The club was empty, and the faded glamour was even more marked by that sparseness of people. The place was designed to be seen only in half-light, with a crush of shimmying bodies filling the too-small space, and the loud jerky rhythms of saxophones and trumpets making conversation difficult.

"They've only recently left," said Pasha, finding a cigarette still burning in an ashtray at the bar. Dmitri guessed that whilst they'd been at the hotel waiting for Heinz and Sable to pack, Gennady had returned here and encouraged the Communists to leave as the hideout was no longer safe. He walked across the dancefloor to the stage, hoping he'd find Erich waiting in the basement dressing room, but fearing he probably would not.

A few tentative notes from a violin crept up from below where Dmitri was standing. Those first cautious notes quickly formed into a coherent piece of music, the classical arrangement of which seemed incongruous in a place more accustomed to the tense, rowdy beats of jazz. The gentle music called for the four of them in the club to follow the notes to its source; Dmitri was glad his friend had been left behind.

Frau Renfeldt's fleshy mass was lying face down on the floor of the dressing room. The entry wound at the back of her skull indicated that she had been surprised by the shot, this was some small consolation.

Erich had dragged himself over to the far wall to be with his mother's corpse, leaving a smear of blood on the already filthy carpet. His stomach wounds continued to pump out gushes of blood as he took shallow breaths.

The airless room left a metallic taste in Dmitri's mouth. He could smell the lingering cordite from the recent gun shots.

With the bow held uncomfortably in the remaining fingers of his left hand, and the full complement of fingers on his right finding the strings, Erich faultlessly played the antique violin which the Nazi torturers had assumed he'd never do so again following their mutilation of his hand. Erich watched over the body of his mother as he played Mozart's Lacrimosa requiem. This was her funeral.

"The Communists?" asked Dmitri softly, not wanting to disturb the power of the music. Erich gave a small nod. Another gush of blood leaked from his evisceration wound. His arms began to weaken, and the notes to falter.

"The Nazis didn't realise …" Erich's sentence was interrupted by a wheezing, followed by a cough of blood, "…that I'm left-handed." His small laugh became an uncomfortable cough, which then developed into a painful choke. The violin and bow dropped from his hands as the fluid in his throat suffocated him.

Dmitri and Pasha rushed to help, but there was nothing they could do.

The sound of voices and the thud of boots from the floor above then reached them.

"Damn it!" exclaimed Heinz. "We're trapped." His expression was one of fear and cowardice; Dmitri recognised it from the night on the terrace at the hunting lodge.

"There are other exits," said Pasha. "The stage door is along the corridor."

Heinz took Pasha by the arm pushing him forwards, encouraging him to lead the way quickly. Heinz left Sable behind.

"If we live, they live, Mitya," said Sable, touching the shoulder of her friend, who was crouching by Erich's body. "The only truly dead are those who have been forgotten."

"The Communists are no better than the Nazis," said Dmitri. "I've seen too much death."

"We must go, darling," urged Sable.

Dmitri laid the violin and bow across Erich's chest, hoping the police would ensure the great musician would be buried with his instrument.

At one end of the long corridor cluttered with costumes and props the SA brownshirts appeared, at the other end Dmitri and Sable were dashing for one of the exits used by the performers.

Someone gave the order to shoot. Dmitri pushed Sable aside and the bullet came between them, piercing into a heating pipe, the explosion of steam from which surprised Sable. She lost her footing and fell down the three steps that led down to the exit.

"Mitya, I don't think I can walk," said Sable. Her ankle was badly twisted, and putting any weight on it was agony.

"Try for me, darling," said Dmitri, holding open the exit door.

Sable took two steps forward and collapsed against a rail of costumes.

"Leave me," she urged.

"Like hell I will." Dmitri scooped Sable into his arms and carried her through the door into an alleyway behind the club. He put her down in order to wedge a metal pipe against the door, forcing the brownshirts to make their way back through the club, and giving Dmitri and Sable a head start.

"Damn it!" he exclaimed. "Where are they?" He'd carried Sable through the alleyway and around the next block, bringing them out further along the street where Heinz's limousine had been left. The car had gone.

Sable couldn't walk, and Dmitri carrying her would be too conspicuous. They were trapped. Dmitri reached into the pocket of the overcoat for the gun he'd taken off

Gennady. Not finding it, he remembered that Pasha had taken it when they were in the limousine.

"What are we to do, darling?" asked Sable.

"If I run, they might chase me," suggested Dmitri. "You can hide and wait for Heinz and Pasha to return."

"But what will happen to you, Mitya?"

"I'm a fast runner," joked Dmitri.

"I don't doubt it. But I mean, if they don't catch you, how will we find you?"

"Where's the French embassy?"

"Oh, yes, good idea, Mitya. It's at Pariser Platz. From the Adlon head towards the Spree river and it's on the left."

"I don't like to leave you here, Sable, but I can't see any other way out. They're already searching the streets."

"Darling?"

"Yes?" asked Dmitri.

"I think there's a man waving at us from the doorway over there." Sable gestured to a building on the main street.

Dmitri glanced to where Sable had indicated, but there was no one there.

"It's nothing, darling," said Dmitri.

"Just wait, and watch."

"We don't really have time."

An elderly man then poked his head out from the doorway of the building Sable had pointed to. He gave a quick wave, unmistakably beckoning Dmitri and Sable to join him, then disappeared back into the doorway and out of sight.

"It could be a trap," said Dmitri.

"Aren't we already trapped?" asked Sable. She steadied her shoulder against the wall to take some of the weight off her ankle, and hobbled slowly out onto the main street towards the doorway.

"Sable, for Christ's sake," hissed Dmitri, but he stayed back and watched for a reaction from the SA brownshirts further down the main street. He readied himself to run towards them and surrender if they should notice Sable.

Only once Sable was out of sight in the doorway did Dmitri push his shoulders back and slowly step out onto the main thoroughfare. Knowing the Nazis were only a couple of streets behind him made the hairs stand up on the back of his neck. He stopped himself from hurrying, instead browsing in shop windows and meandering slowly towards the doorway.

"Herr Schacht has a place to hide us," said Sable. She was already inside the building, holding the door open for Dmitri.

"You are English?" asked the elderly man.

"Russian and American," said Dmitri.

"Jewish?"

"Well -" Dmitri began to speak.

"Yes," interrupted Sable, adding, "and in very great danger."

"This way," said the old man.

In his kitchen he started to move the electric stove. "Please," he said, "We must push."

Dmitri easily manoeuvred the stove across the floor and Herr Schacht lifted up the first of several loose floorboards.

There was a loud knock at the front door, followed by the command, "*Achtung! Achtung!*"

"Our friends will come looking for us soon," said Sable to Herr Schacht as Dmitri lifted her by the shoulders and lowered her into the space under the kitchen floor. "Two young men in a Mercedes limousine." Herr Schacht nodded his understanding, glanced towards the door that was being hammered on by several fists, and waved for Dmitri to get into the hiding place.

"Thank you," said Dmitri as he moved the floorboards back over his head.

"We Germans are not all like the devil," said Herr Schacht.

There was just enough space under the kitchen floor for Dmitri and Sable to crouch, but they chose to lie side-by-side. Herr Schacht had lined the crawl space with blankets, and, in the darkness, Dmitri could feel bottles of something and packets of food. Sable took Dmitri's hand and clenched it tight. They heard Herr Schacht's laboured attempts to replace the stove over the top of them and Dmitri wished now he hadn't pushed it so far away from its usual place.

Neither Dmitri nor Sable dared even whisper. They lay like corpses, listening to the thud of footsteps above them, and each waiting either for Herr Schacht to give them up or for them to be discovered, arrested, or shot.

Even when the footsteps had gone, neither Dmitri nor Sable dared to either move or speak. Each could hear the other's shallow breaths. Dmitri occasionally squeezed Sable's hand and she responded in kind. Time lost its relevance; seconds could have been minutes, or minutes hours.

More heavy footsteps stamped across the kitchen floor. The unmistakable scraping of the stove prompted Sable's grip to tighten, crushing Dmitri's hand.

The first of the floorboards was removed, and the occupants of the crawl space blinked at the sudden burst of light which distorted their vision.

"This is hardly the time for a game of hide and seek," joked Pasha. He extended a hand down to Sable.

XXII
Essen.

DMITRI HAD wanted to continue the escape out of Germany completely, but Heinz insisted on going to his family estate at Essen in western Germany instead. His argument, being that a border crossing now would be too dangerous if he and Sable were already under suspicion, carried enough weight to get Pasha and Sable's agreement to their temporary stay in Essen.

Villa Alleinstein was the gilded nineteenth century mansion that Heinz proudly called 'the Versailles of the Ruhr'. Dmitri saw it as a theatrical attempt at noble pretence by a family of common financiers who'd struck lucky with some mining explorations eighty years before. Every piece of Chinese porcelain, each ornately framed picture of a plump naked goddess by a stream, and all of the classical depictions painted on the walls had been purchased in bulk as set decoration for the house when it had been built by Heinz's newly-rich grandfather. Dmitri disliked the pretension of it all and wanted to rescue Sable from its self-important posturing; she deserved substance, which neither Heinz nor his property suggested.

Dmitri had reluctantly acquiesced to the delay, but two days had now passed in Essen and he was uneasy with their remaining in Germany any longer. He was restless to get Sable and Pasha to safety across an international border.

Pasha, who continued in the disguise of chauffeur, and Dmitri were housed together in one of the two hundred rooms of the grand mansion, being in the area reserved for the other servants. They had all decided that two new staff members was less suspicious than two house guests; staff came and went frequently as workers realised they could earn more money from industrial labour than domestic service.

However, this pretence kept Dmitri and Pasha apart from Heinz and Sable and reduced the opportunities Dmitri had to add pressure on the argument to leave Germany. The opportunities for all four of the Berlin fugitives to be together were limited, as Heinz and Sable convincingly conducted themselves like two young people engaged and due to marry soon, with Heinz introducing his fiancée to his friends in the northern Ruhr city at nightly soirees.

Dmitri had already suggested to Sable that perhaps her betrothed was not the man she thought him to be. Sable had refused to hear about what led to Isaak's death, and maintained that she loved Heinz. She wanted to leave Germany, she'd told Dmitri, but with Heinz not without him.

"Beckendorff told me before I left the hunting weekend that he'd asked me to buy the dossier from the Austrians to blackmail Hitler, not to protect the Führer from its contents," said Heinz. He showed Dmitri the obituary of General von Beckendorff in the newspaper.

"Then I don't imagine the old soldier's death was from natural causes," suggested Dmitri, glancing at the report. The Russian prince was dressed in the livery of Heinz' valet, and remained standing when in Heinz' presence, just in case another member of the fifteen-strong household staff unexpectedly entered.

"His wife, Hedda, was the real Nazi, not the general," said Heinz. "I assumed he wanted the file to advance his wife's standing in the Party."

"It seems he wanted to humiliate her instead," replied Dmitri, "and the new chancellor." He passed Heinz a dinner jacket. "Knowing the contents of that dossier leaves you with a target on your back, Heinz."

"Only if the Party thinks I can't be trusted," said the industrialist as he put on his jacket.

"What if they don't care?" asked Dmitri. "I think we should leave for the Dutch border, or the League of Nations protectorate in Saar, tonight."

"If I am a target, then running away in the middle of the night is only going to make things worse."

"I don't like this," urged Dmitri. "We're not safe here."

"Trust me, Mitya," said Heinz. "I love Sable and won't put her at risk."

"If I didn't trust you, Heinz, I wouldn't have agreed to us staying here," said Dmitri. "But Sable and Pasha need to be told about Beckendorff. His death changes things."

"No, it doesn't," insisted Heinz, confident that he had the upper hand in the decision-making process that their small democracy of four people seemed to have developed into. "I have to introduce Sable to more of Essen's high society at dinner, so perhaps we can all meet afterwards?" Heinz checked his reflection in the full-length mirror. "We'll go when I'm sure the Nazis don't suspect anything." He smiled back at Dmitri as he left the room.

The confidence of the young industrialist did not ease Dmitri's worries. The Russian prince was a man used to being in charge of his own destiny. Since his escape from

Siberia he'd led a life on his own terms rather than following other people. It had been his father's instruction for him to come to Germany, the first such parental order since the grand duke's return from a mental wilderness. That decision had proved a disaster for Erich and his mother. Nothing good had come from Dmitri's journey to Berlin, and he now regretted not trusting his instinct to go back to Paris with his family and help his friends in Germany from there.

Now he was putting faith in the assurances of a man who had been so weak as to fire a gun at the head of his own chauffeur just because a failed teacher dressed in the new uniform of political power in Germany had told him to prove his loyalty to the Führer.

Heinz had shown little remorse, despite the gun he'd fired being empty, for the eventual fate Isaak had met at the hands of the brigadeführer. In fact, Heinz seemed to be enjoying himself too much, having returned to Essen as master of the expansive family estate he'd inherited upon his father's early death five years before. He presented Sable to his associates as one might show off a prize he'd won, and a trophy he intended to keep. His time was occupied making decisions about the management of the estate, a building he was soon to abandon, and his business interests, endeavours which would surely be confiscated by the National Socialists when their owner's betrayal and flight from Germany were made known.

Heinz did not appear to Dmitri to be simply biding his time before escape, but a young man relaxing into life at his country estate with a beautiful woman who'd promised herself to him.

Dmitri had seen Heinz quickly turn down the volume on a large Bakelite radio receiver when he'd entered the dressing room. The faint noise from its speakers could still be heard now that Heinz had left for dinner, even if what was being said on the radio was unclear. Dmitri was about to turn it off completely, when his fingers moved the volume dial up instead of down.

After only a few minutes of listening, it was clear to Dmitri that Heinz had the set tuned into a frequency dedicated to the propaganda of the National Socialists. He smashed his fist down on the console table, bruising his hand, and cracking the geometric marquetry of the wooden tabletop.

"HE WAS listening to a Nazi radio station," said Dmitri, intercepting Sable as she made her way to dinner from her own suite of rooms on the first floor of the villa.

"Stop it, darling," she replied. "You're being jealous. Of course he'd listen to that station, to hear if any news about us was being broadcast."

"I don't like us being here," urged Dmitri. He adopted the appearance of a servant, staying a step behind Sable. She hurried along one of the many corridors in which she'd frequently gotten lost over the two days she'd spent in residence under the pretence of betrothed lady-of-the-manor. "Let's all leave now," urged Dmitri. "We can be across the Dutch border in an hour, and before anyone raises the alarm."

"And if they're already watching us, Mitya? Waiting for us to do just that?" She didn't look back at him but glanced in a gilt-framed mirror as she passed it, admiring herself in the latest of many new frocks by designer Annemarie Heise that she'd brought with her from Berlin.

"If you want to stay here and be his Madam Pompadour, then just admit it."

"You're being childish, Mitya."

"Beckendorff's dead," he said. Sable stopped walking. She inclined her head to one side, as if trying to place the name. "The general," clarified Dmitri. "The Nazis are cleaning house, Sable. And we're a large stain on their new carpet."

"I'll be late for dinner," she replied, tossing a swathe of ivory taffeta over her shoulder. She started to descend the stairs of the grand hallway. She smiled at the guests awaiting her arrival at the bottom.

Dmitri stayed at the top of the stairs in the shadows.

"I'M HANGED if I'll chuck up the sponge on this one, Pasha," said Dmitri, throwing himself back on his own bed in the small room he now shared with his childhood friend. "I don't like trusting my fate to a man like Heinz."

"He does seem to be taking the whole charade of being back here for the wedding a little too earnestly," replied Pasha. He was polishing his shoes and demonstrating very little skill at a task he'd never had to do as a younger man, and never bothered to do as an adult.

"This all feels like hooey to me," said Dmitri.

"I drove Heinz and Sable to one of the collieries he owns today," said Pasha, "and he told me to go and meet the mine workers." Pasha put down the polish and brushes and moved over to Dmitri's bed so he could speak in a whisper. "I understand why showing his fiancée around makes things look legitimate, but why am I being told to show myself to more people than is necessary?"

"Did you?" asked Dmitri.

"Hell no. I wandered around out of sight for a while and managed to get my only clean shirt covered in coal dust doing so. I beat it back to the car and waited there feeding handfuls of grass to the pit-ponies. I watched the winding wheel bringing the cages up and listened to the crusher grind away until Heinz and Sable came back."

"Was anything said?"

"I told him on the journey back here that it had been a stupid idea, and he looked a bit deflated."

"There's something queer about this, Pasha." Dmitri stood and paced around the small room. "Even if the Nazis know Heinz is planning to leave, what's to be gained from staying? I'd rather make a dash for it and catch the Nazis off-guard." Dmitri picked up one of Isaak's shoes that Pasha was now using as his own and helped to clean it properly. "When we see them later, you'll support us going for the border in the morning, won't you?"

Pasha thought for a moment, then replied, "I trust you more than him."

XXIII

THE MERCEDES-BENZ grosser-pullman limousine
was waiting outside the decorative pastel-painted church.
The pediment above the pillars had a carved depiction of
Apollo in his chariot that looked out across a frozen lake;
the main villa was farther up the hill.

The bride and groom left the church and paused under
the late Baroque-styled portico to receive the applause of
the well-wishers who'd just witnessed the lengthy
Catholic ceremony.

Sable was wearing a sweeping white tulle gown with
fringed beadwork and silver detailing below the hips that
shimmied and sparkled in the late winter midday
sunshine. A floor-length diaphanous veil draped down
her back, attached with a silver clip to a beaded cap that
framed her face. Sable's expression was one of disbelief
rather than joy. Next to her, his face beaming with pride,
stood Heinz. He was dressed smartly in a three-piece suit
with double-breasted waistcoat, wing-collar shirt, and
white bow tie.

Heinz opened the door of the limousine for his new
bride.

The powerful eight-cylinder engine purred into life. The vehicle slowly moved forwards with the newlyweds settled in the plush seats of the car's ample interior. Heinz enthusiastically waved to the guests, who would all have to walk up the hill to the villa for the wedding breakfast.

Sable feebly tried to mimic her new husband's enthusiastic gesturing. She was still in shock from his announcement earlier that morning that the wedding would provide the assurance needed to shift any suspicion away from them with the National Socialists. Her pleas for Dmitri to be present had been ignored; the risk of him being recognised by those police and National Socialist officials from Essen who would be in attendance was too great. That was why, Heinz had explained, he'd sent Dmitri to Essen on a lengthy errand, knowing the Russian would be in too much danger if he stayed at the estate.

"Are you happy, my darling?" asked Heinz, taking his new wife's hand in his, as they both stopped waving. Sable's hand was ice-cold.

"Of course," she replied. He ignored the apathy in her voice.

"Heinrich, would you hurry, as my wife is cold?" Heinz leaned forwards and tapped on the pane of glass that divided the rear compartment from the front cab. Had he paid more attention Heinz would have seen that it was not Heinrich was not driving the limousine.

The vehicle sped up, coming to a halt at the double staircase façade of the graceful Italian-inspired villa. A valet was waiting to open the door on the bride's side of the car. Instead of letting Sable get out, the valet jumped in and slammed the door behind himself.

"Congratulations Herr and Frau Langer," sneered Dmitri. Pasha accelerated away from the villa.

"Mitya, it would have been too dangerous for you to be there," said Sable. Heinz relaxed into his soft leather

234

seat, letting his wife explain matters. "This makes everything look more plausible. Oh, say that you understand," she implored.

"And I suppose you worked all this out for yourself did you, Sable?" asked Dmitri.

"Don't be angry, darling," she replied. "Heinz thinks this really is best."

"For Heinz, maybe." Dmitri kicked the German's shin indicating he should join the conversation.

"Who would argue with newlyweds going on their honeymoon tomorrow and taking two servants with them?" suggested Heinz. "Turn around before anyone gets suspicious."

"Pasha's driving us to the Dutch border," said Dmitri.

"You're being foolish, Mitya," said Heinz. "And this is my car, so turn around!"

"And I suppose the SS guards I found searching mine and Pasha's room were just there to help us pack for tomorrow's escape?" Dmitri took a revolver out of his jacket and pointed it at Heinz. "You're the one who's been foolish, Herr Langer."

"Heinz?" asked Sable. She edged away from her new husband.

"He's making it up, darling," said Heinz. He reached for Sable's hand, which she pulled away from him. "Trust me, Sable."

"That's another mistake you've made," said Dmitri. "Sable trusts me. Pasha trusts me. And I trust both of them. Who trusts you?"

Heinz, with a half-smile, contemplated what Dmitri had said. He looked across at Sable, but she'd turned her face away from him. She watched the grounds of the estate she was now mistress of dash past, as Pasha continued to speed along the track that led to the main road.

Heinz looked back at the revolver, and at Dmitri's expression, trying to assess his options.

"That acrid smell is from the revolver. It's missing two bullets," said Dmitri. "Don't make me fire a third by trying anything reckless."

"If you let me and Sable get out here, I'll stall any more SS coming to arrest you until you and Pasha are over the border," said Heinz, watching Dmitri's eyes for a flicker of hesitation. "This car should get you there in less than an hour," he added.

"It's true then?" asked Sable, turning to her husband. "You weren't going to leave?"

"I hate the Nazis, my darling," said Heinz. "But I detest the Communists more."

"That hardly explains this …" Sable paused to find the right word, "…this sham." She removed the wedding ring that hadn't yet been on her finger even for an hour. She placed it carefully on the tan-leather seat between her and Heinz.

"I love you, Sable," said Heinz. "I've wanted to marry you since we first met in Paris." He looked at the ring but didn't pick it up. "That has nothing to do with the Nazis."

"It has everything to do with it, Heinz." She reached across for Dmitri's free hand. "Mitya is my friend."

"A friend who helps Communists like him." He nodded his head towards Pasha.

"The Communists killed my mother, my godparents, and many of my family and friends," said Dmitri.

"Then join me and fight against them, with the National Socialists!" urged Heinz. "Join us," he added, reaching a hand across to Sable's shoulder. She shrugged it away. "It's not too late, Mitya."

"Your brand of politics isn't to my taste either," said Dmitri.

"Tastes change, Mitya," said Heinz. "They become more complex over time." Heinz leaned forward, enthusiastic to the prospect of converting the Russian prince to the cause.

"You mean they become numb, surely?" said Dmitri. "Numb to torture, to death?"

"My family was persecuted by the Communists as well, Mitya. They kidnapped my mother and arrested my father here in the Ruhr in nineteen-twenty-three. It wasn't the workers from our factory who did that, it was foreign agitators. Bolsheviks. All you've done in Germany was help your friends, that can be forgiven if you join us now."

"But I'm not asking for forgiveness, Heinz," said Dmitri. "You're the one who's —"

"You've spent time with Pasha, Heinz," interrupted Sable. "You even encouraged him to speak with the workers at the colliery. Surely you think there are good Communists?"

"Darling," replied Heinz, "I wanted him to speak with the miners to expose the traitors here in Essen. I hoped someone from Red Orchestra would recognise him and reveal themselves."

"You could have raised the alarm at the book burning, but you didn't," she replied.

"We want the leaders of Red Orchestra," said Heinz. "Not the dumb followers."

"The man with the gun that night was Gennady Bunin," said Dmitri.

"He's just Moscow's errand boy," said Heinz, sitting back in his seat. He glanced out of the window. "We want the German leadership. We need Marianne Lázár. I'd hoped she'd still be at the club."

"Do you know what your friends did to her fourteen-year-old son?" Heinz ignored Dmitri's question. "And the camera film I burnt on the bonfire was fake I suppose?" asked Dmitri.

"You should have checked it first," said Heinz. He turned to Dmitri with a smile of self-satisfaction. "Wouldn't you prefer to be a part of something magnificent, the new European revolution, rather than being France's lap-dog, Mitya?"

"I have a prince's dislike for all revolutions," said Dmitri.

"You're no longer a prince though, are you?" Heinz gave out a sarcastic chuckle. "You're playing at being one, seducing silly women with your defunct title. I'm a real prince, a prince of industry, and I will help build the Reich!"

"You almost wet yourself when Vogel gave you that gun at the general's house," said Dmitri. "That wasn't terribly princely."

"But I pulled the trigger, didn't I *Prince* Dmitri Romanov?" asked Heinz. "I wonder if you can now."

"With quite some ease," replied Dmitri. "And *this* gun has bullets in, be sure of that."

"You'll be stopped at the border, arrested and hanged." Heinz leaned forward again. "I hear piano wire is the noose of choice for traitors."

Sable slapped her new husband hard across the face.

"I HATED not wearing nail polish," said Sable, glancing at her hands as she helped Dmitri adjust the bow tie he was now wearing as part of Heinz's wedding outfit. "And I miss my blonde hair."

"So do I, my darling," said Dmitri. He reached down between the seat cushions and retrieved the wedding ring that had fallen there. "You'll need to put this back on I'm afraid, in case anyone notices."

"I suppose I don't mind." She took the ring but hesitated to slide it back on her finger. "Especially as you're the new Herr Langer, darling." Dmitri eased the gold band along her finger and leant down to kiss where is rested against her knuckle.

"At dinner last night, Heinz was talking about his hope that I would soon bear a child for the Führer," she said. "I shudder now, realising it wasn't acting."

"We have more immediate worries than damn Heinz Langer, Sable," replied Dmitri. "We have to get across the border."

"Will we make it?" she asked.

"From where we left him Heinz had a pretty long walk to the villa. I doubt he's back there even by now." Dmitri checked his watch. "I wish you'd let me shoot him."

"We may need the bullets," said Sable.

The border post for entry into the Netherlands came into view. On the other side of the German guard box and barrier was a café and customs house, beyond which was the Dutch border and the safety of Venlo.

Pasha slowly edged the limousine along the tree-lined approach road. The wheels crunched on fresh snow as he brought the car to a stop at the side of the road. A bus had just pulled up at a stop opposite them.

"I'm leaving you both now," announced Pasha, leaning back through the dividing window from the front cab. "I must go back to Berlin."

"What do you mean?" asked Dmitri. "You can't. We're so close, Pasha."

"We look more plausibly like newlyweds with you here, Pasha," added Sable. She then realised how selfish this sounded. "And Germany is not safe for you."

"I have to stay and fight," said Pasha. "Mitya, get Miss Nash to safety. Goodbye to you both, and good luck." He got out of the vehicle and crossed the road to join the line of those waiting to board the bus for Dusseldorf. Dmitri pulled his friend out of the queue.

"You'll die here, Pasha," he whispered. "And for what?"

"Many of those Communists are my friends, Mitya," said Pasha.

"Then help them if you must, but from the safety of France."

"Mitya, don't you feel more pride for those nobles we knew who chose to stay in Russia after the Revolution, than us who ran away?"

"I've been back to Russia since," said Dmitri. "The former people, as the Bolsheviks call our kind, have achieved nothing in Russia apart from their own suffering and entertainment for the new leaders."

"But they stood up to the revolutionaries and refused to give up their own country without a fight. My father knew he had to fight for Russia, regardless of the consequences, as do I. Germany is now my country," said Pasha.

"There are smarter ways to defeat an enemy than just getting killed, Pasha. Your father's noble gesture left you an orphan, and the war he fought for Russia destroyed everything."

"Hitlerism hasn't taken complete hold yet." Pasha accepted a cigarette from the case Dmitri found in the pocket of Heinz' jacket that he was now wearing. "It's only been a few weeks. The chancellor can still be defeated, but not if all of his enemies leave Germany."

"There is no opposition strong enough now, surely you can see that?" asked Dmitri. He lit both cigarettes. "Swastikas fly from every other house. And children say a Nazi Grace at dinner."

"That can still be reversed."

"Books can't rise from the flames of a bonfire," said Dmitri. "You and I see Hitler as a ruthless fanatic, Pasha, but the majority either believe he's Germany's saviour, or are willing to let him become that."

"You have your family in Paris. The Communists are mine, and they need me here, to defeat the Nazis."

"That's what Hitler wants, Pasha. Every attack makes the Nazis look like victims of a Red terror. You're helping fascism by staying and fighting."

"I'm getting on that bus, Mitya, and don't want to say goodbye in anger." He held out his hand. "Sable needs you. Good luck."

Pasha, the romantic dandified teenager, the gentle-faced young man who had been orphaned, the aristocrat adored by both men and women at the grand balls held all over Petrograd before the revolutions, had become a man with the same heroic decisiveness of the father who had left him alone in the world. Dmitri desperately wanted to drag Pasha back to the Mercedes, to not let his friend board a bus to a battlefield he would so obviously die upon. But the pomaded hair and character of mischievous fun from those winter balls were in the past, this Pasha was no longer fighting against the heroism so many had suspected was in his character, he was embracing it.

"At least take this," said Dmitri, discreetly passing the revolver to Pasha.

"I'll be sure to make use of it." Pasha tucked the gun into his jacket. "Sooner rather than later."

"Good luck, my friend," said Dmitri, taking a firm grip of Pasha's hand.

"THEY'RE GOING to get suspicious, Mitya," said Sable from the back of the Mercedes. "We can't stay here like this. The bus has left, and Pasha on it."

"I know, Sable." There was an edge of rebuke to Dmitri's voice.

A car sped past them. It came to an abrupt stop by the small guard house, from which a border guard emerged. Four men got out of the vehicle; all were dressed in the familiar black uniforms Dmitri now despised.

A barbed-wire barrier was drawn across the road underneath the border pole.

Dmitri was already in the driver's seat of the Mercedes limousine, and reversing the vehicle slowly along the road, when he saw a second car approaching from behind him. The speed of this vehicle indicated a threat.

One of the occupants of the first car was pointing at the limousine.

Dmitri and Sable were trapped.

Dmitri cursed himself for delaying even a couple of minutes to gather his thoughts about Pasha's departure; otherwise they would now be safely in the Netherlands.

He stopped the car.

"What do we do?" asked Sable, also seeing the approaching car in the rear window.

"I hope you can run, darling," said Dmitri. He got out and opened the door to the rear compartment. "Give me your shoes." Sable did so.

As Dmitri whacked the satin shoes against the car door to break off the heels, Sable grabbed the hem of her floor-length gown and, with one mighty effort, tore the fabric up to her knees. Beads from the fringe flew off in all directions. She buckled the shoes back on and jumped down from the car.

"Run as fast as you can through the woods," said Dmitri. "After a few minutes, come in towards the border and try to find a gap in the fence."

"Surely, you're not going to stay here?" she asked.

"If I stay, they won't chase you," he replied.

"If you stay, I stay."

"Sable, I've had enough heroic recklessness from Pasha already. If you're free, then you can help me.

Otherwise we'll both be caught or killed." She stepped back into the car.

"Why are you so bloody stubborn!" he barked. He grabbed her arm before she sat down and pulled her back out of the vehicle.

"Are we running or staying?" she asked.

"Oh, very well," he conceded.

Dmitri guided them both away from the snow-dusted parts of the forest, choosing the leaf-carpeted areas which would make following their footprints more difficult. They zig-zagged through the trees.

"Keep up," called Sable, surprising Dmitri with her decent pace. "You forget that I was the Bryn Mawr sprint champion."

They stopped after about five minutes of fast running. Dmitri had kept his bearings despite the circuitous route he'd tried to take.

"The border's that way," he advised, pointing to his right. "Let's head there and try to cross."

The sound of dogs barking cut short their rest. There was now no need to plot a route that would confuse their pursuers. With dogs on their scent, they had to run straight, and hope the head start they had was sufficient. Sable tucked the ends of her torn skirt into the silver waistband, but Dmitri didn't run until she was also ready.

They found the fence quickly and followed it, hoping to find a break.

Looking ahead, Dmitri couldn't see any obvious crossing point.

The sound of barking was getting much louder, and even the cracking of tree branches could now be distinguished.

"Wait!" called Sable. Dmitri came back a few paces to join her where she'd stopped. "I hope even Russian princes learnt how to climb trees as children." She pointed up at the branches of the tree nearest to her.

Dmitri saw immediately what she was suggesting. The sturdy branch of one tree almost connected with a similar branch of a tree planted on the opposite side of the fence, forming a bridge.

As Dmitri gave Sable a boost up to the first branch, his jacket ripped down the seam across the shoulders. Sable secured herself and reached down to haul Dmitri up.

"Keep going, goddam it!" he urged. "They can still shoot us on this side of the fence." Sable stretched her arms and legs in unnatural positions to navigate the branches, climbing up to the one which would act as a bridge. They could now see the approaching dogs and Nazi handlers.

She edged along the branch, hoping it would take her weight. She reached across and transferred on to the branch of the other tree.

Dmitri followed Sable, sitting on the log, and edging forwards. His greater weight made the wooden beam begin to creak and start to lower. He knew it wouldn't hold if he edged further along. Sable was safely down in the neutral zone but could see the difficulty Dmitri was having. He slid back to the trunk of the tree on the German side.

Sable ran along the fence shouting to attract the attention of the dogs and handlers, drawing them away from Dmitri.

"Sable, don't!" he called, worried the Germans might still fire through the fence. She was risking her life while he hesitated. He took a deep breath, looked ahead instead of downwards, and from a standing position rather than seated, he ran forwards along the branch.

It broke away from under him.

He threw his body forwards with his arms outstretched.

The branch disappeared from underneath him, crashing to the snow-dusted ground below.

His hands grabbed at the bare branches of the other tree. He lost his grip, fell, then tried again, until a branch took his weight. He landed in a crouch, his left knee reminding him of its weakness with a sharp release of pain. But he was on the safe side of the fence.

Dmitri called to Sable, but she didn't hear him over the sound of the barking dogs. He ran forwards along the fence, heading towards the approaching danger. He lost a shoe in a patch of wet mud but left it and hobbled onwards. He grabbed Sable's hot hand and pulled her towards him.

The Nazi's gathered on the other side of the fence, only a few feet away.

"Hold me tight, Mitya," said Sable. "I'm scared." Dmitri raised his chin and pulled her in close.

"Well?" he asked of the guards on the German side of the wire barrier.

An enthusiastic SS guard raised his rifle and aimed it through the fence.

"No!" commanded an officer. He put his hand on the barrel and lowered it.

Dmitri turned Sable around and, still holding her tightly, they walked away.

Crawling under the Dutch border fence at a point both he and Sable could squeeze through, the two refugees emerged on the other side in wedding outfits now torn, muddied, and wet. He was only wearing one shoe, and hers no longer had their heels attached. They each had scratches on their faces, and sweat made Sable's make-up streak down her face.

They looked at each other and laughed.

"Well I don't think much of the honeymoon so far," joked Sable.

XXIV
Paris

COUNT MISHUKOV opened the door to the drawing room of the villa on the Bois de Boulogne and announced the unexpected visitor, "His excellency Heinrich Carl von Brandt, the German ambassador."

The distinguished ambassador walked a few paces into the room, then stopped, placed his arms by his side, and bowed, firstly to the elderly grand duchess, then to Dmitri's father, Grand Duke Andrei.

The ambassador had been appointed by the previous government. There was a Nazi SS officer waiting in the car outside who would replace him as the Reich's representative to Paris; this was the ambassador's last official duty before boarding a train to Berlin and to early retirement.

"Welcome, your excellency," said Andrei. He indicated a chair for the German ambassador to sit in. "Can we offer you some refreshment? Tea, coffee?"

"Nothing, thank you, Your Imperial Highness," said the ambassador. "I'm not anticipating being with you for long, and I'm sorry for not having made an appointment.

I was informed this morning of being recalled to Berlin, and I was keen to discharge this duty before I leave."

"And what is the matter you have come about?" asked Andrei.

"It's a personal matter for Frau Sable Langer, whom I believe is staying here?"

"That's correct," said the grand duke. "*Madam* Langer has been with us since her return from Germany. We are all guests of Her Imperial Highness Marie Mikhailovna here at the villa."

"Might I be able to meet with Frau Langer?" asked the ambassador.

"About what?" asked the grand duchess, affecting the most imperious tone she could adopt.

"Something rather tragic has happened in Essen, Your Imperial Highness," said the ambassador.

"Your excellency, this family knows a thing or two about tragedy," said the grand duchess. "There is no need to be *diplomatic* with us."

"Heinz Langer is dead."

"I see," said the grand duchess. "Unfortunately, we here are also all too familiar with death."

"Sergei Vasilyevich, would you ask the ladies to join us, please?" said Andrei. The equerry, who had been waiting by the door, left.

"Ladies?" asked the German ambassador.

"My daughter, Princess Anna Andreovna, has become a close companion of Madam Langer's," explained Andrei. "Considering the news you are about to impart, I think she might be needed for support."

"HOW DID he die?" asked Sable. She reached for Anna's hand, surprised and excited by the news.

"It seems your husband shot himself with his own revolver," replied the ambassador, his voice revealing the incredulity he held for the explanation sent to him from Berlin.

"Suicide?" asked Sable. She tried her best to feign sadness at the news of Heinz's death, which actually made her feel as though a heavy weight had been lifted from her shoulders.

"Unfortunately, Frau Langer, that's all I've been told." The ambassador shrugged his shoulders as he repeated the explanation he'd been asked to convey. This was the first time anyone had called Sable by her new married name, and it sent a shiver down her spine.

"Doesn't that seem a little odd to you, your excellency?" she asked. "That my husband would shoot himself instead of coming to join me on our honeymoon?"

"We live in strange times. You have the condolences of the new Reich." The ambassador shifted uncomfortably in his seat, keen to leave now that his duty had been carried out. "The embassy can help you with all matters. Please use the telephone number on the card I left with the equerry."

"Matters?" she asked.

"Your husband had no other family," said the ambassador, adding, "You are now a very wealthy woman, Frau Langer."

Sable forced down the edges of her mouth, which were twitching into a smile.

DMITRI HAD decided to walk back from his meeting with Tao Chen at which he'd handed over the list of witnesses copied down from the dossier. In the interests of fair play, Dmitri had made sure Emile-Jacques received a copy of the same list that morning; the French and Chinese could race each other to Austria to make their enquiries about Hitler's Jewish ancestry.

At the entrance to the villa, Dmitri stood aside to let the vehicle leaving the driveway join the traffic on the main road. Dmitri glanced across to the French policeman who'd been posted by the entrance gate of the villa by Emile-Jacques to check all visitors. The policeman nodded that everything was fine.

The car came to a stop as the driver waited for a fruit truck to pass by. Dmitri lifted his fedora by the tall crown so that he could see more clearly in the back window, checking who had just been visiting his family. Despite the police presence, Dmitri was still worried for them, even in their own home.

Next to a distinguished elderly gentleman, the half-bandaged face of Brigadeführer Vogel turned and glared back at Dmitri, who was crouching down to peer inside the diplomatic limousine. Some of Vogel's face and neck around the edge of the bandage showed red scarring.

The Nazi's expression changed from irritation at the intrusion of a passer-by, to one of primitive hatred towards the culprit of his permanent disfigurement once he recognised Dmitri.

The car pulled quickly into the traffic, leaving Dmitri momentarily dazed by the unexpected encounter. This shock quickly turned to fear; he was reminded of Anna's abduction by Bolshevik spies in Istanbul the previous summer, just when he thought they had been safe.

He ran into the villa, bursting through rooms, until he found Sable and Anna in the drawing room. Sable was laughing.

"What happened?" asked Dmitri, "Why was Vogel here?"

"Mitya, it's wonderful news," replied Sable, coming over to take his hand and calm him down. "Heinz is dead."

"Dead?" he asked.

"Yes, that was the German ambassador. He came to inform me. Heinz shot himself with his own revolver, not that I believe that of course." She went to pour them all a drink. "The Nazis must have killed him."

"With his own revolver?" Dmitri thought for a second. He took the glass from Sable, then he remembered saying goodbye to his friend at the border. "But I gave that gun back to Pasha."

"In which case," said Sable raising her glass, "here's to courageous Pasha!"

Dmitri Romanov will return.